SINGER

BOOKS BY IRA SHER

Gentlemen of Space
Singer

Ira Sher

SINGER

Houghton Mifflin Harcourt

2009   BOSTON   NEW YORK

Library of Congress Cataloging-in-Publication Data
Sher, Ira.
    Singer / Ira Sher. — 1st ed.
        p.   cm.
    ISBN 978-0-15-101413-2
    1. Traveling sales personnel — Fiction. 2. Male friendship — Fiction.
3. Southern States — Fiction. 4. Nineteen eighties — Fiction. I. Title.
    PS3619.H463S56 2009
    813'.6 — dc22   2008016214

Book design by Melissa Lotfy

PRINTED IN THE UNITED STATES OF AMERICA

DOC 10 9 8 7 6 5 4 3 2 1

for Asher

SINGER

DID YOU EVER HAVE A FRIEND? Someone you knew, while likely never admitting as much, that you'd meet in whatever capacity he was willing to extend himself? From whom any request might become an invitation? It's wonderful, that request — in whatever form it comes. And in my case the request arrived, literally, as a call for help:

"It's Charley." A pause, a tumble of thoughts compressed to a space the width between two words. A diamond in a hill of coal. "Charley Trembleman." And then a cough, as I collected his voice out of the snowy night. "I've had an accident, Milty. Do you mind coming down here? Do you mind coming down to help me straighten things out?"

I forget what immediately followed, exactly or approximately what was said, but everything was there, really, in those first words. For though I, too, paused and reflected in my lamp-lit living room in dark New Jersey, it is no small thing to be chosen from among a man's many friends to aid him in his time of need; and the request *was* wonderful, the sort of request I myself would have found impossible: to rely on someone so entirely, and to tell him. I would be certain, in advance, that he'd say no. I was envious, and I felt again how little I understood Charles.

It strikes me, too, how little of Charles's situation I understood when I flew to Memphis — only that he'd been burned in a motel fire; that he needed, specifically, someone to drive him around, because his job with the Singer Sewing Company required that he endlessly travel — or so he'd explained from his bed in the cinder-block infirmary where I found him slumped twenty-four hours later, hands bandaged, wearing one of his late-model cotton suits and resembling a colonial governor under benevolent house arrest. The walls perspired in the chill air. Someone was raving down the hall. I was unprepared for the relief, frightening in its intensity, that resided in those hands that took mine; and then an awkward silence descended.

If I recall correctly, I'd told Charles I could join him for a week, two if necessary. As we drove south, he beside me, chain-smoking and watching Memphis — bare, taxonomical, and dreaming in the February sun — I thought of how he'd kissed a nurse upon her sanitary fingers as we left. She'd laughed, but hadn't taken away her hand. He'd fumbled from the room like a drunken man, addled — *that* was the thing, because I'd never known Charles to be addled. For a moment I hadn't recognized him, and then, for a while, I failed in various small ways to recognize the man I knew. Despite this, some part of me felt we knew each other well enough that we didn't need to go through those preliminaries that normally attend a reunion. If only that part weren't struggling dimly with another, less-celebrated region, which couldn't help but feel he thought I had nothing else to do.

The truth is, even now I have few obligations awaiting my return: I have no *job* as such, being of independent means; moreover, I was, just then, at ends in my life. I'd been half expecting another call when Charles found me. Hearing his voice freighted with the intervals of painkiller, I understood for no reason but the accumulated certainty of a week that the other call wasn't coming.

I've begun learning to sew, after acquiring a sewing machine —a Singer, naturally, the 221-1—a portable electric nick-named the "Featherweight" by a generation of presumably brawnier Americans, and probably the largest-selling home machine ever manufactured by that company. With its primitive outboard motor and bulbous, hooded light hovering beside the lacquer-black body, it looks like a model of a steam engine—an enormous-gauge toy with gold filigree and an embossed plate upon its front—and it had belonged previously to Charles.

I feel I should mention at the outset that while I've enjoyed studying the machine and pressing my foot on the rubberized treadle that drives the needle up and down in its eyelet and fills the room with the smell of oil and cloth-cased wiring, I haven't much liked sewing. I'd suspected this would be the case, and after several nights spent poring over the manual and dandling the tiny objects that make up a sewing machine's anatomy in my less-than-delicate grasp, I've now confirmed my suspicions; but as has frequently, even gra-tuitously, been pointed out to me by my wife — a nonsewer, herself quite tiny, yet a person I once grasped with some fa-cility — there are so many things I dislike; and after all, there are things we dislike that we do every day, for no other reason than because we want to.

It was Charles who had once "explained" sewing to me; and I found the essence of sewing, at least as he described it, not only plausible but appealing enough psychologically that, perceiving I'd torn the tail of my good shirt — *the* good shirt currently in my possession — and having fidgeted here in this godforsaken place for ten days with no one who might be able to help (my host is a nonsewer, while his wife suffers from a mild arthritis that discourages her continued prac-tice), I opened the black leatherette carrying case in which the Singer was enshrined. The metal parts winked up at me. I reached in my hand and drew forth the glossy engine, placing it on the secretary by the window, where it has since remained.

"Sewing," Charles had said, laying a newspaper across his knee and a cigarette in the pop-out ashtray of his '79 Im-pala, the thought sparked, no doubt, by an article in the lo-cal gazette, "is the process by which you thread together with a single strand two otherwise disparate objects. I think, Milty, this realization was what first attracted me to the busi-ness. The essence of metaphor, isn't it?" he'd added by way of conclusion as I engaged the turn signal and smiled, unsure whether he was joking.

In my perusal of the manual that accompanies the 221-1, it has since become clear that beyond this strict definition of sewing lie all kinds of decorative sewing methods (and attachments) that have bastardized the essential into a field of technique onanistic and little removed from typing, often instead requiring both a single object and multiple strands. But if I haven't enjoyed sewing as much as I'd hoped, if not believed I would, I did also suspect from the outset that such generalities are ruinous. I *have,* for example, borrowed a typewriter from my host for typing. I can understand how Charles, fobbing himself with epistemology in the seat beside me that day, could have identified these latter-day uses of the sewing machine as the first inklings of what would eventually become its domestic decline. Perhaps even the decline of the Singer Sewing Company.

Across the room from where I lie is a tall, narrow mirror that reflects in its modest ripple the stippled wall and ceiling above my head. Beside me and to the left is a second bed, scattered with a few articles, including a road atlas, and regarded by a sibling mirror, each set in a plasticated gold frame on either side of the television stand. With the window curtains drawn — they're made of fine nylon netting, embroidered with enormous, colorless flowers — the room maintains an almost uniform feeling of impending rain or dusk, regardless of the hour. Upon the secretary, before the window, sits the Singer and the borrowed typewriter, and upon the television, around a photo of my wife taken during our last trip to Mexico, lean several postcards: "Lost Battle Cave, GA," "The Artiste" motel, and the monotone brochure for a pile of classical idioms that constitute a nearby museum.

In this country of encroaching roads and a mounting anxiety to remain connected, my first impression of the Idyll motel was of a place slipping *away* from all fellow habitation, though this is not particularly true: I know of a highway not far from here that within the hour would carry me east to Tuscaloosa, Alabama, or west to Meridian, Mississippi. Given a little more time I might wander on to Louisiana, to Texas — even Mexico isn't out of the question. One need not, of course, flee so far: My point is that there's an excitement in opening the atlas and turning to that first state — Alabama, "the Alphabetically Precocious State" — if simply in imagining the manifold possibilities that lurk ahead. I am reminded at a glance that even the old post road running past my door would take me in little more than an hour to the museum on the brochure's face, and I'm reminded that I should pay that elusive collection another visit. I've never driven that particular stretch of road, a road Charles once spoke so highly of; and there is, after all, something cheering about excursions.

I must admit, however, to another sensation that overtakes me as my thoughts play across the prologue to my atlas — the national map, ground of all journeys, map of all themes and broad arcs — for grasped at once, one cannot help but comprehend a deepening mass of roads as a darkening net. Particularly in poor light. There is, as I've described, a small incandescent lamp on the Singer — the "Singerlight" — positioned on the flank of the 221-1, its upper side shielded and shielding the operator with a small chrome fender. About an hour ago the bulb in the lamp burned out, and since then I've been shuttling back and forth between bed and typewriter, unable to sleep, unable to read the words I write, waiting for dawn to go outside and replace it. I am, you see, afraid of the dark, but one makes allowances. My room is at best dim, even during the day. At night the bathroom light trembles in the mirror above the vanity. The fluorescent in the ceiling, if you can bear it, fills the room with corpses. It's hard to believe, sometimes, that I came here to save someone.

FOR A MOMENT HE'D TAKEN MY HAND, and his was full of wild life. But of course one can't live that way, let alone think. "Don't you find it strange," someone once asked me—and I suppose it would have to have been Charles—"that in living we should grow farther and farther from life?" Yet it seems true.

Breaking free of Memphis that first day, we entered fawn-colored lands, winter down here like age, a tiredness. As the smell of bandages and vinyl faded, we began to talk of disasters: the proliferation of leaks in nuclear plants in Tennessee, in Japan, and just a few weeks before in Rochester, New York; the impending sense of nuclear war. As if, he pointed out, we were menaced from both within and without by the tiniest thing of which we could conceive, by the alphabet of the physical world; though I also understood that if this alone excited him at the moment, it was because, as a man who'd just escaped inferno to be cradled in narcotics, his mind reverberated with apocalypse.

I was naturally curious about Charles's fire, but one doesn't ask a man gasping in a lifeboat how it feels to drown. The fire seemed to lie always at the tip of his gaze; out the windows, we followed the flattened countryside folded in brown, trees like scorch either side of the highway, and the knowledge that we were embarking on this together, of his confidence in me, threw a kindness over the hesitations of the day and the people we passed on the road, the man in overalls who pumped our gas with a hand tattooed with the word "LIAR." Charles put on his sunglasses and mentioned a mutual friend, Harvey Partner.

"I meant to ask," I said, reminded by the name, "whether you were able to get into the museum, to see that painting." I was referring to a work by the celebrated nineteenth-century American painter of the Cumberland School, Alsby Kennel, which I myself had tried without success to see on a previous occasion in the Southlands. For while I don't have a *job,* if I can be said to have a profession, it's as an enthusiast — particularly of Kennel's work. It's something that we shared, back when Charles and I were in school together.

"I was able to visit the museum," he affirmed after a pause, reflected light rolling over his features, "but your painting . . . the caretaker told me he'd never heard of it" — and to my look of perplexity — "not even when I found the card I sent you in their gift shop. He told me it was a reproduction of a Turner night scene."

My jacket pocket held the inscrutably rendered postcard he'd mentioned — it could just as easily have been a Rothko — along with several others from him I'd shuffled through on the plane. I said, "We were, you know, only there that day because of Harvey."

"I was thinking about him last night," Charles murmured. "How it didn't really surprise me they couldn't find or even remember the painting—no one ever believed Harvey. It was cruel, at bottom, but that was the thing with Harvey—people were cruel to him. You'd have thought he'd never had a bad day in his life . . . but people were cruel all the same. Maybe they thought it would be a novelty."

"*I* wouldn't have believed him," I conceded, "except for that postcard. It was an unlikely painting on whatever authority for a man whose whole life was spent on small canvases, portraiture. There would be *books* about such a work."

"Well?"

"Well—there would . . ." And seeing the look he gave me: "Oh, you know what I mean—Harvey saw it as a child. Maybe he imagined it was larger than it was . . . maybe he imagined it . . ."

Charles glanced away. Even unshaven, torn up, there was something sharp in his face—"disconcertingly handsome," my wife had gushed after first meeting him. I'd missed it when we met in the hospital, but now I began to see that his face had in fact changed very little; it was his expressions that seemed uncollected. He said, "It hardly matters at this point."

"Of course," I agreed. "We'll have to see for ourselves . . ."

And then, for a moment, we again passed into silence.

"Where," Charles said suddenly, changing the subject, "is the bag that nice woman gave me in the hospital?"

I glanced at him. "The nurse? It's on the backseat."

"It's full of samples, she said"—by which I understood he meant those little blister packs of pain medication. He made a stiff turn, motions stunned.

"What are you doing, Charles?" I asked, although of course I knew—I can see now that from the very first he was trying to evade me.

"She said I should have something every four hours."

"Two hours ago," I chided, moving the bag out of his reach with a free hand, directing him back to our conversation: "And you know what I *mean:* You've wondered about this painting—you've gone looking for it. I was curious enough to look for it *despite* the fact that Harvey claimed to remember it."

"I think you better leave him alone," he said sourly; yet I'd succeeded in raising a glint of the Charles I remembered. It was in the tilt of his head, the way he pulled on his ear.

"That's right—forget Harvey. But to think that a work like this could be lost . . . *in a museum*—" All the same, I let him rummage now in the paper sack until he had what he wanted.

Something about his injuries made him look childlike. He has black hair, surprising in someone our age; and while Charles isn't small, he's quite a bit smaller than myself. Before I knew him, long ago, when I only knew *of* him and thought he was a bit arrogant, I'd nearly hit him one night, at a party. Perhaps he'd sensed where my thoughts had drifted. Catching my glance, he said, "Don't ever do that again."

For whatever I might say elsewhere, we *didn't* know each other so well, Charles and I. We both understood this. He was a man I'd spent time with at parties in college, and on rare occasions we'd met to play chess or Go, both of which he developed brief manias for. I would strain and scratch over the board, periodically forcing a draw, and he would talk voluminously about Kennel: Had I seen his portrait *The Thief*? Had I noticed where, in the landscape *Fear House*, the canvas had been cut away by Kennel's own hand, the house laid down from another scene like a piece broken from some fire-lit world?

I don't know exactly what I expected now from Charles, except that there was a time when we'd both had a kind of reverence for the antebellum painter. It was something Charles had felt *as* a painter (for he was, back then) — one could see in his own work Kennel's ancestral landscapes becoming urban and mathematical, and infused with Kennel's sense of the offstage: the figure vanishing, the hasty grave — and that I'd discovered, in a different way, when I first understood in Kennel the duration of time in a painted instance, a labyrinth that must have been very much what America felt like to someone fleeing European history in the nineteenth century. Whatever reserve existed today, whatever its motivation, though, clearly it was left to me to overcome — such, I recalled, had always been our relationship:

"Charles . . . what would you say if I told you that of the eleven Kennels presently in the country, I have in my possession three? *Woman Bathing,* for one — I'm sure you recall it, because you claimed, once, it was your favorite canvas." I continued only when I recognized, even in his silence, apprehension: "I *have* that painting, Charles. It's on the wall of my study, though I believe it was on loan when you came to visit. So you see, there's nothing rhetorical in my interest — and to find that a little county museum could through its own ineptitude have hidden away another work, of whose value they likely have no conception —"

"Milty —"

"It could be mural-sized or as big as a postcard, it doesn't matter —"

"Yes — *it doesn't matter*," he repeated impatiently.

"But *of course it does* — it matters to *you*" — wishing I could shake him. "You can't seriously pretend it doesn't mean anything anymore, just because you happen to sell sewing machines this year —"

He reached for his cigarettes and mangled the pack until he got one out. "What's the word?" he said quietly. "Milty — what's the word for someone who comes late to the party, and then won't leave? Or better . . . the word for that insufferable pledge, *you* remember — the one who becomes the tiresome authority on every rule of whatever little club they must join . . ." At which I lost my temper — for an instant my hands left the wheel — as it occurred to me we were fighting, idiotically fighting, as we always did.

Today, of course, I see that he was a sick man; but at the time I could only be astounded that he'd given up everything brilliant in his life, everything, I would claim, that he loved, for . . . and there, I suppose, was the issue. He'd been an exceptional painter, an artist I admired. I still admired him as he sat in his ocean of leatherette, chasing pills across his shirtfront, even if I couldn't pretend to *get it*. Not that I'd *gotten* Kennel when Charles first introduced me to his work, but there was an electricity. I felt as if Charles had slipped out of focus, become a lesser version of himself, receded by time. I had to squint to make him out. Still, the distance felt too deliberate. He was jealous, I grasped as his voice exploded in the car:

"I am not going to hold your hand, do you understand? There will be no galleries down here. There will be no chit-chat or cocktails. No hot ticket for the season, and no one to laugh at your *wit*. And if you came here under the delusion that we're making scenic trips to whatever shrines you've been fussing over for the past twenty years" — his voice edging higher as I thought there, *there* — "unless the truth is that all this, everything down here, just *looks* like a Kennel to you, and so now what you want me to do is join in your schoolboy choir and aestheticize — aestheticize the whole thing —"

"But don't you see? You are — you *are* —" I cried, though half turning, the car weaving on the blessedly empty road, I caught the mildness in his face, as if, I felt belatedly, he wasn't excited at all; though I believe he meant everything he'd said, because it was true, at least the part about the landscape resembling a Kennel — those deep and hovering skies, clouds opening canyons of light, and below in the valleys, a surface like mold in which rivers fork from low hills into floodplains. Down to the blasted oak in the foreground along the roadside ditch, like a folly, our altercations acts of nature: The world rendered clearly in their wake, as in the wake of a storm.

I felt a great relief, nearly a sob. I'd feared in the hesitations of the day — in the way we'd both, like librarians, run our fingers over those familiar titles in the stacks that comprised a safe and mutual ground — something only apparent once I understood I'd nothing to fear: the possibility, the seeming inevitability in the world of business with its piles and self-help manuals full of schemes determinate as money, that Charles had grown dull, and the years had beaten him down. I was remembering that I admired him in school as one admires an opponent, a chess player, who pleases precisely because he might beat you at the game you'd believed your own. It was a side of Charles that retreated in the company of others — something I wasn't sure others perceived — yet during brief moments of social amnesty had arisen between us like a conspiracy.

"*You're*," I at last amended myself, "the thing that reminds me of Kennel, Charles — the painter as country gentleman, the man with the buried past, losing his mind in a velvet carriage as his lackey ferries him around lands fallen to carpetbaggers. I came down to help *you*" — my breath cavernous in the wake of my words.

"And I'm not ungrateful," he replied. "But I am no longer," he reminded me, as if he'd followed none of these mental volutions, "a painter." Then he allowed, almost as an afterthought: "I guess this *is* a kind of vacation for you, though, isn't it, Milty? And I guess we'll have to go back and see this museum of yours, won't we?"

The car passed beneath a darkening portion of sky, a moment of overcast, and we quieted amongst the motels streaming by. They're some of the many things I see now with Charles's eyes, one of those places in which his thoughts have eclipsed mine: glass beads strung down our nation's highways (Diamond Court, Pearl's, The Falling Star); a gentle shift from state to state, a dialect, a narrative of sites and dreams — places to wake and sleep, places that are the footprints of other journeys (Robin's Rest, Tennessee Lamp, Mountain View) —

until you come to the one whose journey most coincides with your own.

The Atlantis is a yellow brick horseshoe, two stories high, hard against Route 22 — a relic of some caravan route to the Gulf, with its painted boxes of plastic flowers hung from stacked galleries, a sorrow of swimming pool behind a chain-link fence. We parked in the lot out front, and Charles lit another cigarette. He examined himself in the passenger mirror. His face looked bloodshot, as if he hadn't gotten the hospital out of his system. Wherever the fire had left a telltale on his arms and hands, they'd wrapped him like a boxer.

"How do I look?" he said.

"How do you feel?" I asked, filled with quiet joy.

"Ever burn your hand at the stove?" He plugged the lighter back into its fiery cave and I let the engine die. There were only two or three cars in the lot besides our own.

"So you've been here before?" I said of our motel.

"The wallpaper," he recalled, "has a mythological subject matter"; and then for a moment he seemed to see the Atlantis as I did. "When you're living in exile," were, I think, his words, "you develop routines. Did you ever try not to step on the cracks when you were a kid? Leave bread crumbs behind you on the forest floor? When you were a visitor in the land of adults?"

"I still feel like a visitor," I replied.

He turned to me, then, and that childhood glittered in his eyes. "I'm usually even farther south than this . . . moving all the time. You lose things: It's been three years since I saw snow," he said. "So you develop routines . . . though I guess it's a magical protection" — as if to apologize for the digression, or the unmagical though colorful sign for COLOR TV, the black and yellow stencil of a telephone on the Plexiglas of the motel office.

Glancing at the hand he'd placed on the dash, I remarked, "It doesn't seem like much protection." But the drugs were flooding his gaze with metal.

I asked so little, it occurs to me. Perhaps I asked little because from the very beginning I'd wanted to tell Charles about myself — this is, arguably, all I ever wanted. Yet standing in the parking lot of the Atlantis, it seemed my life was opening now into those whispered corridors of friendship I'd believed existed only in mythology passed down from fathers to sons. I might have asked where to begin — where to find the door — but I dimly recalled: one looks for commonality, waits for a thought to coincide, as if we had each simply to paint our door at the same point on opposite faces of a wall. I'd heard him, I'm sure, in the passenger seat, listening — as if listening for breath upon the other side of that partition.

"What was the name of the little town, with the museum, where we met?" I wondered aloud as we stood before the concierge, but Charles shook his head.

It began raining as I took the keys from his hands and turned them in the tumbler to his room. He sat on the edge of his bed. He looked suddenly haggard — after all the shouting, I found myself speaking quietly to him, as if he might be hurt by loud noises. I asked if he needed help, but he told me he'd manage, and so I left him and opened my own room, next door, before coming out and standing under the veranda to watch the rain spot the asphalt until everything was black and new. Once, weeks later, he would kneel in a burning room and tell me, "Everything they say will come true, comes true"; yet this was such a mute and minor time. The day had fallen back into the West, and the air smelled like wet highway; at some point — I'd dozed off a little, leaning there — it wasn't raining anymore.

I've wondered at times if that museum — *the museum* — is never open, though I've come to see this as a quality that in no way detracts from its value. Isn't the very earth beneath our feet, after all, a museum that's always closed? And isn't this also, with a few dazzling exceptions, exactly what our minds are to each other? Yet I've not always found it possible to accept the situation so philosophically. A year and a half ago, in the summer of 1980, these same considerations had led me to wonder, deridingly and aloud, what function such a place might possibly have.

"The Earth or your mind, Milty?" my wife had asked, disembarking my train of thought.

"The museum," I reminded her. "What is the function of such a *museum*" — but I was being taunted.

How exhaustively hot it felt outside the domed, marble edifice, stuck (another folly) in that anesthetized backwater to which we'd traveled — Carthage is our little town's unassuming name. I'd remained staring at the ridiculous assemblage of Egyptian columns and Roman friezes long after my companions — my wife and old Harvey Partner (another nonsewer) — snickered and turned away, ambling toward greener conversational pastures. My hand dangled from the elaborate crosses of a wrought-iron gate through which Harvey had pulled a sword of grass he was now playing between his fingers and lips. Caroline was laughing like a hog. In the shade of a gnarled oak, we'd read and reread from a brass plaque the hours of the museum, consulting afterward a pamphlet collected earlier from a billet of tourist information at our Memphis hotel. We'd been arguing — or I'd been arguing with an imaginary representative of the museum — about the small but significant differences between the pamphlet and the plaque affixed to the fence until Harvey readjusted the plastic harness on the vinyl cowboy hat he'd picked up at a gas station, pulled for emphasis against the lock adorning the gate, and then, together with Caroline, wandered back down the grassy slope of futility. It was a bitter pill — giving up my imaginary argument — and I took a moment swallowing it.

"Well," I mumbled, loosening my tie and letting go of the warm iron as I stumped after them, "it just seems like a shame, after coming all this way" — glancing at my watch yet again. "The curator's probably stepped out for a drink —"

Harvey turned and looked up at me. The museum was already miles away in his mind. "Sure, Milty. Though you know I saw it years ago, and heck, it might have been a loaner. It might not be on display anymore, this Kenner of yours."

"Kennel," I corrected. "And believe me, if that pillbox has a Kennel, it'll be strung up front and center. Unless of course," I added, glaring into the brim of the hat he'd tipped back between us, "it *is* Kenner you meant all along"—for I hadn't ever believed the painting was there to begin with; I didn't believe Harvey had the slightest idea. The whole trip to this town had been precipitated by a discussion Caroline and I were having about the beloved painter, during which Harvey had unexpectedly announced from behind the cover of a powdered donut: Kenner!—Oh, right, Kennel!—he'd seen one of his paintings (the painting in question) in a county museum (the one I'd just turned my back on) not far from Memphis, where we all happened to be. I was already a bit tired of Harvey; I'd endured a welter of his harebrained notions while trapped indoors by bad weather the previous day. To my incredulous stare he shucksed that his mother's family hailed from a nearby town called, of all things, The True South.

We found on the map, open between us, the freckle of The True South, and then, proximate and precancerous blip on the nation's underbelly, the town of Carthage. As surprised by the inference that Harvey had been inside a museum as by the claim he made to differentiate between paintings, I jokingly suggested that we take a drive; but finding myself on the road twenty minutes later committed to a potentially odious afternoon, I reflected that perhaps Harvey had an insufficient grasp of my familiarity with the subject—the enormous surprise and pleasure that would lie in really finding such a work—as well as the depth of my doubt, for while I consider myself an amateur expert on the master, I'd never even heard of the "mural-sized" painting Harvey claimed, when pressed, was entitled *The Fall of Atlanta*. During our expedition (it turned out to be nearly three hours along a fidgety black line, half washed out by flooding) I'd prepared to settle for the lesser pleasure of watching Harvey blink and scratch his way through a quaint collection of deer porn; yet standing before the darkened museum, I was, it seemed now, to be deprived of either joy.

Caroline stepped from the shelter of a tree and shaded her eyes to sweep the diminutive green in the lap of the museum. "The problem is," she informed me superfluously, "I just don't care anymore. You know what I mean?"

She turned back in our direction but looked at neither of us. It is a thing my wife does: turn her face in profile to her interlocutor while she talks. She has black bangs and a lovely ear, riveted that day as most days with a chunk of gold, and I suppose she wants you to notice these things rather than the slight narrowness of her face and eyes, or the little upturn to her nose that makes her look so feral when she's being covetous or, in this case, vindictive. When I first met her, she'd described herself as an actress; gestures such as this seem to be the last vestige of that occupation.

"Now what was it you were saying a minute ago, Milty — something about drinks? Maybe," she suggested through a willful misappropriation of context, "we should all just cut our losses and get that drink. We can write the museum for a monograph," she concluded to Harvey, who probably thought a monograph was a type of antique plane.

I looked over my shoulder for the last time at the offending building. It was, according to the pamphlet, the product of an "un-schooled local genius and original mind," as so much had been since we drifted south of Virginia and the colleges and universities were replaced by churches of diminishing proportions and ballooning ambitions. The street and square before us were empty. The sky jammed down against the roof of the town like a glacier of tin. I put my sunglasses on as a dust-colored sedan nosed around the corner of what comprised the whole urbanity, trickling past darkened shops until it came to rest halfway down the block, where the door opened and divulged a man in a blue suit defending himself against the sun with a newspaper. For a moment we stared at one another, and then I returned to my pamphlet with its frequent recourse to the words "treasure" and "posterity," or as Harvey had put it, "treasured posterior." When I looked across the green again, only the stranger's feet were visible, jutting from the door into which he'd fallen back.

"Like there. What's in there?" Caroline drawled to Harvey, who was fiddling again with his repulsive cowboy hat. She pointed just beyond the solitary car to a dim set of windows, possibly a bar. Like so many things in the town, the sign above the door was illegible from a dank, pouring light. She began walking.

"What if I just wait here," I said quietly, and then, louder: "I'm just going to wait."

"Don't be silly," she threw over her shoulder, Harvey already following into her wake. "It's hot and there's nothing to do" — motioning laterally with her handbag. I watched the teeter of black heels on the cobbles of the path. She was, of course, right.

Caroline is often right. I wasn't surprised, for instance, to find within the shop a long zinc counter backed by bottles, a handful of tables and chairs. My wife has a nose for these things; her knees sag naturally in the direction of cocktails. When the bell that jangled our entrance seemed to disturb no one, she rapped with her rings on the bar. Hearing a scrape, some sullen motion, we made our way into the thin, brown room and sat down.

The laconic proprietor had just shuffled off with our order, and Harvey was in the process of resuscitating the piece of grass with which he'd regaled my wife, when the door chimed open again and our man from the sedan stumped in, newspaper in hand. Daylight was all over his back, and he seemed to pause and stare at us for a moment in the darkened interior — as blindly, no doubt, as we stared back — before, as if on cue, a brass band, fusty with age, burst from the farther recesses. I craned around for the jukebox, then returned my attention to our cohabitant, but he was already engaged with the bar, face averted, suit dark at a spot between his shoulders. Caroline and I exchanged looks, while Harvey, half turned, continued to watch the stranger seated in the one place a golden foil of sunlight penetrated the papered-over windows.

"Can't we leave now?" she said to me under cover of Mr. Partner's transferred attentions, opening her bag and clawing through the contents for her compact.

"They haven't even brought our drinks —"

"No — I mean, can we go someplace else *afterward*?" — speaking in a low voice, making up her face. She has a small mouth that she does in an almost orange shade of red, and appears to sharpen like a pencil. "If we go back to Memphis, we can catch that parade" — and to my smile — "I know it's *stu-pid*, but anything's better than —"

"I want to wait," I insisted, bringing on a dispirited silence during which the barman fetched me and Harvey each a drink, and a drink that my sweetie inhaled nearly before he could get safely back behind his counter. She called to him in the childish voice of entreaty she uses to ask for all alcohol, and then, a moment later, out popped the guidebook within which she meant to sulk. The barman came and went with another round. The grass, Harvey announced to no one, had been damaged during transport. Setting down his instrument and again removing his headgear, he rubbed the pink welt just below the greasy blond dome of his hair.

"I forgot how hot it gets," he began, perhaps explaining his use of the terrible hat.

"Thankfully," I remarked, "I hear it's quite a bit cooler in the museum. Even if it turns out to be devoted entirely to the memory of the late Kenner —" to which Harvey gave me a blank stare.

"I told you there's a Kenner —"

"Kennel," I corrected again. "But what do you think, C — as I've asked everyone else, should we ask our friend over there at the bar for his thoughts on the local landmark? Perhaps, luck be a lady, we in fact have before us the legendary Kenner himself, miraculously preserved through the absorption of cadmium red —"

"Oh, stop it," Caroline burst out, forsaking her travel guide. "You just don't like people."

"Should one?" I laughed.

"Should one what?" she mimicked, prodding unhappily at her ice.

"*Like people.* But that isn't the point," I concluded, turning to Harvey, who'd slouched back in his chair, hat held defensively in both hands. "You're being hyperbolic—because it isn't even true. Example: Harvey Partner." Harvey watched me like a wary prizefighter. "I like Harvey here just fine, don't I, Harv?"

"Sure, Milty."

I'll be the first to admit, however, that he didn't look convinced. Harvey, with whom I'd gone to college years ago, had grown during those same years, I suspected, into the sort of person who liked Caroline more than he liked me; which is not to suggest there was anything funny going on—Harvey has a face that droops with loyalty—but he felt sorry for her, and it was this I was playing to when I said:

"What I think, Harv, is that Caroline's decided that I'm some sort of *bad man*"—noticing Caroline's glass was empty and raising my hand bar-ward on her behalf. "But before I unbutton my heart any further, maybe I should ask if *you've* given up on me, too."

"We're your friends, Milty," he said. "It's our job to take you for a better man than you are."

I laughed; Caroline, however, bristled: "Oh no—you might be his friend, but I'm his wife, and it's not my job—"

Fortunately, the bartender came over and handed her a fresh cocktail. My laugh frosted the room. I was glad a few seconds later when she added, "I *do* wish he'd stop staring."

"Who, me? Or our friend," I decided, following her eyes.

We were certainly making enough noise that anyone with an ounce of curiosity would have taken notice.

"Maybe he wants to ask you to dance," I suggested, as the rusted hiss of a trumpet began a new song. It's not uncommon for men to check Caroline out in a bar — she's a pretty Mediterranean woman who does like to dance, and people can tell such things. She stared back across the room in a way that probably seemed insolent to her — wide-eyed, with periodic battings. Have you ever really seen someone bat her eyes? I thought it was just a figure of speech, encountered in books, until I met my wife. She's the only person I know who actually does it, though she must have learned it somewhere — and when I think about it, she must have read it in a book, likely a book on acting.

"He looks just dreamy about now," she warned, as his head returned its profile to us.

The barman trotted over to my rival and became engaged in a low conversation over the newspaper he'd spread on the counter. Beside him was a briefcase, and periodically he reached inside for things — documents he took from sheaves of clipped or stapled papers, licking his fingers to separate the pages.

"Well, I'm guessing with those big, wet hands, he's no ballerina. And he looks far too organized to be our curator," I said, watching him paw across a tented map, directing the bartender's attention to a leaf from his files. "My suppositions are those of a layman, naturally, but he seems a stranger to these parts —"

"I think he's handsome," Caroline opined as she set down her glass.

Harvey, in the position least suitable for viewing the topic of discussion, and who, while gifted with a pleasant demeanor, had no particular gift of mind, slipped back farther from the table, saying, "You two just let me know when you need me."

The stranger and the bartender were slouched into their conversation, the stranger's dark head nearly touching the barman's gray; and I wavered, for perhaps the man *was* a local. One could have sworn they'd met each other before. I remember thinking how old-fashioned he looked: the broad lines of the suit he had on, cut from thirty years ago, pants suspendered high around the waist. He took his jacket off, revealing French cuffs. His shirt was wrinkled, a bit fatigued by the heat, but the overall effect wasn't unstylish, merely antiquated. Giving the matter more thought, I considered that such people likely took their cues from a different time — the bartender would certainly have appeared dated if spirited to an urbane location — but there was something else I couldn't place about our friend. I said merely, "I shouldn't be surprised — you've always liked them old."

To which Caroline retorted, "He's no older than you," and once again I took a closer look. While it was also true I had a good dozen years on her, and it was partially, even affectionately, of myself I'd been speaking, when he next turned his profile to us, I saw that despite the existence of a honking pair of reading glasses he was younger than I'd assumed. It was this I'd been unable to place.

"Then why is he dressed that way?" I asked. Caroline, however, had renewed her sulk.

"I'm a bit out of shape if you want me to play all by myself,"

I said momentarily, narrowing my eyes at the stranger. "None-theless" — peaking my mouth — "we can begin by assuming he's a spy. A Soviet spy. I understand the textbooks are out-dated over at the Kremlin, written as they are in the Khru-shchev era —"

"Now you're being stupid," she murmured. Yet she added: "It's *obvious* he's from here. He hasn't been around in a while, but he just got back to town and he's waiting for his friends. They come here every day after work. He's explain-ing a thing or two to this fellow who didn't even recognize him at first —"

"But he has a briefcase full of paperwork," I protested. "Is he planning on sharing that with his friends? Isn't it more likely we're dealing with some form of tax assessor?"

Caroline gave me another look. "He's come back after a dozen years," she said to Harvey of all people — he stared at her like an ox. "He made his fortune while he was away, but now he's given up on all the fancy people . . . back in —"

"Let us say New York."

"He's come back to his hometown today, to build some-thing."

"*Of course*," I exclaimed with budding comprehension, "he's had plans drawn up for a museum — a real museum, with hours and everything. That would explain the paper-work. The museum will be his gift to the mouth-breathers of his childhood — a gift of culture" — still, I could see I was los-ing my audience. Complicating matters, the old-young man now removed and displayed for the bartender a ring from his finger. The more I examined him, the clearer it became that if he'd just returned from the Big City, he'd merely pulled an old suit from a trunk in the family attic, stuffed a briefcase full of bad debts and rubber checks, and taken to the highway again. Locust swarms of these beings arise from the mud each spring, breed, and expire at the touch of winter — my brother, of a somewhat hardier stock, was hatched from such a riot; though to be honest, my brother's personality is perhaps only a subset of those qualities I least admire in myself.

"He's a salesman," was what I said.

Caroline actually snorted. "He couldn't sell a peanut to a squirrel," she quipped. And as if to prove her point, the barman handed him back the ring with a fond twist of the head.

"Well, he didn't come in here just for suds at two in the afternoon. He came in following *us*," I said, "and I believe he *is* following us. He smelled the Italian leather in Caroline's handbag from across the green. And if you think this little patter at the bar isn't part of our friend's —"

"Stop calling him that," she snapped.

"— game . . ." I leaned in toward my wife. "You just don't like people, do you? I mean, I'm not your friend, he's not your friend . . . what about Harvey here? It's a sad state of affairs is what it is, and if you ask me, it's a good thing our friend over there takes us for better people than we are — don't you think, Harv?"

But Harvey had turned around, and I followed his gaze, which was when I saw the stranger's face clearly for the first time. He'd removed his spectacles. I'd just admitted, grudgingly, that he *was* handsome under all that Bakelite, when Harvey said, "It's Charley."

"Who?" Caroline asked, hailing the bar for another drink.

"It's Charley Trembleman, isn't it?" Harvey repeated to me as, as if hearing our voices for the first time, the man swung fully around and came across the room.

"Charles," I said, rising in astonishment. "What the hell are you doing down here?"—before it stole over me: "But it's true, then . . ."

In the miscegenation of hands this seemed to go unheard. "What the hell am *I* doing here? What the hell're *you* doing here, I could ask—" He laughed, eyes flashing over us, resting finally on Caroline. "And I don't imagine you'd have much of an answer."

"Oh, no—we don't have any answer at all." Caroline sighed, glass half in her mouth, earrings suddenly garish and huge, like lamps on either side of her head. "We were just trying to get into one of Milty's boring museums."

To his look of incomprehension, I said, "The place with the dome across the street."

He smiled. "So that belongs to you."

"But you *are* here about the painting," I insisted.

His eyes, however, barely caught mine. "Aren't you," he said, "going to introduce us?"

I glanced between Charles and my wife. "Oh, right—sit down. Sit down. This is Caroline, my bride." I drew forth one of her rigid little paws where it peeked above the table. "Charles went to P——— with Harvey and me," I explained. "He was the only other kid from Elizabeth."

"I guess that's true," he said. "I forgot all about that, that we were from the same branch."

As Caroline reached happily for a newly arrived drink, an idea dawned upon her.

"But you're Charles Trembleman *the painter*."

Harvey's laugh punched the room. I felt myself redden. It was surely obvious in that moment that Charles loomed larger in my cosmology than I in his.

"Well, a long time ago . . ." Charles said.

"The poor man had to eat, after all," Harvey chimed in.

"Oh," Caroline purred, speaking to Charles as if they were at a garden party. "I know *lots* of painters that do just *fine*."

"That's *because* they do just fine," I corrected, feeling my wife to be something of an albatross. But let us again be fair: Though there are people through whom a native stupidity shines forth past any varnish of education or acculturation, Caroline is not such a one. If anything, I feel that some agency — I suppose it would have to be me — has thrown a pall of foolishness over her thoughts in recent years. "And yes," I admitted, seeing things would need clarification, "this is Charles Trembleman *the painter*. And a very good painter at that."

Caroline smiled and wrinkled her nose. "You should send something to Milty's gallery."

"Museums, galleries . . ." Charles continued to regard me. "Thank you all the same, Mrs. Menger, but I don't do that anymore. Haven't I, though" — turning the conversation — "seen you before? Harvey mentioned a girl a few years ago, an actress . . ."

He had the face of someone who cares too much for his face, but you forgave him. He seemed, moreover, less changed by the years than either Harvey or myself: lean, youthful, especially around the eyes. Kind eyes, I recalled, seeing them again. They were green, and they commiserated with whatever they touched.

"I *like* you," she said cheerily, taking her glass out of her face — a little too cheerily for my taste. "I like him." And then we had a moment where we all sat grinning at each other with stupid goodwill before I decided it was time to get the conversation away from my wife, collecting her thoughts in quivers between her teeth.

"So, if it's not the museum . . . what *are* you doing here?" I asked.

"I am," he told us, taking a seat and folding his hands on the table, "an area agent."

"Is that a baseball thing?" Caroline asked. "Are you like a scout?"

"Yes and no," he replied carefully. "I'm a bit like a scout, but not of the kind you're thinking." It dawned on me then what he was talking about. "I'm a regional agent for the Singer Sewing Company."

I was starting to remember the sort of a guy Charles was. I winked across the table, and he returned the wink: He was pulling their legs. His dad was a Singer man, my father was a Singer man. And even if mine was a company lawyer and his a machinist, it was a club. Harvey's face assumed the vague look it took on whenever his intelligence was in question, while Caroline, glancing at Harvey and finding him poker-faced, played with her earrings.

"But really," she said, taking shelter beneath a kittenish goggling, not liking games she didn't understand. "Really," as I waited for his expression to shift, and she looked sadly into her suddenly empty glass. He was unmoved.

"So you sell sewing machines?" she asked at last, perhaps afraid by now she'd hurt his feelings. Charles leaned forward across knotted hands.

"Mrs. Menger, not just sewing machines," he said with slow conviction, further unnerving her. "There isn't a finer machine made anywhere in the world, for any purpose, than a genuine sewing machine manufactured by the Singer Sewing Company."

For a man who'd appeared to be flirting with my wife a moment before, he'd certainly dropped the ball. Caroline tittered, glancing at me. The moment stretched, and I was about to say something, to rescue her. She'd been fiddling this entire time, however, with those earrings, and as our glances met, she succeeded in fiddling one off her ear; in an instant she'd lost her hold on the piece altogether, and the noise of it rankled across the table and onto the floor, where we heard it warbling at some remove, then silence.

"Shit," she exclaimed, rising from her seat.

It's a turn in our lives I've had occasion to think of since. The opening and closing of a little door, like the flutter of an eye. For several minutes we were each down on all fours on the warm, old boards, between the legs of the chairs. Time turned to gum, and I was caught up in that physical madness such moments hold, as if a thing could "just disappear." The bartender, coming in to find us so abased, was kind enough to join us.

"What does it look like?" he asked.

"A chunk of gold the size of my hand," I grumbled, while Caroline, turning her head to show its lonely sibling, murmured, "They have sentimental value"—despite which, after what seemed an impossibly long interval, I came up for air amongst the rustlings of my compatriots to discover her seated, brooding with her finger on the sweat of her glass.

"It's gone," she said simply.

"It can't be gone," I replied from my knees.

"It rolled down a crack—"

"It was as large as my hand," I insisted, feeling a pause in the shufflings and scrapings, the eyes of the room upon me, suddenly ashamed of both of us with this "sentimental" earring that likely cost as much as Charles's car. "And," I said, standing and coming back to the table with the desire now only to have this behind me, "I suppose you're right—it's gone."

What satisfaction could be found in such a denouement? I would have opened the door and driven away from everything right then if it could have been managed, though of course it could not. One by one, everyone rediscovered their seats. When Charles finally gave in and sat down, Harvey said, "Well, after all, it was just a little thing"—the ass.

"What *were* we talking about?" Caroline said. Patting her ears, finding them mismatched, she put the remaining earring in her purse. "Oh, yes—you were a sewing machine salesman," she told Charles, her voice rising in fresh disbelief. It was unbearable.

"For Christ sake," I exclaimed. "He isn't serious—" appealing to Charles, relieved to watch a smile touch his face. Funny guy, I recalled with irritation, taking a drink. It hadn't been entirely out of the question, somehow, his working for *The Company.* I laughed, I think. Charles leaned across the table to her again:

"You're a good sport, Mrs. Menger," he said, producing a pack of cigarettes. "I'll tell you what—let me buy you a drink, for being such a good sport."

Charles stood up, and in the shadow of that motion I looked

at Harvey. I don't even know why. Caroline caught my glance and said, "What? What is it?"

She was smiling at first, as Charles strolled toward the bar. I remember Harvey telling her it was nothing, but she wouldn't believe him; and then I remember she began crying as Charles came back with her gin and tonic. "Why are you crying?" Harvey kept saying, and she was saying, "I don't know, I don't know." Charles put the drink down and lit a cigarette, trying to make out what was happening. He glanced at me, but I shook my head. I called her name a few times, but she wouldn't look up.

"I think you've had enough," I said.

"Yes — I have," she replied. "Haven't you?"

"You've had more than enough," I told her.

"Well, who wouldn't?" she said in a gritted voice. "I can't stand it, Milty — you have no idea" — appealing to our friends, everything ugly about us suddenly magnified in that little space. It was Charles, of course: Harvey didn't notice such things, he seemed to nest in a certain amount of ugliness through no fault of his own, but Charles's presence felt like a light switched on in a private darkness.

And so, I thought, watching my wife's face dissolve into mush, this was to be our reunion. At least it was realistic: We were people who'd dried down the years to skin stretched over ticks, delicate bones grown thick. Still, what made it unbearable was that in my mind we persisted, those people we'd once been, like old Muybridge shots, overexposed as if through the power of our own light. Hadn't Harvey, for instance, been a slight yet vital man? A wrestler, actually. Hadn't we met on the school team, when he was one of those whippet fellows?

Two-thirds my size but with a wiry strength, he had a way of looking at you that made you feel he understood, something a little fierce in him; but maybe he never did, and maybe there never was. When I gazed backward, into the years, it seemed there was a day we'd all exploded from a gate, feet flying above the ground in every frame of memory. We loved those ghosts in one another. When I met Caroline, years later, myself tired and she so much younger, I thought I'd found them again in her. And now here she was. We could imagine anything might await us in that light to which we galloped; anything, of course, except this: that it was never us at all, that ghost-liness — only our youths. As if to corroborate my intuition, she grasped the drink Charles had set before her and swallowed it neat, sputtering.

"I don't feel sorry for you, do you hear?" I said quietly. "Everyone else might, but I don't."

"I don't care," she sobbed. "I feel sorry for *you,* if you want to know the truth." But then, just as quickly, it all seemed to be over.

Charles sat down at the table again. Harvey looked at him. Something — some moment — was occurring between them, and then Charles said, "It's digital."

I didn't understand. He extended his left hand, and on his wrist was a watch — black plastic, ferociously ugly, with the dead-looking face such watches have.

It occurs to me now that Harvey was killed not long after — maybe two months — in a bar fight in New Orleans. Someone shot him in the face, after they'd happily spent the evening together, it seemed, buying each other drinks and pickled eggs and at least to the eyes of all witnesses acting like fine, old friends. Lately, I think Caroline could use someone like Harvey around.

There was something frozen and shaking in me, but I tried to forget it. I'd never seen a digital watch before. Even Caroline leaned forward in her seat.

"Not to insist . . . but what *are* you doing down here, then?" Harvey asked. It's funny, now that I've remembered he was to die in the near future, how it looks to me in the glass of memory as if he's already dying.

"I don't really know," Charles replied, eyes flitting over mine. "I got lost. I had a few days to kill, and I was just following a road—I don't even know what it's called." I wondered if he was speaking metaphorically, but that turned out not to be the case: "Just a county road, with a number. If it has a name, no one's ever told me. It's my favorite road, though, anywhere—prettiest road I've ever seen. I've taken it a dozen times," he said after a moment, "only never all the way here. There's a motel along the way, and I make it that far. I stayed there last night, but I thought as I had the time, for once, I'd come up here and look around."

He was deliberately soothing us; still, my wife and I looked to Charles as people might look to a savior.

"What do you think?" Caroline chirped, wiping her eyes.

"Well, I just got here, and like I said, I was lost. I turned onto some other road, and this was the place things petered out, so I stopped. Odd thing was, fellow at the bar knew exactly what I was talking about with my 'prettiest road' bit. He told me if I kept going down Main"—motioning—"I'd wind up back on that road . . ." Charles had become lost in his explanation, and smiled. "Somehow it's all better back there, back toward The True South" — feeling his way. "Out here isn't bad, but the fellow at the bar said so himself: The closer you get to The True South, the prettier it is. It's curvy. There are these hills" — and his hand molded a wild, feminine form in the air. "It's the sort of road you want to drive fast. Just as fast as you can," Charles said, glancing at me. "You like to drive, Milton . . ."

"Milty loves to drive," Caroline put in. "He *already* drives too fast." I hadn't expected to hear my name, but I knew she meant nothing unkind — by then I wanted to believe that neither of us ever did.

"You just follow Main right out of town," Charles repeated. "It *is* my favorite road, I'm sure, anywhere, though I imagine people must die on that last stretch all the time, because I always find myself driving faster than I should. And really, if it came down to it, it's the kind of road I might not especially mind dying on," he told Harvey — I'm fairly sure it *was* Harvey he said it to. "I mean, a man could do a lot worse."

"You're so morbid," Caroline said when he'd stopped to take a drink. And to us: "Isn't he just morbid?"

"Not at all," Charles protested without caring, putting out his cigarette. "Anyway, I'd never have run into any of *you* if it wasn't for that morbid, beautiful little road."

"You said The True South," Harvey spoke up.

"Hey," Caroline said, "wasn't that where your mother was from?"

"That it was a pretty town . . ." Harvey murmured.

"The road — but yes, the town, too."

"I remember it that way," Harvey told his hat. "Of course I was just a kid — I've wondered if it wasn't my imagination."

"Don't you want to go see?" Caroline suggested brightly, the idea bubbling out before it reached the rest of her head. "Why — we're right here, we should just go." But I recalled, at the back of everything, that something was wrong with Harvey's mother. She was very sick, or had died, or been cruel to him. I think it was the last — yes, of course: It was Harvey who died. We each understood.

"See it?" Harvey tested the plastic hat again. "No . . . I don't think I'm ready for all that." For a moment he fell silent, and then he smiled. "Doesn't it make you feel *old*, Milty, seeing Charles? Seeing you alone out here," he added, for we knew him as such a social creature.

"Do you know," I found myself telling Caroline, "to propose marriage, Charley got *twenty people* to lift him up to Joan Peebles's third-floor window." It was the sort of detail my wife loved.

"How ro*man*tic! And she said *yes*, I imagine . . ."

"Actually, she wasn't home," Charles replied dryly.

"But what happened?" she asked.

"Let's say it was just as well," he assured her, and we laughed.

"You're a bad man, Mr. Trembleman," Caroline complained happily, wagging her finger at him, her face the tear-streaked face of a person who's forgotten she was sobbing a moment ago; and then, right as I was about to say something — I have no idea what anymore — Caroline gasped, "Oh — what a lovely ring!" grasping his wrist. "It's much nicer than your class ring, Milty."

"Is it?" I said, feeling I'd had enough jewelry, but leaning forward for a better view of the small gold band with what looked like a ruby in its face. He was dazzling us. He could always do that.

"It's funny," I added after a moment, bending closer to the hand that uncurled obligingly, and seeing there the small capital *S* in what he would later tell me was ivory—the slender, serifed double-curl of the Company insignia. I'd seen it ten thousand times if I'd seen it once, whenever I glanced north from the street on which I was born, above the trees and the peaked roofs to the Singer Sewing plant, its logo poised above and nourishing the town it birthed.

"I've been the area agent down here for seven years," Charles said as I sat back, and he put his hand away. "It's not exactly door to door, but it's a lot of travel. I'm the man who visits the showrooms, brings in the new products, talks shop . . ." Then, more cheerfully: "It must seem like a sort of exile to you."

I suppose he was right—it would have been exactly that; but it wasn't exile I was thinking of that day. What seemed most important, and would become only more so over the following months, was that this was the beginning of the friendship Charles and I would otherwise never have had. I admit, before that afternoon, that I often thought of friendships as the sort of thing you shed as you advance through your thirties into the suburbs of your forties. As your clothes improve and your hair thins, you replace friends, I might have said, with other things: with jobs, with wives.

We all stayed late that night in Carthage, falling back into the past before going our separate ways. We received occasional calls or cards from Charles afterward, posted from the land of his self-described exile. He even visited us, once, last

Thanksgiving, when he was up North to see his mother. In general, the cards were noteworthy only for the world of camp and nostalgia from which they sprang—motel souvenirs in tri-tone color schemes, reproductions of a dream—and I imagined Charles traveling amongst these things, a free man at large in the paradise of others. Then, back in December, he sent me a thank-you note: a postcard with an inscrutable image of what claimed, on the reverse, to be *The Fall of Atlanta*. It is one of many things I wish I had with me, today.

FOR A MAN IN MY POSITION — alone for more than a week in a desolate and decrepit motel in rural Alabama — it might seem strange to say, but I was more lonely in the days leading up to Charles's midnight call, and my subsequent arrival in the South, than I'd ever been, or believe I ever will be again, although at first I didn't realize as much. Perhaps it's difficult to feel isolated within the continuity of busy days of writing checks, appearing early at the gallery and not leaving until well into the evening, circulating at openings. Yet there was the gradual awareness, like a journey into the middle of nothing, that this time Caroline was truly gone. By then — and it was two weeks before that she'd left — every human voice had fallen out of my life. What nervous chatter remained was no more human than the wee-hour sounds emitted by the chair beside the desk in this motel room, devoured from within by a minute and voracious inhabitant.

I'd initially been too angry to take note, but as the weeks settled, and no one came by the house, and no one called, and I found my own calls to people I'd considered our *mutual* friends unreturned, I became aware of this encircling silence. My days at the gallery grew so long that Patrick, my business manager and an unbearable social companion, asked if I was all right. I went back home to sit in the cavern of my living room and wait. Surely the silence had been there long before, unremarked in the general conversation of our life. She had, however, in leaving, drawn attention to it. Now it was all I could hear.

The morning I arrived here, at the Idyll, Thales ("rhymes with nails") appeared in the door of my room, a paper bag held uncertainly in his hands. His attention wandered to the Singer, as yet untouched, shrouded in its case on the table.

"That's Charles's," he said, "isn't it?"

I replied that it was.

"He found it in the field out by the well-house — long time ago." He looked at me, then, with his mild, erased eyes. "This land," he added, "is full of remains of the Civil War. It remembers everything."

"I have a terrible memory," I replied.

"As do I," he agreed. "But that's the thing: I just stay here, and it all comes back to me" — by which I imagined he meant nothing might ever happen to escape him. I watched as he gazed about, half visitor, half auditor. He recalled the bag beneath his arm:

"I suppose I should give this to you, to give to Charles."

"What is it?" I asked, taking the bag, finding it weighed little.

"One of those dandy suits he wears." We both smiled.

I peeked inside, into a nest of blue. Thales went across to the television and picked up the photo from the top of the stand.

"Is this your wife?" he asked.

I nodded.

"She looks," he said, "like she's lost something." He handed the picture to me, took a final tally of the room. "You must miss her."

I awoke at the Atlantis that first night in the South from a black slumber—a shapeless thing full of dread—and momentarily disoriented, believed I was home, and that Caroline was asleep beside me. I at first even mistook for a shutter clapping in the breeze the dull thuds of passion in the room above. In the twilight, I'd conjured for myself from nothing a whole life again, but the sound went on without word or comment into cold understanding, like an act of carpentry.

It was dawn, or shortly thereafter—a slovenly light. The room leered back at me. The wallpaper seemed bacterial rather than mythological, and contained at intervals the flattened ruins of mosquitoes, like fossil archaeopteryx. Putting on my pants, calmly fleeing a nascent claustrophobia, I emerged to find Charles dressed, bags stowed, perched and reading the paper on the back of his car. He'd shaved, ironed his antique suit, and become again that old-young man I remembered from the bar in Carthage.

My disorientation must have persisted in some corner of my face, for taking me by the shoulder, he led us into the diner across the parking lot. It was an unusually warm gesture for the Charles I knew, and it struck me that a long time had passed since anyone had been very kind to me, or truly happy to see me, as Charles had so clearly been the day before in the hospital. The night's dreads, vaporous yet so oppressive they'd congealed to an incident in my mind, shifted off like the bad dreams they were — only dark fears in a dark room, after all — and I allowed him again to soothe me. He idly flipped the paper about, reading aloud, showing me the face and backside of the local *Herald-Monitor-Republican,* with its ubiquitous rampant eagle, poorly kerned gut, and incongruous illuminated logo; reading from this rolled small-town megaphone stories large: about the discovery of a new disease, AIDS, whose little slate calling card was susceptibility — a disease of susceptibility itself; and small: the repellant and embarrassing gas-huffing craze that had crept from the rural subterrain like a half-wit cousin. Gently he read me from the diner into the car, and charmed by these dreads — other people's, after all — I put the car in gear and sailed into the day.

Our ride, I should mention, was that same almost cream-colored sedan Charles had parked opposite the museum in Carthage — the same now parked outside the Idyll. I hadn't been in a truly American car like Charles's Impala for going on two years. Not, in fact, since we'd had Caroline's destroyed amid tears. In such a vehicle, one lies in a heartland of red leatherette, a chariot napped in faux threads to mark the soft arm and leg and sustain the long, cumulative life envisioned for you by the manufacturer, because unless you or your fiancée had been given such a car by an elderly relative mandated by law from ever again taking the wheel ("No, dearest, we can't give it back — she's legally blind, my love"), this was an old person's car.

"Weren't you once a reader of the *Times*?" I asked, shutting the book on this vignette.

Charles folded over another page, murmuring, "I don't follow the nationals anymore." He gazed out the window of his car. "I like viewing the country from the windows of a train, so to speak, instead of a plane."

And then I took a little chance. I sent some slightest piece scurrying across the board begun yesterday, carefully preserved by sleeping hands through the night, a little figure of curiosity as much as fun: "Wouldn't you say," I continued, "that you're playing a bit of a part? With the historical clothes and the car and the newspaper?"

He might not have heard me — he was momentarily lost in wrinkling the paper. But something softened the corners of his mouth. He laid aside his reading and began a minute task with one bandaged hand and a pencil, hunched forward and squinting at his watch. "Singer had a contraption that might have been more to your taste," he said finally. "A 3,800-pound, nine-horse-drawn carriage, capable of seating thirty-one and containing a nursery and smoking room in which he would parade up and down New York's Fifth Avenue. We might have used it to travel to and from your various museums . . ." He swore softly at his timepiece. When he saw me dart several unilluminating glances in his direction, he held up a newer, elaborated digital watch, acquired, I assume, since the one he last displayed in Carthage. It was a mass of indecipherable buttons he seemed to reconsider before saying, "Are you uncomfortable?"

"No — not at all. I don't mean the car, particularly — but the car, then: Don't you think this is a funny car to have, for example, for someone in the prime of his life?"

He removed a pair of reading glasses from his shirt pocket, and armed with these and the pencil, continued prodding until, accomplishing whatever it was he wanted, he braced the watch against his leg and returned it to his wrist.

"So we're going to fight again," he said.

"*No.* No. The car, the clothes . . . they aren't the point. It's just that none of this seems very much like *you.*"

His mittened hand ran along the windshield. "Look around, Milty," he said, "here in 'Prime of Your Life' Alabama. Let me put it this way: If you were a long-distance runner, would you be wearing what you have on? Or, better, if you were a preacher, coming into a town you'd never been to before, wouldn't you want people to recognize you? Wouldn't you want there to be no doubt in their minds about what it is you represent?'"

Beneath my denim jacket I was wearing a gray oxford shirt and a pair of more-or-less new jeans. I'd packed lightly and planned on few formal occasions. I had a sweatshirt to keep out the cold at night. But this was, once again, irrelevant:

"I'm driving a car for a sick friend," I said after a pause.

"What if someone were to see me, pulling up in front of their store, with you at the wheel, as you are now?"

"They might ask if you were all right—"

"They would not," he assured me with a shake of the head. "It isn't their place to ask if I'm all right. We aren't here, after all"—he gestured out the window toward the flat fields beyond the road, the little aluminum houses scattered like dirty shoes across the glorious land of Kennel—"to receive comfort. We are here to give it."

Charles fell silent. I glanced at him for a smile, but instead the paper rose back into place. Did every traveling salesman see himself, in the darkroom of his mind, as a missionary? There'd been, though, an excitement in his voice, a tremor in the hand that shored up the paper wall. He was telling the truth, inasmuch as he wasn't playing a game. He'd never been a humble man, and he wasn't now. It was then I perceived we'd entered the gray matter of suburbia around Birmingham, and a few minutes later the white bulk of the Meadowview Mall sprawled into view.

The Meadowview is a mall of the new philosophy: Its windowless façade, veneered with pea-granite, encloses a 68-degree fluorescence. I parked as near the doors as I could while Charles put on his jacket, and then together we strolled the squeaking and reflecting floors beneath anticipatory banners of Easter. Giant planters of steroid-flushed houseplants lay in symmetrical islands, crowned by novelty rabbit-egg baskets. Women clustered in pods around baby strollers or seating opportunities; men gazed through windows and itemized their solitary ventures. We passed a sewing store, but Charles guided us on until at last we arrived at "Archie's for Men."

"Get the two best suits for yourself you can find," he said.

"The best?" I asked, examining the display windows, a sort of homage to departed styles. It was as if we'd come to a barn and he'd told me, "Go on in and win yourself a bride."

"That's right. You can do no wrong in Archie's," he explained. "They won't let you.

"You think I'm joking," he added when I hesitated. "But after you've found your suits, put one of them on — they do on-the-spot alterations — and then come collect me from the Modern" — the sewing store we'd passed. "I'll be waiting for you." At which he left.

I stared after him, half expecting others to do likewise. He was a ridiculous man, I thought, seeing him fade among the garish colors of his fellow shoppers. He was an insolent man. In the moment I wished I'd said as much—at a distance he didn't seem hard to ridicule—yet there was something unshakable in Charles. It was perhaps the only thing that kept me from leaving him there: the intimation that some significance awaited me; that he was, in fact, the agent of something besides buttonholes. His entire manner in the car, I reflected, wasn't unlike the silent preamble I was given during college when he chaperoned me to something he was certain I'd find an aesthetic *treat*. And then as soon as I entered Archie's, I felt I'd taken my place in a formal composition—that I was to be dressed for my role. The feeling began quietly, but had become unmistakable when I emerged forty minutes later from the hands of the cataracted old men with their tape measures and pins.

For I did perceive, circulating through the arcade back toward Modern Sewing, past the same clustered ladies (did they not, for the first time, look up mistily from their lunches, as if at the distant call of a stag?), past the glazed eyes of the singular gentlemen shoppers (moving aside, as if recognizing within me the secret shield of Junior Partner), a certain personal invisibility. Not to say I was, in any conventional sense, unseen—if anything, I felt festooned with glances. But they looked upon me now as one of their own. In the apportionment of polyester to cotton, the ampleness of an ample suit upon an ample man, they knew me. I was, as we all must be and as Charles himself had suggested, one amongst their beloved typologies. I was no longer that creature of oddity and superstition: the stranger.

And it was in a mist of such sensations that I stole into the Modern, granting the salesgirl who joined me at the door a knowing turn of the head, making my way between the blue and beige plastic backs of the machines — a field of praise, a crèche for industry — toward the rear of the store, where Charles and a portly, sad-eyed fellow lounged by the Culligan.

"This must be your man," he said to Charles, heaving his face into a smile as he reached for my hand. "I feel as if I already know you."

"Mr. Leigh's an old friend," Charles explained. "A non-sewer."

"*Eliot,*" Mr. Leigh suggested. His eyes fell, I noticed, continually upon Charles, whom he referred to as "Chuck." "Chuck tells me you're helping him out, Mr. . . ."

"Menger. Milton. That's right," I said. Seeing that something more was incumbent upon me, I added, "Nice shop you have here."

"I was just saying how I miss the days of the old Skyview Sewing Center" — his soft, slightly gray hands streaking out to smooth a pile of folded cloth samples. "Back when people sold their wares in town. I supposed I'm old-fashioned, but I'm getting used to things, isn't that so?"

"It's a business of change," Charles agreed.

"And you're not kidding," Eliot hooted, eyes going far away. "When you think back to those first machines — made of wood, Milty. By tailors, of all people" — shaking his head.

Charles smiled. "Yes, the fine-grained imagination of the Frenchmen, Thimonnier and his people. Milton here has just come from the tailors, actually."

There was a polite pause. Eliot continued: "Sad, really, when you think about it — destroyed by their own wooden demons," adding, "Have you seen the new models?"

I glanced at Charles, who merely raised his brows. Eliot, meanwhile, tripped back several steps to stand beside a machine like a medical device — a baby-blue, high-tech microscope. "I guess I haven't," I said, selecting a tone shy of mockery. What I knew of sewing machines at the time could be lost in a thimble; I saw, however, that the engine in question had none of the wasp-waisted elegance of the Victorian models. It was vulgar, carbuncular with membrane keys, the slick, anatomically vague body adolescent and even repulsive. I was about to remark on exactly this, yet something stayed me, and I leaned closer for a better look; for it was as if sewing machines were made for an entirely different purpose than I'd been led to believe, that I had no previous inkling of — or just an inkling.

"Well, isn't that something," I murmured, finding my companions' eyes upon me. But let me explain:

To resort to memory again, that developing tank of the mind, I recognized the sensation I felt in confronting the sewing machine as akin to one I'd known shortly after college when, on a rare occasion, I'd visited Charles in lower Manhattan and found him sketching a model — a woman our age I remembered from literature classes — who sat nude and still beneath the windows of his kitchen. Beside Charles, there were several other young artists, gathered like bees around a queen. I'd had a very proper upbringing (my mother would have said "We didn't *know* naked people"), and at that time my experience with women existed under only the most furtive conditions. I took a seat in the hall and waited for them to finish, glancing now and then into the brightness. Twenty years later in the showroom, I felt the light of that distant hall wash over me, as if I'd seen *through* for a sliding moment, as when you catch the reflection of your own eye in an unexpected mirror. There was, I saw, a place on the blue plastic Singer, where it curves over from the column rising from the machine's base and begins the long horizontal traverse, that to touch would be like laying a hand in the hollow behind a woman's knee.

Perhaps my perceptions are shaped by subsequent events, but all the same, since then I've come to see something of this in every Singer sewing machine, even the dark and corseted creatures of the nineteenth century; the difference, though, in the new models such as the one before me in the Modern being that of the girl, for she's become a nylon girl. She's the girl no one wants, except once. A flush crept like a rash on my face. There emerged a thing suddenly terrible and knowing in the very word *showroom*.

"I told you he had an eye," Charles remarked to Eliot. I caught, though, no hint of lubricity in Eliot's face when he beckoned a sales assistant from where she loitered at the front of the store—a handsome, bucktoothed brunette of perhaps twenty, wielding fingernails that seemed to preclude manual labor. She arrived before us a moment later, inquiring in a raw voice, "Mr. Leigh?"

"Lilly," Eliot said, "would you give Messrs. Trembleman and Menger a tour of the 1411?"

"Oh," she replied with a look that further discomforted me, "I'm sure Mr. Trembleman knows all about it"; but she wheeled around in her polyester skirt suit, and slipping into a seat, removed from the cabinet below the machine a length of white satin.

I've found in recent days that hours seem required to commit to the grave and irreversible action of binding cloth to cloth, but placing her fabric lightly, nearly thoughtlessly beneath the presser foot, she sat up very straight and, touching the machine gently in several places, commenced to sew. Throwing a glance at us over her shoulder, she hit a button or two on the side of the 1411, prodding it lightly, and the electric whirring in which the room was now laved ground down several tones.

"Did you know, Milton," Eliot said, eyes flickering to Charles, "that after the Second World War, employees returning to Singer factories in Germany accepted handfuls of needles instead of paychecks? It was, in fact, pure kindness: They were worth more as objects of trade than the devalued mark."

I replied that I didn't.

"And can you imagine that during the war," Charles now informed us, "German flyers avoided bombing Singer plants in France and England, believing the company was German-owned?" He laid his hand upon a nearby machine. "Generations of their countrymen had worked in Singer factories under domestically recruited management, and the Germans, as did Singer employees in most parts of the world, believed that they were working for a local concern. The Company and its people were everywhere, *came* from everywhere. It is the ubiquity of the Company that is, perhaps, its greatest success. The manual alone has been translated into fifty-four languages."

"Admiral Richard Byrd," Eliot noted, touching my sleeve, "brought six Singers on his Antarctic expedition."

I glanced into Eliot's face, the thick bulb of his nose. His hand sank away. I'd recovered sufficiently that I sought

Charles's eyes for an acknowledgment of what I felt must be a game they were playing, but Charles's attention was upon Lilly. She was oblivious to the chatter around her, working in a more concentrated way, as if advancing toward some grand theme. Periodically she'd stop and take a scissor like a garden shear from the cabinet, cut another length from her hoard, and fold this, too, beneath the shimmering needle. Allowing my eye to stray over the body of the machine and her haunch, closely clasped in her skirt and moving with the rocking of her foot on the electric treadle, once more I thought of the nude seated in the window of Charles's apartment; and it seemed to me that this woman and her machine were together like the model, but it was within the machine, strangely, that the nakedness resided. I looked up to find Eliot addressing me:

"What a man he must have been!" he suggested.

"Singer or Byrd?" I asked.

"Yes, past centuries teem with men who seem larger than life — but Singer, Singer of course," Eliot replied.

Lilly held up and appraised her creation. I could not see, yet, what it might be, but it had appendages like those of an animal.

"The first machines he made were home machines," Charles mused into this moment of examination. "A humble undertaking in its way — though he was not a humble man. He began by changing the lives of women — the disenfranchised — yet when he died in 1875 he was worth $13 million."

"In 1875, the average manufacturing wage," Eliot threw out, "was $2.39 a day. And so," he continued, "it would have taken nearly 15,000 years for an ordinary laborer working every day and spending *nothing* . . ."

We watched Lilly hemming a soft edge of her demonstration.

"Older," Charles commented, "than the biblical age of the Earth—"

At which I broke in: "Lilly, what *is* it that you're making there?"—for I felt utterly benighted amidst this shoptalk; but also because she'd paused at her work, and while the object she manufactured seemed familiar, it remained elusive until she rose from her seat, presenting with a cry—"For *you,* Mr. Menger"—a long-sleeved, button-down shirt.

For an instant I colored, newly amazed at the way these people, who to look at knew nothing about dressing themselves, seemed bent on improving my wardrobe. Yet an entire other part of me felt that I'd just stared at this woman during the course of some intimate act. I held my tongue and took the offered garment in hand.

"Thank you, Lilly," I said. "It's wonderful . . ." and reflexively, as one does when given a shirt, I held it against myself. As she smiled this time, I saw she was missing one of her top teeth. It was a dazzling and proud gap one would expect only in a child.

"Go on," she said, still beaming, "it's yours."

Again I thanked her, but her work apparently done, she performed something like a curtsy and stole off into the store, leaving us clustered in the wake of her invention. No one had remarked on the fact that the garment was impossibly small—the shirt of a slighter, slender man—as could be seen as soon as I led the little arms out along my own.

"You've met Lilly before," Eliot was saying to Charles; and Charles said that he had, recalling a slogan that Isaac Singer barked when he first opened his showrooms to crowds of in-credulous observers accustomed to think of sewing machines as massive and dangerous industrial objects: "Even tiny, frail women can operate a Singer!" And although this in no way described our particular girl, it served as a bridge back to reminiscence.

They were, it seemed to me, soldiers of the empire, sur-veying the field of past campaigns. If they'd discussed what I might ordinarily have considered business, it had occurred before my arrival; yet there was, perhaps, an antique form of salesmanship at work here, or a Southern habit: to speak around the subject without ever coming to dollars and cents. I reflected that it was not as if we'd ever, for even a moment, left the topic of sewing machines.

ACROSS THE PARKING LOT that separates the Idyll motel from Route 219, across the road and then across the fields, the sun was germinating in the trees when I went looking for Thales. There was, beside my own, a single car at the far end of the building — a Chevrolet with Alabama plates. At that hour, the air has no haze or taste of gasoline. A mist was rising from the vegetation, and the land being flat in these parts, the road disappears into itself in either direction. Without traffic, it seems more like a sandbar. After a time I came out from beneath the rusting veranda and stood out on the opposite shore.

I was hoping for assistance. In my pocket was the burnt-out bulb from the Singerlight. I think I've already mentioned my host — a nonsewer, but a tremendous handyman. A half hour passed and then I noticed, a ways down, some motion in the margin of shadow where the sun slanted over the ditch between the fields and the eroded blacktop. It might have been an animal, but I was fairly sure already that it would be Thales, who was usually up at this hour, too, and soon enough I made out the orthopedic shape of a man bearing a metal detector.

I watched him creep along the bottom of the ditch, detector in hand, earphones clamped to his gray head, staring alternately at the disk-shaped snout of the machine and the controls on the handle. Besides the motel itself, all these fields belong to him. I'd watched him travel this same track of siding on the riding mower yesterday, perhaps to prepare the ground for today's round of detections. While the grass and weeds in early March were already knee-high in the field above his head, the ditch was a gentle place, like a golf course. I thought he might pass me by, so intent did he appear on the sidlings of his machine, and I was preparing to wave my hand; but when he was directly below me, he glanced up and pulled the meaty vinyl muffs around his neck.

"Good morning," I said, smiling down at him, supremely conscious, as I always am when I see Thales after any length of time, of my white teeth. He has what Caroline would term a "bad mouth." I have a broad, what my wife has judiciously described as "hearty," face, at which people usually smile back.

"Yes," he agreed, maintaining his anticipatory demeanor, blinking but not smiling. "We're lucky, aren't we" — though in the three or so weeks that I've known him, he's never struck me as *lucky*. I wondered if he was a religious man, and I asked. He shrugged and stooped to pick something up.

"After two hundred years," he said, "you'd think there'd be more down here than automotive debris."

His eyes twitched out across the road at the motel, little of which would have been visible to him save the green asphalt roof. Thales is a mousy fellow, like a maquette for a larger, handsome man. He walks with a slight limp, from an injury sustained while serving as a mine sweep during the Korean War. Shaking his head, he turned to look behind him, along the ditch, then put whatever it was he'd found in his pocket.

"I was going to drop by later," he mumbled. "I found something else of his, you see" — speaking now of Charles. "When did you say he was coming?" He allowed the detector's head to swing from the straps that yoked it to his back, stealing a glance at the gauges.

"He said sometime next week," I replied, putting my hands in my pockets and wondering if this was exactly what I'd told Thales when I'd first arrived — "sometime next week" — a week ago. It probably was. "But you know how he is."

"It amazes me," he noted, staring up from his wallow, "that he ever sold anything to anyone." I had to agree.

For a moment we stood opposite each other among the fine new fingers of sun, Thales in his overalls, myself in my shirt with the torn tail that I'd failed to repair, which I'd put on simply because it was in my hand when the light went out on the Singer.

"Speaking of Charles," I said, when he looked ready to move along, "I burned out a bulb on that little 221 of his I've been running in my room."

"Working on something nice?" he asked.

"Is there a hardware store nearby where I could pick up another?"

"Do you have the bulb on you?" he suggested.

I removed it from my pocket, descended the slope, and placed it in his diminutive hand. His palms and fingers are yellow and slightly flattened. They remind me of raccoon paws. The bulb rested there like an egg, an arc of burn inside the glass.

He murmured what I took for an affirmation, and I followed him back up from the ditch and then across the road and over and behind the motel, along a deer track through the weeds. From the rear, the motel looks abandoned. Tiny windows peer from the bathrooms and rust runs down the cinder-block wall. An old Coke machine lies turned on its side, together with the carcass of an air conditioner. It all vanishes around a small, dirty hill, likely dug out to make the foundations. Thales had placed the headphones back over his ears, checking the path as he went; and though he was exploring a piece of land he'd been over, surely, thousands of times, once he stooped and lifted something from the fringe of the path. After glancing at it, he slid it into the chest pocket of his overalls and continued on his way. He pulled the headphones off again only when we'd reached the door of one of the corrugated sheds that lay on this side of the riot of old privet hedge that surrounds his house.

"I don't know," he said, opening a padlock with a large mangle of keys, "but I think we must have one like it in here somewhere."

I've noticed that Thales, perhaps from having spent years as a night owl — something to which I'm a relative newcomer — can see, or behaves as if he can see, in nearly any sort of light or lack thereof. I stood in the doorway, trying to adjust my vision to the interior dimness into which he'd climbed. It was, however, as if I were staring at a sheet of brown paper, not an inhabitable, three-dimensional space, and eventually I resigned myself to wait for a light to be thrown. I heard him pawing among boxes, the rustlings of fine objects of glass and metal, and I sat on the doorstep to regard the sun again, which had grown to be something the size of a thumbprint, throbbing and turned horizontally among the higher branches of the tree line. When he emerged a few minutes later, I wasn't surprised to see between his fingers a little bulb like the one I'd given him, but with a brass-colored screw instead of a silver-metal one. He took his spectacles out and matched the figures on the glass, holding the two together for me to corroborate, the new bulb still powdery with dirt that he blew off before parting with it.

He left me then and disappeared back inside the dark shack, and after waiting a moment for his return, I sat back down with the bulbs in hand. There was a heavy quiet. On a day on the edge of spring in this part of Alabama the air seems a suspension of pollen, stirred only by the murmur of insects and punctured at intervals by a soft clatter of pans from the house. I was so fixed upon these things, smelling the reek of earth and moldering wood, that I didn't hear Thales come up behind me until he spoke:

"A shame about the inner state."

I didn't understand, and then I did. Listening more carefully, I discovered that I could hear a high and distant whine—I'd thought it might be bees—and knew what he meant.

"I wouldn't have noticed," I admitted.

"You have good ears, don't you, Mr. Menger? I don't know how long the sound was there before someone drew my attention to it, but since I've been paying it any mind, it's as if it grows a little closer every year.

"I've been thinking a great deal of late about the senses," he continued when I didn't reply. "And it's come to seem to me that they must be communicable." He watched my face to see how this sat. I gave my attention to the replacement bulb, and he said, "How many times has someone remarked to you that they've heard or smelled something, and then, lo and behold, you feel suddenly that yes — you, too, can hear or smell the same thing."

"Perhaps," I noted, "what you're describing is more a matter of suggestibility."

He mulled this over. His mouth opened, and remained so. I thought this might signal an end to the conversation, but it did not: "Suggestibility," he replied at last, "implies some degree of irreality." After a further pause, a pause long enough to generally introduce a fresh topic, he said, "You mentioned yesterday that you were having trouble sleeping."

Late this morning, I replaced the bulb in the Singerlight with the one Thales gave me. With the manual's encouragement, I then spent several hours threading the bobbin case, setting the needle, and lubricating the various parts of the machine. My test stitches, however, bore little resemblance to those illustrated for me on page 18 of my guide.

I was reminded that when Singer built his first patentable sewing machine with George Zeiber in 1850, he initially believed that the device was a failure. As the day wore into night, his machinists and assistants had one by one given up, and he, too, had at last in Zeiber's company left the shop, admitting that perhaps, as was proverbially understood at the time, the sewing machine *was* an impossible invention to make practical. Nearly home, he suddenly remembered that he'd neglected to adjust the thread tension—it was just such a problem beneath which I labored.

The lockstitch, de facto stitch among home machines, was created in 1844, and first used in an innovative but unreliable machine patented by Elias Howe in 1846. It utilizes two threads—a top thread that penetrates the material with the assistance of a needle, and a bottom thread drawn back and forth beneath on a shuttle—to interlock and hold. The top thread in this scheme traps the shuttle thread in fresh loops with each advance of the needle, automatically and continuously drawing from the bobbin, and one is left, given a proper tension, with two stitches that appear complete and discrete, top and bottom, but in fact "link arms" within the ground of the fabric, keeping each other in place. It is reminiscent of a formal line dance, and of the necessary interplay between the over- and under-stories in a narrative, relying as it does on the maintenance of tension, on the blurring of a succession of discrete actions into one continuous line.

Until the early nineteenth century, the Western world was still a world of discretion, where the waltz, with its paired couples, was considered in some circles too risqué—too like the conjugation of the sexes. A skilled tailor working at the time might hope to place forty stitches in a minute; pictures were cast with chemicals on stone or paint on canvas; and we looked, soldiers and murderers all, at the people we killed. It's a world difficult to imagine now: The rapid superposition of nearly identical moments, allowing change while maintaining continuity, has entranced us, relegating that world and its actors to antiquity. Change in its smallest form in the end changed everything. The first Singer sewing machines could place nine hundred stitches in a minute. The movie camera, the combustion engine, the machine gun — each used a series of points to create the illusion of a line; each rested on the precision of the machine age, whose parts were made to coincide to perfect effect, again and again. But the sewing machine was the first.

WHEN HER AUNT FUCHSIA DIED three years ago, Caroline's tears were doled out like pearls —you might have made a choker for that poor woman, parted first from her car by the state, and then from her life by a progressive loss of vision that elided the distinction between "walk" and "don't walk" at the corner of Bird and Bride. But how my wife loved her '68 Pontiac, the first thing shed on the old woman's path to the grave! Theorists and readers of popular magazines alike have claimed that we've left behind the machine age and are entering something new — a nuclear or silicon age — which is perhaps why we love our machines as we do. They are to us, after all, what the draft horse and the spinning wheel became during the industrial era: at first merely antiquated; later rediscovered, at a safe distance, as antique. I would go so far as to say that Caroline believed her aunt had given up life itself so that this car might endure. Yet some months later we stood on a promontory of dirt above a pit of car chunks and watched the wrecker lift the old hulk and drop it into the compactor — or I watched; Caroline wetly buried her face in my shirt.

"We couldn't very well take it into the yard and shoot it, could we?" I soothed. Someone below pushed a red button on the side of the yellow iron box, and the walls moved in. To where we stood came a delicate sound. When at last Caroline looked back around, a crane had placed her little car-cube amidst a vast pile of white, red, and blue. It was now one of many blues, the ones uppermost glistening in the sun. She put on her aviators.

"I want to leave for Memphis next Saturday," she said, with the understanding that this had been our deal. She felt a trifle guilty, I would guess, as she knew I'd hated that car, and she had, knowingly and in exchange for a vacation, just allowed the transport of her beloved to the knackery, as it were.

For my part, it's true I'd hoped for something more exotic, but after all, we'd just witnessed a death. Her family lay in Memphis — in my mind I saw them like crabs scuttling over carrion — and deaths often pull us toward the cradle of our people. Caroline sniffed and held on to my arm as I steered us from our lofty perch.

"We'll visit Harvey," she said unexpectedly, brightly, turning from the vehicles.

"Harvey," I repeated. One can never be sure at certain times exactly why one says the things one does. Perhaps I was irked at how rapidly she'd converted her currency of sorrow to pleasure, though I'd sensed this subject might arise. He lived in Nashville, not far from our destination, and of my old friends he was Caroline's favorite — he'd become a fixture of our trips to the Metcalf homestead, domain of her ingratiating ancestors and siblings.

"What," I asked, "does Harvey have to do with anything?"

"Well, we *know* he'll be there—"

"But you can't mean," I said, trying to separate her gently from the idea, "that we'd have to spend another trip with Harvey?"

My wife regarded me with confusion. She shook her head and her bangs swung around above those vast gold earrings —the size of small fists, really—as she said, "You *told me* he was the only thing that made the entire state bearable."

"Let's not be hasty—"

"It was your idea," she exclaimed, not without truth. I held up my hand. For when the possibility of a trip to Memphis had reared its head a week before—at first, I believe, in veiled rebuff, during the initial phases of this latest and most successful campaign for the destruction of the Pontiac—it *had* been I who'd drawn consolation from Harvey's name.

"It's just," I told her, picking our way along an avenue of cars in various states of devastation, "that I think it would be nice, for a change, to have some time alone, the two of us, when we're not giving alms to your family."

Which was also true, though of course it's further true that having begun any argument, there's a sadness in abandoning it to the untrained yet numerically superior forces of one's adversary. I had opted for the path of coherence over historicity. Caroline, choosing to view this in a different light, has often instead remarked that my arguments proceed by drafts.

"I mean," she said on this occasion, in that shrill voice she gets when she feels she has the high ground—the voice of a cocktail waitress, which, incidentally, she was, once I'd peeled away her nominal claim to the stage — "you're saying the exact opposite of what you said five minutes ago."

"Sweetie, what were my *exact* words?" I asked, allowing her to present her journal of conversational clippings until she admitted, as she inevitably admits, "I don't know — *you* know. It's different, that's all. It's not the same."

It is a tactic — what she sees as *my* tactic — that she finds inherently slippery, though this is to miss the beauty of an outlook such as mine, where the argument becomes a thing to be crafted. Such dialogues are, I've reminded her on many occasions, the very image of our shared life together: an initial impression not merely corrected but perfected by the other party. Keeping within reasonable bounds, the impression is revised, and then, within the confines of the correction, the process repeated, until the statement of theme, variation, and repetition yields a result that is absolutely classical: Perhaps in a slightly different form than the original conjecture, but in a form inseparable from it, rooted in it, we arrive at a statement of facts that may be accepted as true by both parties. When I consider it now, it's like the process of memory itself — the way no figure of the past ever appears except within the ground of the present. Caroline, however, seems to find little solace in this — or she pretends to remember a golden moment (tricky, memory) when this wasn't the case.

"Your difficulty, dearest," I told her, "lies in your belief that just because one comes to a truth late in an argument, it's any less true." But things had clearly taken a bad turn.

"It's dishonest. Look, you're doing it right now," she said unhappily as we reached my German machine–undestroyed car in which I'd accompanied my wife on her own vehicle's fateful voyage. "You're just making this up as you go, waiting to see what I fall for. It's not right," she concluded with a final shake of the head when I climbed in beside her.

We drove for a time in silence. I was aware that some sort of scene lay ahead, an iceberg of hostilities, but I was cheered by the recollection that at the end of this particular journey, at home, was the first of what I hoped would grow to be a collection of Kennel's canvases — purchased dearly only two weeks before, and arrived that morning by courier, a benediction cast over my errand of destruction. It was small, containing in a rectangle the size of a dinner tray a somber view of a still, dark creek, overhung with willow, pricked with the points of water lilies and a great stroke of sun. Upon the near shore, laid out on a miniature bank of sand, were a woman's clothes, though as for the onetime wearer of the clothes, there remained no trace. The painting had taken me months to track down, and longer to convince the seller to part with. It was marvelous to think that this treasure awaited me uncrated in the hall.

"Do you know what I love about you?" Caroline said suddenly, into my pleasures. "It's that you can't even be honest with yourself. From minute to minute you don't have any idea what you're trying to say. You don't have any idea," she screeched, "*what* you think."

I'd averted my face, but felt her stare upon my cheek. I replied very slowly: "What I think, is that one of the last true pleasures afforded me in this thankless and mistaken world is the consolation of excursions. And I do not mean" — turning toward her now where she moved her pointed little jaw from side to side, trying to determine in what direction I would mislead her — "exclusively in the sense of all the many 'trips' we make together, though these aren't unimportant. It is, more specifically, the idea of collaboration I wish to draw your attention to. Collaboration on all of our excursions, be they spatial, intellectual, or otherwise. I can be quite concrete if you wish: When, for example, we went to Mexico last year," I inquired, "who did all the planning, found the hotels, arranged the tickets?"

She continued watching with narrowed eyes. "Me," she replied after a waver, tone defensive, as if she feared I was plotting to take even this away from her.

"And who always lays out intricate schemes surrounding the local festivals and the resurrection of whatever regional dead saint?" I asked.

"Me," she said more quietly.

"Yet who," I said, having brought us to a conversational overlook not unlike the breezy plateau we'd just abandoned at the dump, "who is it who gets us lost because he loses his watch and catches the wrong ferry; and who leads us through some swamp of a back road, along what was never truly a shortcut, on a bus powered by mosquitoes, to a tiny town right on the ocean, where we spend the rest of the trip — amicably, if I remember anything?"

"You," she said after a pause, contrite, even beginning to smile, staring out the window at the blur of fields that would accompany us home. She was, I expect, reflecting on the trip to Mexico, but it was shading into thoughts of Memphis, and from there into the field of all excursions, and that consolation that remains in these miniatures of lives to be lived long after the larger life has looked back one too many times upon itself and turned to salt. There is often, I reflected in the seat beside her, little to choose between travel and flight.

By the late light sweeping the summer lands, I saw her face was turned toward the cream-colored past—less true but kinder, I suppose, than an age of gold. The glow still hung among the strands of hair blown about her mouth as she glanced from the window and said:

"Does this mean I can call Harvey?"

It was growing late when Charles and I left the Modern Sewing showroom and drove into the ahistorical Alabama evening. We hadn't chosen a busy or crowded road, but we stopped at a dozen lodgings — permutations of the Atlantis — without luck, until in the end we were forced, due, as it turned out, to a local birdwatchers' convention (and to Charles's refusal, I should add, to stay in any of the many chain motels), to not only share quarters for the night, but accept accommodations undesirable even by Charles's standards.

For while I myself found little difference between this evening's and our previous night's choice of shelter, I noticed that my companion instantly regarded the Piney Lodge with suspicion. It was understandable that whatever superstitions — or *routines* — he operated under had surely intensified since his recent escape from the fire. But shortly a more precise reason for his anxieties became clear: After asking to see the one available room, he'd returned in a froth to the front desk, enumerating vexations both vague and particular yet impressive in the cumulative impression they gave of irrelevance. By the time I began exchanging looks with the concierge, I was certain that unfamiliarity alone—in this case coupled with a sense, amidst the unfamiliar, of being forced into a singular decision—offended Charles. The concierge attempted to reason with him:

"Mr. Trembleman—please, Mr. Trembleman, remember yourself," he repeated melodiously. "I cannot give you another room, for it is under reservation."

"But I've taken this road a hundred times," Charles returned—it had been his refrain—again stretching across the counter his bandaged hand and a business card. "How can I *not* know you? And now you insist you've only got *one room*?"

Charles glanced at me, then back to the man. "Let me speak to the manager."

"I *am* the manager, Mr. Trembleman—"

"*How* can you be the manager?" Charles cried, running his hand down his face as if he'd been over this. "*If* you were the manager, *then* I would know you." He was sweating; there was something feverish in his eye. He'd become over-excited.

"We'll take the room—it's fine," I told the concierge, realizing I had to save Charles from himself. "He's not well," I said of my friend, though it struck me that Charles simply appealed to those values most cherished by the exile: the meticulous, unshakable missionary among the heathen; the British governor stationed in his tropical outpost, approximating tea by steeping a local root vegetable in tannic river water. Through a half-open door at the back of the office I glimpsed sleeping mats and a candled shrine to the Blue God. The concierge, realizing he was engaged with a divided body of colonists, concentrated his efforts upon myself—a betrayal that didn't go unnoticed:

"I know every inn and motor lodge between Birmingham and Walton," Charles exclaimed, turning to me and then staring about the room. "I could *never* stay anyplace like this. It's too . . ." But in the midst of this pronouncement, he grew suddenly calm; as it turned out, he'd recalled that some years ago he *had* stayed at the Piney Lodge — a scrap of motel stationery sporting the establishment's former name reminded him — and apparently assured in this way that we weren't straying entirely outside the roof of habit, he was able to endure all of the particulars that only moments ago seemed anathema. He went quietly off to smoke and await me while I completed the registry. By the time I was finished and came to our room, I found him asleep on a bed, and went out to lean on one of the pillars of the veranda.

I hoped, I think, that a forced cohabitation might present me a better occasion to share my domestic disasters — the sort of revelation that occurs more easily under cover of darkness, in the wings of sleep — considering that if he laughed, blamed me, even treated me to the indifference that came so naturally to him, what of it? The trance of our strange afternoon in the showroom had worn away, and his obsessive harangue with the concierge had again diminished him in my eyes. Yet a feeling of mild desolation also returned, similar to what I'd felt the night before. Perhaps there's something biological in the onset of darkness that pulls at a man far from home. In my disheartened state, I was coming to agree with Charles that the Piney Lodge was decidedly inferior: Before me lay a parking lot and a small pool not unlike the one gracing the Atlantis, but half full of water, black with leaves, and separated from the surrounding pavement by what could only be described as dirt. Across the way, beyond the parking lot, a windowless slab appeared on closer inspection to be a gentlemen's club.

The air contained a meager warmth, the grass and enervated shrubs lining the road a meager color. Aware of the motion of cars on the road as one is aware of the ticking of a clock in an otherwise quiet room, I was regarding the parking lot and pool, looking into the pen of green rubberized chain-link and its hollow blue-and-black-fouled bowl, when from this reverie I was pulled with a start by the consciousness that upon one of a handful of white plastic lounge chairs beside the pool, a person was reclined and watching me. I'd been staring directly at him or her without noticing. Finding the sensation of sudden communion unpleasant, I involuntarily stepped back into the dark of the doorway.

The moment came and went like a chill. The transparency of my retreat, however, left me embarrassed. I hesitated in the shelter of the room, then casually strolled out again, as if I'd meant only to duck inside to check on something. The person in the chair—a woman with peroxide-blond hair, in a business suit, I ascertained rapidly—was still watching from her seat; or I presumed as much, finding her in sunglasses. And then she smiled. Carried by the momentum that had swung me back outside, I returned the smile and ambled over to stand at the edge of the fence.

"It's a beautiful day," I said, not untruthfully.

"It was. A bit cold for a swim," she replied. Excepting her misapplied wardrobe, she looked as if she really intended to catch a little sun. She turned slightly from me and angled her chin back toward the matted sky.

"You're here with Chuck, aren't you?" I thought I heard her say.

"Excuse me?"

"Charles—Trembleman—you're here with Charles." She turned to me again. "I don't remember you from Singer."

"I'm not—I'm just giving him a hand. His hands"—the pun was garish and she seemed to sit up a little and pay attention—"he was burned, you know, in one of those motel fires down here."

"I heard something about it. Shocking, isn't it," she said, not sounding at all shocked. I felt, suddenly, that I'd intruded upon her, and let go of the fence. She was the sort of person I wouldn't have expected so far from taxis and martini bars. She spoke rapidly, like a typewriter. Beyond her Wayfarers, I couldn't see her eyes, and I gave my attention to the highway, with its caravans of trucks and various rural transports.

"He didn't burn his face, did he?"

The question surprised me. "No."

"He's lucky then. He couldn't give money away without that face." She paused for an instant. "Have you ever seen a man on fire, Mr. — ?"

"Milton," I answered. "Milton Menger. I'm sorry if I—"

She smiled. "My name's Jane. There are piles of us."

"Excuse me?" I said.

"Milton's an unusual name, Milton. There are piles of Janes. My husband, or ex-husband, told me so once." She raised her hand and checked the time on the inside of her wrist. "Are you married, Milton?"

"I am, actually . . ." although I trailed away into complexity.

"That's a pity," she said. "Otherwise, I'd say we should have a drink. There's not really any sun left."

"I'd like a drink," I told her.

"I'm not making a pass at you, if that's what you're thinking."

"No, no," I said, although this had been pretty much exactly what I'd believed.

"It's just you're a friend of Charles's —"

"Yes, we should all have a drink —"

"And Charles doesn't like me very much, Milton. I have to say, I'm surprised to find you traveling around with him. You look all wrong." She didn't elaborate.

"How do you know Charles?" I asked.

"I'm an area agent — for the Central South."

Now it was my turn to smile.

"What?" she said.

"Oh, nothing" — and as she continued to look at me — "I just never expected to meet two of you, let alone in one place." I might have pointed out that the very nature of the job, each agent granted an exclusive territory, seemed to forbid such a thing; but as if to demonstrate the fallacy of my thinking, Charles emerged at that moment from our room, and lighting a cigarette, slouched across the lot toward us.

"Ms. Garnet," he said, parking himself beside me at the fence.

"Hello, Charles," she replied, sounding pleased. "You poor thing. You must be in pain."

An hour later, we reconvened at a converted fast-food restaurant a short distance down the highway. A peeling reflective material had been laid over the windows of the yellow brick structure. It looked like a blind head wearing a red hat.

Charles, at my suggestion, had changed into the shirt Lilly made for me. It fit him so well as to be indistinguishable from what he'd worn in the showroom, save that it had a sort of disco sheen. When he complained about this—a glance into his suitcase revealed a uniform stack of white, button-down garments and a warren of identical blue ties—I pointed out that there was little call, otherwise, in changing from one white shirt into another. Half to simply nettle him, I'd put on a green Hawaiian print on which orange flowers made optical feints. Both of us, though, stared in genuine surprise when we arrived at the bar and discovered Jane waiting in a leopard-print pantsuit.

"I thought," she said, seemingly by way of explanation, "we were having Chinese food."

"This was, at least the last time I came through, a Chinese restaurant," Charles told me, no less unilluminatingly. "You know—with a tiki-bar thing." It wasn't a great leap of the imagination: The tables were partitioned from each other by fish tanks containing gigantic, solitary carp, the walls were papered in black and gold, and the man who approached us for our order was Chinese, though he wore his hair in a mullet.

As soon as he'd gone, Jane, rubbing her hands in a facsimile of excitement, said, "Well, I'm sure you're sick of the gory details, Milton, but you have to excuse me—I'm just *dying* to hear about the fire."

I think I can be forgiven for believing Charles's silence on the matter thus far could be taken as a tacit request to approach the subject gingerly. In fact, the better acquainted I became with my friend's ways, the more hesitant I'd grown, perceiving that the fire must have entirely disordered the carefully regulated life he'd created. I wasn't, however, unhappy she'd brought it up. Charles put his hands on the table, the left bandaged into a club to which he'd fastened his watch; the other, apparently more fortunate, having the fingers exposed. The bandages ran up into his sleeves.

"You can't imagine," he said to both of us. "It was like drowning in fire. I couldn't breathe. I was trapped in my room because the fire was outside, but there was nothing I could do—it was all around—until everything became so hot I panicked and decided they wouldn't find me in time. The doorknob was burning. The whole door was smoldering, but it was the only door. Then the fire broke the windows and spread up the curtains. In a few seconds it was all over . . ." There was a candle, like a toy fire in the middle of the table. It seemed best to blow it out, and I did. "I had to use the blankets on the bed to open the door, and while I was fumbling with the knob, they burst into flame—the whole place was made of plastic and sawdust. The covers just turned to syrup on my hands—"

"Oh," Jane cut in, reaching to a neighboring table for a fresh candle. "Just the *thought* of syrup on my hands . . . I mean I have to say, Charles, I was surprised to find you back. And I suppose we have *you* to thank for that," she said to me, adding, "You seem like fascinating company, Mr. Menger"—though giving neither of us a chance to respond: "Now forgive my curiosity—Milton here probably thinks all kinds of things about me—but I've been following your tragedy at a distance. All the conjecture about the fire in the news," she whispered to Charles; and then glancing my way: "Do you think it was *him*?"

"Who?" I asked.

"Why, the Arsonist of course"—batting my hand—"don't you watch TV?"

I had to admit that no, I didn't.

"Oh. Good for you, Milton." She smirked. "But then Charles already explained . . ." Until, seeing from our faces this evidently wasn't the case, her smile deepened. *"Charles."*

He took out his cigarettes. "All right—so I haven't told him," he said with the air of one being scolded. "Milty *just* flew down. There was everything to catch up with—"

"Charles," she repeated, "does someone have to light a fire under you to get you to talk?"—but she didn't sound either serious or surprised. I had the feeling she was baiting him. She turned to me. "So, your old friend didn't want to burden you with the thought that someone's going around the South, right around these parts—your parts, in fact, unless they've changed your territory, Charley—burning down five, six?"—Charles shrugged a yes. "Well, you get the idea, Milton. *This is a dangerous place.*"

"And yet here you are, tonight," Charles said.

"Yes." She smiled, taking one of his cigarettes. "Look at that."

For a moment she waited, cigarette poised before her mouth. I thought she might say something more—there seemed no end to what she might say—but then I realized what she wanted—I grasped the matches from the table and gave her a light. Her teeth were very white. Her eyes, now that they weren't behind sunglasses, were gray and deeply white, her brows heavier than I expected, as she was otherwise so finely made. She was beautiful, it occurred to me.

"I'm still a little thin on the details," I said, finding I was staring at her. "So . . . perhaps someone can tell me, what is this thing, exactly, about an arsonist?"

"The thing?" Jane said. "He burns down motels. He's probably chasing Charles—"

"How do they know it's one man?" I asked.

"I don't know—how do they tell that stuff?" she said to Charles. "I guess they look for patterns."

"Yes, he likes old motels, apparently."

"Charles likes old motels, too, in case you hadn't noticed, Milty"—and to Charles again, "I thought maybe you two might meet up—"

"Would you please stop it."

"Well, what's a little fire between friends? Maybe it's just a coincidence—fire, fire, fire," she said, stabbing out her cigarette. "I have to tell you, though, I *am* disappointed"—turning to me—"I could have—and *did*—get as much of a thrill reading the papers as I got just now. 'Inferno at the *Cozy Rest*'—wonderful. I mean, what else can you tell us, fresh from the fire? Paint us a picture, Chuck, of our friendly Arsonist."

I must have stared at her again, for if I wasn't mistaken she actually mouthed to me, soundlessly, *"All kinds of things."* I wondered, too, if she'd accidentally lit on her choice of words about painting. Had Charles struck her I wouldn't have been surprised, but he simply said, "I don't know. What am *I* supposed to know? Beside this"—holding up his hands—"I don't have any more experience with fire than you do. The police probably have tests . . ."

"They would look," I suggested, feeling I was stepping

between two people about to start swinging, "to see if they can determine where the fires began, and with what —"

"Very *good*, Milton," Jane said. "You seem to have a bit of experience with this, yourself."

"And," I said, ignoring her, "they would try to find a motive, to tie the fires together."

"A *motive*," Jane repeated. "I *love* crimes of reason. You'll notice I already gave you a motive, but of course Charles didn't care for it. Lately my motives are never good enough. As I explained to you before, Milton, Charles doesn't like me — please, Charles — at least not anymore. He's ceased to put stock in my suggestions."

"And yet here you are," Charles said again.

"Coincidence, coincidence," she replied. "Which is" — she rose, placing her purse over her shoulder — "the opposite of motive, when you think about it. Just a minute, gentlemen."

I tried to catch Charles's eye after she'd stepped to the back. For a moment he pressed his forehead to the table, but he was smiling as he straightened up.

"Is she high or something?" I said.

"Maybe." He shrugged. "It wouldn't make any difference. She's doing this for you, you know."

"What do you mean?" I asked. "She came to see *you* . . ."

"Oh, she certainly did. But she's trying to impress you. She wouldn't wear that getup for just anyone."

"She's awful," I murmured, unsurprised she'd think Charles didn't like her — she was one of the least likable people I'd met in a while. That they knew each other quite well, though, was clear to see — they had, I felt, known each other better at one time. But more than this, I was warmed by the feeling of being on the inside of something with Charles. I wasn't sure of why Jane might try to impress me, short of the flatteries of my ego, yet I felt Charles had invited me into his confidence in that interval in which Jane left the table. I felt I'd said the right thing, too, even if, as I'd pronounced the word *awful*, I knew it was true in the broadest sense. I was watching her now as she came back across the room. The whole bar turned to follow her.

Tonight, as happens most nights when I'm lying in bed past four, I can hear the phone ringing in a remote part of the Idyll. There's usually no other guest, and the phone just rings itself into silence — a wrong number, a transposition of digits — though sometimes the phone rings only briefly, and I get up and go out onto the veranda to look and see who else is parked in the lot. Tonight I found it empty, and stood for a while in the unexpectedly cool air, watching a distant electrical storm play in and out of pockets in the clouds.

Directly to the right of my room the lights of the lounge shine on the wet ground. The lounge contains several padded chairs and a TV; a tiny office is delineated from the carpeted area by a Formica counter. If a person arrived at the motel, entering the lounge by way of the exterior, diamond-paned door, and found the office empty, as it often is, he might ring the brass buzzer on the countertop. And if he was possessed of a superhuman patience, a theistic trust in providence, Thales or Eileen, signaled by a bell wired under the yard and into the house out back, would eventually appear through a little door in the rear of the office — nearly a cat door — to show the intrepid visitor a room; which is, I imagine, why the Idyll is generally vacant of guests besides myself. Many a night I've lain in bed or sat slumped at the Featherweight, listening to the phone or nothing at all, kept awake by the simple idea that the Idyll, unlike a house, but like many motels with their mono- or biplanar wings flanking a lounge, remains generally vacant of tenants at its center.

Now, by center, I do not of course mean to indicate a purely physical location, as in the case of this motel. I am thinking of a center in all of its senses — in all of those many senses, together, to which Charles was to introduce me. It is often the location where one finds oneself spending one's time when alone in an unfamiliar house. It is the place in which you discover yourself taking refuge from a party you've thrown in a vague honor, with little desire to greet the guests. It is never the laundry room; nor is it a guest room. It may be a hall. Such a place is usually, I have found, not in a cul-de-sac, but a location arteriole through which the house, in the language of real estate, flows.

Let us begin, in this case, by saying there is no "flow" in a house like the Idyll. It is, many would have it, properly speaking not a *house* at all — except when we view the edifice as a whole. When I returned here alone last week, being advised to take any room I cared and finding everything unlocked, I spent several hours going from room to room, thinking I might even spread my activities over a wide space to introduce more variance into my days. I was mistaken. The only collectivity

I've succeeded in establishing is the gathering together of every piece of motel stationery—I seem to be going through more paper than anticipated. No doubt it's no accident that I chose the same room I occupied and shared with Charles several weeks ago—it is, in Thales's words, "the best room."

Yet while it's proven impossible to inhabit the entire motel as a home, it shouldn't be surprising that the rule of centers I spoke of with respect to houses applies equally to motel rooms or suites, those tiny houses in those great houses of the highway. The heart of such a space is found in most cases to lie, as here in my little room, at the juncture between the carpeted area of the bedroom and the area—tiled or grimily carpeted, it matters little—containing the washstand, with its hollow-core door opening into the more private recesses of dirt and nakedness in the bathroom.

If, as I've already claimed, motels are the footprints of past journeys—and like so many personally cherished notions I can follow the idea back to Charles—and in choosing a motel one chooses the motel that coincides most exactly with the steps in a journey of one's own, then the center of a motel room is the place where one would stand to discover which of those many rooms, those hived houses, coincide most closely with oneself. Every time you check into a motel it is a winnowing; and it is, when you think about it, as if every traveler is a key, though few ever find that room for which they are, if not destined, then at least made.

As I write this, it's at last growing light. Perhaps I'll be able to sleep now. A riding mower erupts into life as the old man prepares some new patch of ground. The traffic, what there is of it, will soon pick up on the road. There's a state park,

Foible Creek, a few miles away, and Thales must have imagined, coming home from the Korean War, that this would be a fine place for a business.

He came by, as promised, yesterday evening. Again with something of our absent friend's: shoes, now. A pair such as a mailman might wear—or, I suppose, a priest—and of course they might have been anyone's, though I don't see enough traffic here that Thales might become confused. I've never understood, myself, how someone can leave anyplace save a shoe store without the shoes he walked in with. I said as much, but he replied that given the state of my footwear, I might try them on.

I'd forgotten that I mentioned my sleep troubles to Thales —yet I do have a terrible memory, and so I've been writing things down. I began early yesterday, discouraged by the failure of the Singerlight and momentarily unable to recall what it was that Charles had said about sewing and metaphor. There is, I might as well admit, something in what Thales told me: I *am* susceptible. I acquire accents that aren't my own, borrow words. Ideas work on me, quietly, perhaps only at night, without my knowledge or consent—and then one day they're mine, or I'm theirs. They are a mob I know well, my ideas, but individually, I don't remember from where; though I realize, sitting here, that many of them belonged to Charles. Lately I've been thinking a lot about Charles—that there are other things I should have written down. When one doesn't sleep, it's amazing how much time there is to think.

I *am,* after all, a poor sleeper. There's some help in Charles's pills; and as I hinted above, it's comparatively recent, my career as a reluctant night owl. Which is why it's also only lately that I've devised my technique for sleep, and perhaps why, thus far, I've encountered mixed success. The technique itself is simple, and therein lies its beauty:

I approach the land of sleep with an emptied and stupefied countenance, as if hoping to be taken unawares by one of sleep's intelligences. I imagine my face — my helpless, immobile face — tied on the end of a long cord, sinking through the subterranean as if into a well or cistern. And it is like cutting someone before throwing him overboard into cold and shark-infested waters, or like abandoning some drunk but well-dressed man alone and disoriented at an intersection in an unknown and dangerous city. Knitting my fingers across my chest, I lower down, down the stupefied face.

I nodded off, briefly. I see I was rambling before I laid the pen aside, and then I found myself sleeping. I had a dream — one I have fairly often these days, and which I had, I recall vividly, the second night of our tour together, Charles and I, when we returned to the Piney Lodge from our evening with Jane. The dream is always a little different, but each time I visit it not as something I'm beginning anew, but rather a thing the details of which I'm endeavoring to remember, as though on each occasion approaching the same half-familiar and twilit city from a different direction.

It is a faint light that I follow, yet I've been here many times before, and always illuminated by this late light — late in the summer, late in the day, when the sun kneels beneath the horizon; a cumulative light thrown from ground-floor windows over the deepening lawns of urban yards, yellow rectangles upon porch rails and flower beds, hedges of black-soaked green, deep trunks of trees, and a child's red bicycle, over-turned and glossy as candy; all these lights together — the lights of a city raised at once — make a larger light, a music in the air above a town slipping into night.

There are people sitting upon the damp lawns beneath the trees, as if in caverns of leaves that stretch in monotone chambers down the street. In a neighboring yard another group is camped, sprawled on the grass. A woman in a white cardigan whistles and inscribes some instruction in the air toward a girl silhouetted in the doorway of a house, and the girl glances back, her dress soft as a moth, before she turns and goes inside.

In the grass, a boy thinks what it means to "go inside," but his words are so new they separate from their objects and cure in the air. He looks slyly up at his mother, at these women, like a spy. The women sit in a loose ring above the boy, a few steps from the sidewalk where girls in spring dresses run. He watches the girls dart and swim in the dusk, into the street this evening devoid of traffic, and then between lanes up across the broad median on which yet more people sit or lie, freckling beneath the emerging stars. There are hundreds of people reclined or running in childish games, or ambling down the block toward a light that grows and gently throws itself upon all of them. His eye lingers, then withdraws with a catch as something dawns on him: Where are all the boys? Where are the men, even? His own father?

He stands, a shaky tower, and his mother clasps his hips. She points down the street.

"You were asleep — Daddy took your brother to see the fire. Do you want to go look at the fire?" she asks the quick turn of his head.

He nods and regards the crowd.

"Do you see Daddy?" his mother says. "Milton?"

He turns and smiles at her, and she smiles back. Gently, she releases his legs, and he begins his journey across uneven terrain.

He's jealous that his brother should be together with his father, without him; he's often suspected that they prefer each other's company. His mother's words settle upon him, distracting, and perhaps this is why his eye wanders from the waving figure in the blur of children and arrives instead upon the fixed star of a girl in the street, rolling a hula hoop round her waist. She's wearing yellow, the hoop glowing like a halo in the evening. Other girls move in flocks of light on all sides, but they pay her no attention, and she pays them the same mind, staring down at the ring in which she's contained. He rambles on, nearer to the median now, watching the girl with the hoop, until he grasps the slope in his hands, and it fills his vision.

When he stands, the children—all these girls with their jump ropes, their marbles, and their dresses each a tiny house with porches and gardens—stare up at him from the street like frogs. Looking back, he sees his mother and he waves. She waves, and then turns to her friends. Below, the girl with the hula hoop sways in the dusk. She might be ten. She's separated by her magic circle from everything in the world. His attention falters, and he looks back toward his mother, but she's still speaking to someone. If she would just turn, he thinks—and then he looks around.

The girl has moved. Not so very far, yet it makes him anxious. She stands at a corner where a little street emerges like a creek from between the houses and joins the avenue. He feels himself a bark drawn in the current of a secret entrance to the sea, and he makes his way toward the glowing ring, descending the bank.

Down amongst the young again, the world is a tumult. The girls have long brown hair; their games have girl-rules, which relate to animals, as if girls are, themselves, more like animals. The girl with the hoop drifts as she twirls and slips down the little street, between the homes and darkened lawns. He follows. She isn't far, turning slowly without looking up or around; but one of his shoes has untied itself, and he bends down to grasp the loose lace. Only in rising from where he concentrates does he realize that he's wandered some distance from the picnic activities on the boulevard.

At the next intersection, where a lamp makes a small, dirty pool, she's stopped, still turning, still oblivious to him. He draws nearer, and with each step she seems to grow brighter. Perhaps now, he thinks, he'll finally catch her; though what, he wonders, would he do? And in so thinking, without warning, she comes loose from her pivot, rounds the corner, and disappears behind a hedge. It is as if a needle has lifted from a record. Trembling a little, he hears the sound of leaves shushing in the trees, and once more glances about.

There is a prickly quiet to the air, the voices of the picnickers failing amongst the rasp of leaves, the ticking and rustling of watered grass. A cricket speaks to him from the fringe of a lawn. Behind, the excitement of the avenue has dwindled to almost nothing, and the yards on either side of where he stands appear deserted, the boles of the trees emerging like pillars in the inner structure of the night. Thinking again of the girl, he walks a little farther toward where she's vanished; even when he hears a brisk crack, and notices a movement where a shape detaches itself from a tree — the shadow of a large man, waiting quite still — he walks on. There's something familiar to the boy in the shape and stance of the man. He has less the feeling of walking into him than of catching up, after an absence.

"Are you looking for something?" the man asks, his face a block of darkness beneath the brim of a hat; and then, after a moment, when there is no reply:

"You're lost, aren't you?"

The boy hesitates, regarding the hand the stranger holds down to him.

"It's all right," the man says, "if you don't take my hand." His voice isn't unkind. There's an odor of alcohol. "I'm going to look at the fire. Do you want to look at the fire?"

And so they set off, the man keeping gait at the boy's side.

"Is your father with the Company?" the man inquires after a time.

"Aren't you with the Company?" the boy replies.

"In a manner of speaking."

Nearing the avenue, the man comes more into view. He has a strong, bearded face. He's dressed in a dark suit that's been rumpled from sitting in damp grass. He looks, the boy thinks, like a president from another century, or a grandfather, the wrinkles around the eyes soft and oiled.

"You look like someone," the boy says.

"That may be. I have a daughter you might know. Her name is Elizabeth —"

"Elizabeth isn't a name — it's a place," the boy replies.

To which the man smiles, but acknowledges, "I suppose you're right." As they come to the corner, and the noises of the street percolate around them again, he doffs his hat to a passing young woman. She stares at him briefly before her eyes snap away, to other sights. They stroll side by side into the file of stragglers moving toward a brightness ahead, where sparks shimmer into the sky.

"I'd be willing to wager," he says, taking the boy's hand at last, "that not far from where we stand, someone, likely your mother, is worried about you." The man indicates an opening in a knot of people, between whose shoulders the glow condenses and intensifies. "Thank you for holding my hand," the stranger confides as they draw into the crowd. "You're going to laugh — and it's much better here — yet I've always been afraid of the dark."

The boy looks up and smiles. He says, "I don't believe you," unsure if he's being teased.

The man glances down in surprise. "You should never tell anyone" — he shakes his head — "that you don't believe them." But he, too, is smiling. Grasping the boy beneath the arms, he hoists him onto his shoulders; and it is then that the boy sees the fire.

In a clearing normally employed as a baseball field, a small, two-story home has appeared this night. It is like so many others around it, except that it is full of flames.

At first he is uncertain what to think, but the man, carrying him and good-naturedly navigating the clots of people, threads his way near enough that they feel the heat on their faces and see the details of the fire licking the transoms of windows, twining the pillars of the porch, moving about upstairs, through the rooms, like a person looking for something. A great cheer erupts on either side, coaxing the boy from his bewilderment, until he allows himself, voluptuously, to fall into the pleasure of the fire. All around he sees the men and boys he'd looked for in vain only a few minutes before. They are clapping and shouting; it even seems to him they're clapping more for the fire, so large and clear it might be made of colored strips of cellophane, than the firemen in their yellow and black suits, slick with water as they grapple with the fantastical devices of a fire truck. An idea occurs to him:

"Whose house is that?"

"It belongs to the firemen," the man says.

"But who lives in that house?" he asks.

"No one," the man tells him. "It's nobody's home. They built it for the fire — so they could put it out."

Both of them return their attention to the blaze, although the boy is thinking now about what the man said. The firemen push against the flames, advancing. They signal to one another, as if they'd pursued the fire into a corner. A ladder reaches a window, vanishing into steam and smoke where a fireman clutching a shiny hose braces against an invisible pressure. Under cover of renewed cheers, one of the men is beating the front door with an axe. In a flurry they are running, signaling, hoses trained through windows; and then the door is down — men rush in, coats enormous and dark against the furnace of the interior.

But it is at last time to admit that there is a fear that always comes over me, here. I might forget the fear until this very moment, but then I remember, and it begins. I haven't been afraid to see the boy come upon the stranger on an empty street; and I haven't been afraid of the fire itself — although, as I've explained, like the stranger I am afraid of the dark. What fills me with fear on each occasion are the boy's eyes as they rove the cheering crowd.

The people around him make a lush and rushing sound; a man in a felt hat puts both hands to his mouth and whistles, filling the air with a soft cloud of spit; a burly woman hoists her son in two stout arms and shouts through the back of the child's head. The child is raising his hands and clapping, hair in a flurry, and the boy, too, is clapping. For an instant, an older boy catches his eye, but then the youth — perhaps fifteen, acne-scarred and whiskered like a catfish — wipes his brow and returns his broad face to the scene.

And I am afraid — afraid, watching the boy searching among these people for a familiar face, that he will realize that he knows all of them. I am afraid that he will see these are a lifetime of faces — of people he hasn't met yet, but whom he will come to know, and who will come to know him. I am afraid that they've been gathered here from his entire life *because* they know him; that there are people here who have called him by pet names, people he's borrowed money from; people he has made love with, whom he has watched die, and perhaps even people who have watched him die. They surround him, and I can only hope that as long as he remains clapping, unaware, they will not notice him. I tremble to think that his eyes might meet any of their eyes, because I am sure, then, that he will know why he is there, and they will know why they are there, too; and I imagine the things they might say when they see who he is — the terrifying things they might tell him about the life he hasn't had yet, but which they remember, and in which, one day, he will be swept away.

He bends down toward the stranger's ear, as if he were murmuring to a horse.

"Who are you?" he asks to no answer; and again, "Who are you?"

The man glances at him. "Me?" he replies. "I'm no-body—just nobody at all," turning back to the fire.

There is, then, a sound, at first like a fire alarm, of more trucks arriving, until it grows both too large and too small, and I think that this must be it—*the end* I've been dreading, materializing, as any apocalypse, in undreamt-of form, at the hand of a vassal, in the shape of a fly or germ—and then it becomes another sound that surrounds us, arriving, at last, as the sound of the world—*the other world.*

I'd sat bolt upright in near darkness. There was a sharp, chirping noise coming from somewhere in the room—the room, I realized after a long moment, at the Piney Lodge. I'd left the bathroom light on, and staring about, I found I'd fallen asleep on the edge of the bed, fully dressed, much as I did just a moment ago here at the Idyll. Throwing on the bedside lamp, I also discovered Charles, startled by the flood of light, busy with the tiny buttons of his digital watch.

"I'm sorry," he said after a moment. "I don't know what's wrong with this thing. Were you having a bad dream?"

"A nightmare," I murmured as he succeeded in turning off the alarm. Discovering myself still slightly drunk, and luxuri-ating in the knowledge that it was, after all, only a dream, I lay back, kicking off my shoes. "And then, I'm afraid of the dark," I added, feeling brave enough to again switch off the lamp.

Caught for those few seconds in brilliance, the room lay burned in my brain. I expected to fall immediately back to sleep, but instead remained awake, alternately revisiting the shrunken fears of my dream and regarding the ceiling through a screen of sound as I sank into the crinkled, plastic heart of the mattress: the electric purr of the hotel sign, trucks moaning out on the highway. It had finally occurred to me that perhaps this was the time to tell Charles of the terrible turn in my life—here in this confessional darkness, feeling, still, the warmth we'd shared in the bar; I'd just said his name out loud, in fact, when I realized by certain unmistakable sounds that my friend was asleep.

BY DAWN, HOWEVER, all that remained of the night's terrors and charms was Jane: I awakened with the distinct memory of her mouth aslant, saying, "See you boys in the morning," half hoping and fearing that we would — but it was not to be. At a little past seven, while our fellow patrons lay inert, Charles roused and hustled us into the blinking day. And so I was loading the trunk, my mind like Vaseline upon the events of the evening, when I noticed wedged behind the Featherweight and a tire iron a red gas can with a loop of plastic tubing coiled around its spout. My curious hand reached forward, and Charles sprung to force it back.

His green eyes hovered upon mine. "It's a siphoning kit," he said, though his eyes slunk across the veranda, the windows of the front office. He added, "I don't want to have a moral debate, Milty. You just have to be prepared . . ."

I was still somewhat disoriented by dreams and the hours leading up to those dreams. Yet nowhere in my recollections could I find what had made him draw away—what brought on even a hint of hostility. Only the day before, this might again have thrown me, but my friend's moods and habits were coming back, now, and like a bullfighter I knew that they might wear themselves into an entirely different mood. I asked what, exactly, a person had to be prepared for.

"You'll take this all out of proportion," he began, climbing into the car. "It's a nuisance, just *a nuisance*"—but in the end, having no newspaper yet, spinning the dial of the radio through a frightful braying of biblical lore, he reluctantly admitted another complication to our travels in the South: the scourge of *gas siphoning.*

"An outgrowth of the gas-huffing blight, I expect," was what I observed, casting my first smile at the dash; but that was enough. Charles hadn't used the phrase "moral debate" accidentally, and he launched now into what dawned on me was an apology for, or an explanation of, the siphoning scourge as he understood it in the South.

My hold on the details is thin—I was navigating a complicated highway clover when the rant began—but he led me to understand that since the oil crisis, a great part of his territory had fallen prey to a pernicious misdemeanor made infinitely worse—and here we were getting to the root of the shame—because, discovering one's tank drained in the night, discovering oneself essentially *stranded,* one couldn't simply *ask* a fellow driver for gas.

He paused to see if he'd said enough. Slowly, I shook my head.

Due, he suggested now, to the very nature of siphoning— dubious in itself—if we were to ask for assistance, no party would admit to having a kit; and it was therefore impossible to honestly get even an emergency ration of gas from one's neighbor's car to one's own, even though *everyone* had these kits and would be, in any *other* circumstance, entirely willing to assist. Consequently, led the logic, one was compelled to either join in this general criminality or be condemned to helplessly endure a parade of siphonings, which in their humiliating details prevent the very acts of Samaritanism most called for to remedy them.

"So what you're telling me," I paraphrased, "is that you yourself have engaged in this deplorable siphoning behavior" — though when he turned on me, full of recrimination, I was able this time to match him with my most toothy grin. His face relaxed, became pleased even, as I swung the car into the parking lot of a roadside diner. It had been a long time since I'd had a friend — a real friend — and I was remembering now that you move toward a friend as toward a mirror: the person tangible, the friend intangible.

When we arrived at our booth, Charles sat down opposite, and with deliberate insolence flipped open his daily rag, eyes giving mine a last wry glance. Today, however, I didn't let him go:

"Are you going to read to me again from the disaster column?" I asked.

"You prefer yours in dreams?" he remarked.

"Perhaps, but yours are prettier than mine." And I saw immediately I'd been correct in my hunch that beyond any "moral qualms," Jane lay at the heart of his tirade:

"I *would* have warned you," he blustered. "I didn't think she'd be down here — she has no reason in the world to be down here, except she has this *way* of turning up"—putting aside the paper. "This probably seems like quicksand to you, Milty, all this nonsense with the fire and the siphoning and Jane. And yes, it's true—there *are* a few things I should have told you—but you see how it is? Just take the siphoning: It sounds ridiculous . . . it *is* ridiculous . . . and then of course I *knew* we'd run into her"—entirely reversing himself—"because she's constitutionally incapable of minding her own territory, let alone her business. *I knew it,*" he repeated. "I just didn't think it would be this soon. So what could I say? What could I have said, before you met her, that wouldn't sound just as ludicrous?"

For a moment we were both silent, and then he muttered, "It's the tragedy of this business—people like Jane. They're changing everything. Headhunters bring them in buckets, and of course they don't know a thing about sewing machines. Once," he added more quietly, "she admitted that when she took the job, she thought she'd be working for *Swingline*—the stapler company. Unbelievable."

"Do you think," I asked, recalling our dawn flight, "she'll be surprised to find us gone?"

Charles threw up his hands; the humor, however, had returned to his eyes. He drew a postcard from his pocket. "She'll manage. She always does," he said, beginning to scribble some missive. I watched his maimed fingers grapple across the little field. Whenever I'd received one of these cards, I'd imagined him at the center of some radiating universe of thoughts in which I tried to locate myself on an outer ring. Now here I was.

"You and Jane *do* seem to know each other quite well," I let fall from my new vantage.

His hand stopped. I thought for a moment the détente we'd enjoyed was more fragile than it appeared; he looked angry, even, as he said, "Milty, she takes liberties like that with everyone," though an instant later he allowed, "I guess I do know her pretty well"—and at last, bending back to his postcard, he went so far as to say, "I tried—I really thought I could *do* something with her, given enough time—but yes: I trained her."

Which was where we left things. Likely in order to direct my attentions elsewhere, he laid out a brief and meaningless itinerary—he actually produced a list—explaining that while we were merely covering ground today, I should have some better idea of the road ahead; and then we fell to recalling our days at the university, the weather-talk of nostalgia.

I won't dwell on the mundanity of the afternoon. It was irreproachable. By three, we'd taken rooms at The Long Valley Motor Inn in southern Georgia, an establishment dating from the twilight of the modern era, when motels were composed of separate cabins, accomplishing during their first dozen years an evolution that brought them from campground to primitive suburbia. In the case of motor homes such as The Long Valley, each cabin became a tiny house distilled to a visual essence: windows and window boxes, red asphalt-shingle roof, welcome mat; each was nestled within minuscule shrubs and trees, reached by a narrow walk from the circular drive where one deposited one's car. I wasn't immune to such charms, with their wink at the toy life granted the tourist; and Charles seemed put at ease, too. The concierge came out to meet him like an old friend. From the window of my cabin I saw them together by the drive, examining a troop of roses.

I napped, and it was nearly dark when we met across the road at a forgetful little dive, the room cluttered by the sound of a television, a handful of men hunched by the taps. There was a ball game on, or shortly to be on. The men rounded their shoulders toward the screen and hurled invectives at the teams. The bartender called across the room to us, and the men gave a brief, bleak stare before again bowing to the TV.

"What *is* this thing you have with old motels?" I asked directly.

"You don't like The Long Valley?"

"My standards are slipping. But *you* practically live in these places . . ."

"Do I?" he said. "Though you could as easily say I don't live anywhere . . . or I live in *The Territory*. When I first started doing this, I actually liked that my home is any vacant room — I liked the expanse of it. After all, while I don't always like the places I stay, when you have a house — or so I've been told — you *do* want to look in all the rooms."

The metaphor seemed less than helpful, and I pointed out as much: "Still, haven't you noticed they've added some *new* rooms to your home?"

"But that's the thing, isn't it?" he agreed. "That's the problem" — though it wasn't a problem I'd meant to frame. It was like Charles to insist on treating a topic seriously, however I tried to angle things to the contrary: "If I think of it that way, I'm losing ground. Because it's not about space" — and to my polite look of inquiry — "It can't be. You have *five* bedrooms in your house. Obviously, there's a whole other need . . ."

"Oh, I see. This is about inner-outer space — the house as mind," I suggested. "Unless you look in all the rooms, there's always the suspicion that there might be someone else in your house — a stranger?" I could remember in the suburban palace my family moved to when I was nine how if I came home alone near nightfall, I'd comb every floor, turning on lights until the entire house was ablaze to drive from my thoughts such a possibility. Realizing where this was leading, however, I said, "You of course recall that other people stay in these rooms of yours when you're not there?"

"I'm not afraid of strangers in my head, Milty," Charles replied after our drinks came and we fell quiet. "It really is the rooms. You see yourself differently in different rooms."

"The plastic mirrors make me look like a fiend," I joked feebly. Yet I felt a bit lost.

"Maybe it's working in industry all these years. But it often seems to me that progress is an act of forgetting your way from a first impulse to an unrelated conclusion. Or maybe that's what it is to grow older — becoming a stranger to yourself." I shrugged and took a sip. "Isn't it just a little disturbing, though, that a stranger will complete your life for you?" He paused, and I thought for a moment he was finished until he said, "Don't think I haven't noticed" — taking me by surprise. "Don't you ever feel you might have lost the thread? That you *had it,* once? *You* know what I mean," he said, and there was no doubt in his voice. "As soon as I spoke to you that day in Carthage, I knew you'd understand."

And while neither of us, I'd suggest, was thinking at all about motel rooms anymore, I believe that I did. "I've thought for a long time now," I conceded, "that it isn't so much what one loses as one goes on, as that the very simplest things — those things it seemed like nothing to ask for — never come to pass."

He was watching me across the narrow table in the booth. Then something shifted in his eyes, a spasm of green like a motion in foliage. When he spoke next, I wondered if he'd hoped for more in return:

"Well, I am sorry about the room last night — it was enough to give anyone nightmares. I'd forgotten you were afraid of the dark."

I saw that we'd fallen amongst ancillary things to a subject I actually disliked, though I tried then to explain, as I have so many times, the appalling overpresence, the claustrophobia I feel in the dark. It occurs to me now that precisely such an obliterating presence is what I've hoped to lose myself in during the recent, sleepless weeks; but having no occasion to devise my technique for sleep at the time, I had no cause to mention to Charles this fold in my fright. What I did have to relate about nyctophobia, however, he followed with an interest I found surprising, until he explained: "Singer was afraid of the dark" — and when I smiled — "yes, Singer again. I mentioned this afternoon that I wanted to stop and visit some friends in a few days — that fellow Thales and his kin. I actually have it from one of them, a woman named Emily, that he had your same fear. She learned it from Singer personally. She's very old, of course" — I did the arithmetic in my head and found she had to be upward of one hundred years if Singer died in 1875 — "and she only met him once when she was a girl, so she doesn't remember much. But she *does* remember that he told her about two fears."

"Sounds like a queer old man," I said, put in mind of my dream.

"Oh — she thought he was very funny."

I shrugged. "What was the second fear?" I asked.

"The second fear," he said, taking out his cigarettes, "is more unusual"—at which he struck a light, and leaning across the table, stagily whispered a hiss of smoke and consonants.

"What?" I asked, certain I'd misheard him, until he said again, louder:

"Coincidence."

"Coincidence?" I repeated, chuckling. "A *fear* of coincidence? I suppose there are people with a fear of Christmas, but . . ."

"Other people's fears, Milty—the lovely dark, the silky dark." Something in the way he said this disturbed me.

"A fear of the dark is nearly ordinary," I replied. "Isn't it likely she misheard him, or the old man was teasing—or senile?"—feeling that related so long ago, by an unreliable witness, a claim to fear something as abstract as coincidence trod the territory of silliness. "Such a man couldn't hold his life together. I mean . . . if the ordinary events of the world, unevocative, unintelligent, are what make up the raw material of our lives—the flesh, the lumber, call it what you will—then isn't it coincidence that makes the spark? The breath? Are we not all, in the end, ruled by coincidence?" I could feel the eloquence of scotch at work: "It gives everything shape. The entire foundation of religion, and literature, I might add—that feeling of an overarching linkage between events and people—"

But Charles was smiling now. "Milty," he said, "it's an *irrational* fear."

As in Carthage, my first impulse was to assume he was pulling my leg—that his smile, for instance, was an indication of intelligence, even mockery. This, I realized, was what disturbed and excited me: that while we'd begun the conversation discussing my *real* fear, here he was five minutes later, jumbling candor with amusement. When the smile vanished, though, leaving no sign of humor in his face, another thought—two thoughts, actually, entwined—entered my mind: First, I glimpsed that he was one of those people who smile when they're nervous (I, also being such a person, had naturally returned his smile); and second, I understood that he had this fear himself.

On the television, in the center of a baseball diamond, a man—an opera singer by the look of him—was unburdening himself of "The Star-Spangled Banner." The music floated like tinsel through the bar. He had the mouth of a swordswallower. In the crater of the stadium, alone on the pitcher's mound, he seemed a martyr.

"Is it not, instead, a sort of obsession you're describing?" I persisted.

We glanced at each other. His hands, I realized, were shaking as they had when I'd picked him up at the hospital. Noticing as much, he held a cigarette out and I lit it.

"Are you drunk?" I asked. He scowled at me and I apologized.

"It's only that by the sound of it, you're saying that if Isaac Singer, for example—one of the richest men on earth, a household name—walked into a bar and ordered a drink, and noticed that someone on TV was performing 'The Star Spangled Banner,' our national anthem, Isaac would see this and decide that there exists some affinity between himself and *that* singer? And he'd find this relationship, as far as I understand you, frightening?"

But as if to confirm my earlier suspicion he was toying with me, Charles diverted his attention to the screen. Turning, I watched the bar sunk in its sports fable. The singer said his piece, and the teams poured from their dugouts, at this distance impossible to make out except for the redness and blueness of their respective uniforms.

"What are we really talking about, Charles?" I said.

"Do you remember when we met in that town?" he replied.

"Carthage?"

"And I hadn't seen you in — well, since college." At the bar, four or five voices rose for a moment in a squall, then quieted. He paused and stared at me. "I shouldn't be telling you this . . ."

"Oh, *come on* —" I said.

"I hadn't seen you since college," he went on after a moment, "but I *knew* it was you and Harvey as soon as I saw you standing in front of the museum — I knew; but my point is, I followed you inside, and for a long time I just sat at the bar, trying to decide what to do."

"Didn't you want to see us?" I kidded; and then I grasped that this was exactly the answer. It was something I might have done myself.

"Remember what you said before, about things having a 'shape'? Don't you see that I *had* to talk to you, then — I mean, not that I didn't want to, but that I was compelled, by the coincidence?"

"Compelled?" I thought back to our conversation on morality and the compulsions of gas siphoning. The idea seemed too abstractable from oneself, dishonest in his mouth, and I said, "Charles, if you didn't want to see us—" but he snapped:

"You're not listening"—before lowering his voice: "Once you start thinking about it, it doesn't *matter* if it's a 'good' or 'bad' coincidence. It's that it's offered . . ."

"Well—whatever," I said when we'd fallen silent. A helplessness washed over me. Catching my expression, he closed his eyes.

"Look—I'm sorry. That came out all wrong." Then, as if remembering something: "Imagine a house. Imagine your own house, with all the bedrooms. Imagine you're back in Jersey, Milton. What if you noticed, one night, that there was a door in your house you'd never seen before—a door in a room you'd been inside a thousand times; and one night it was just there, as if it had always been there. Unremarkable, almost. A stranger in your house wouldn't know anything was unusual. It wouldn't matter if the door concealed something 'good' or 'bad.' You would be *compelled,* wouldn't you? You'd have to see."

I conceded this was hypothetically true.

"Imagine this happens every day. At first it seems wonderful—every time you open the door, there's a room, a hall, another door. You move into your spaces, you expand. But there's no end to it. If you don't open the door, the door is still there; new doors still appear. Eventually, you begin to forget which doors are old and which new, which rooms are which. And this would hardly matter, too, if you didn't become lost, one day.

"It doesn't last, of course, your confusion over rooms and doors—things aren't so bad as that, you tell yourself—but something's changed. And just as you've succeeded in reassuring yourself, several days later it happens again. It happens again, and again; and while it doesn't last — because you always *do* find your way back in the end — after this kind of thing has gone on for long enough, you're much more careful. You also realize at some point, inevitably, that you're being so careful now because you're afraid."

THREE YEARS AGO, when Caroline and I arrived at La Felicidad, there was a small confusion over rooms, but it only sweetened, in hindsight, the sense of providence that had opened like a road beneath the road half an hour before; for we were initially informed by the matron of the place — a wan smile, fingers among the pages of her registry — "You call ahead?" — "No, I'm sorry, we came here entirely by accident" — that there were no rooms.

The light went out of me. For seven hours (I'd lost my watch, we'd missed our plane, I'd transposed two numbers on a luxury bus to Acapulco to board, instead, a decrepit Bluebird bound for nowhere, ancient swearwords scratched into the seat backs by American children) I had fought — like a salmon I had fought upstream all day, but up the wrong stream. I sank into a chair by the desk and stared out across the porch with its flowers and potted palms, over the dazzling late-afternoon Pacific. Caroline sat down beside me. It had seemed at last our luck had turned when the bus ground to a halt in this village whose name I didn't know. This was the only inn in town.

We'd scarcely had the chance to feel the weight of these words, however, when an older man camped on the porch behind a newspaper began a spirited discussion with Angela — as the matron's name turned out to be. He smiled and gestured to us encouragingly. The registry was opened, a name found, a room upstairs checked. Watching the woman come and go, a raised finger of patience and promise, we sensed the tenacity of possibility. I peered at the name of the occupant-in-question, alone on its fresh page — a Paul Somebody-or-other — just as she satisfied herself of some last detail, and with a complicit glance at Caroline, theatrically tore out the page and crumpled it into the wastebasket.

"We have one room," she said with obvious pleasure, dusting her hands and turning the registry around for me to sign.

For a while, Caroline and I lay on the bed upstairs, watching the sea whiten around an island out in the bay, the unmoving shapes of fishing boats. And when I had wound up and ran down my lovely wife's simple erotic mechanism, we lay entwined again as the sun settled in the sea, feeling — at least for myself — that a certain saintedness was upon us; feeling, as all victors, that as the chances of the day had worked out well, I was basically good. From within my goodness, I said:

"I wish, sometimes, that I could paint."

She lay a damp hand on me. "You always say such funny things — after . . ."

I was looking into the bronze and flaming portions of the sky. "If I could paint —"

"If this is because of what I said this morning —"

112

"No, not at all," I soothed. "I was just thinking, there's a beautiful, small oil by Kennel called *Woman Bathing*—"

"Oh, I see—"

"No, no—there is no woman in the painting at all. Just a dark creek, a bank of willows, and her clothes laid in the shadows. One looks and looks, and at first it seems it's just a matter of time, of oversight . . ."

"Milty," Caroline interrupted, "have you ever really admired someone?"—toying with one of her nipples that had deflated, unexpectedly, more than the other. I gave up my pursuit of painting.

"I see it's your turn to say funny things."

"Seriously, though—have you?"

"If you were paying the slightest attention to me just now, you would have heard that I *was* speaking of someone I admire deeply."

"But I mean," she clarified, "who's not dead."

"Ah . . ." It's very like Caroline to spring a topic in this way—a topic that for an absurd moment I'd assumed shared at least some kinship with the conversational carcass from which it reared—especially if she's hoping, as she undoubtedly was on this occasion, for some postcoital confidence. I was too far along to return to my beloved painting, and more horribly, I saw I would now need to prove something. Fortunately for me, still basically good as I was and thinking as I'd been of Kennel, someone else—someone likely alive—leapt to mind:

"Well, do you remember that fellow that Harvey and I were talking about at Christmas—a classmate of ours back in school . . . a painter, if you would allow me to throw some continuity into this conversation?" She shook her head slightly, her profile turned up to the ceiling and her earrings — those same golden earrings — melting on her shoulders.

"The fellow who made the painting we have over the mantel in the dining room — the sort of urban-landscapish thing?" I said to slightly better effect. "Yes? His name was, is, Charles Trembleman. I think I must have admired him — I know I did." She glanced at me. "And I think if I hadn't met Charles when I did, my world would be a much emptier place. I would never have found Kennel, for example — or painting itself for that matter. I would surely have done something else with my life."

She was now staring intently, so I continued: "If I remember correctly, I'd styled myself a writer back then, the way one styles oneself as this or that at twenty — it *is* the simplest craft, to write in one's native language, and many people never get past it. I was also, I should point out, working under a handicap: Painting was, to me, the sort of ornamental crap with which my parents surrounded themselves. I had no better example, and my mother and father — well, you know — they're the sort of people who were taught as children that 'one's life should be a work of art.'" Caroline smiled, I think because she herself was taken with the idea. "I suppose it was fortunate for them both that they'd identically misconstrued the notion, so that they satisfied themselves by turning their lives into a museum."

"Oh, Milty," she said.

"But hold on — what I'm trying to say is that it was this Charles person who made it possible for me to crawl out from under that and *look* at a painting" — which could in no way obfuscate the fact that Caroline was disappointed. She'd hoped for the mention of someone she knew, or at least a celebrity.

Believing I might still make myself understood, however, I attempted to clarify what exactly it was that I admired, while playing on a quality Caroline prizes and uses to defend her own hypnotically boring friends:

"Charles was, foremost, a *likable* fellow — Harvey liked him, and *you* would have liked him. Example," I offered her deadpan gaze: "I remember, once — we were in Charles's kitchen at a party, and I was looking at a reproduction of Kennel's *Thief* he'd pasted up — he said to me that while it seemed to him most people thought there was no *time* in painting, he felt that in fact it must be the opposite: that as is the case with all things that don't seem to change, that are timeless, such things are in reality much *more* about time than anything else. I hadn't the least experience with painting, and I remember thinking, as he said this, that it was only *because* I liked Charles — or felt I *should* — that I bothered to give his remarks any thought at all. But over subsequent weeks I did give them thought. I took my first art history course. I began thinking about time, and eventually, over time, months and years, I began thinking about time in American painting, particularly — that it was a different time, that there was something a little inhuman in the effort to discard the Old World and the subjects of its past. And then I began to think about painting in general. It wasn't that I agreed or disagreed with Charles, if you understand . . . I became less interested in timelessness, rather than more, as I went on. It was just that one felt free to think with Charles. I'd never been with anyone like that, who wasn't embarrassed, as my parents would be, to be caught *thinking something out.* Charles was always opening things up he was still trying to understand, expecting to be argued with — it became a license to think for oneself."

Caroline, whose interests lay quite far away at this point, said, "So what happened to him? You never introduce me to your friends . . ."

It was impossible, but I didn't care, lying there with our skins orange and apricot in the light. "As far as I can tell he fell off the face of the earth. It's what Harvey was saying over dinner—that painting reminded him. Charles was bright, though—he could be doing anything, now. He might, on the other hand, be as dead as Kennel."

When we came downstairs again, it was night. The moon glittered in the blue above and within the ocean, and we walked along a little path from the porch to the slope of beach sheltered from the dirt streets of town by palm thickets, curving away on either side between the dark foliage and darker water. Far along to the left glowed the festive lamps of a restaurant or bar from which isolated sounds emerged, but these seemed almost to exist in a different time, so quiet was the place we stood except for the pulse of the sea.

There is a trust one must learn when one has a fear — maybe especially a very ordinary fear such as mine. The fear came down around me then in the gathering dark, a roaring in the ear, and I reached for Caroline's hand. Perhaps in this instance the sound was merely the sea, but I was grateful. Is it strange for a large man to seek protection in such a small hand? I don't think so. I like to think it's better to be afraid of something others hold harmless.

We idled there a while, watching wave crests advance. Caroline, who has always liked night walks, knows how to speak to me on such occasions. She relates to me in a low voice all of the things we see together:

"Look way out, there, under the moon. Do you see the line of sand around the island? . . . a white line that looks larger and smaller as the waves touch it. The stars are very bright here. They come down to the sea . . . You can see the island where the stars disappear. There are fish jumping—look—like money thrown on the waves . . ." For a moment we listened to hear if the sound of their skipping bodies carried to us; and then, perhaps halfway between ourselves and the red- and blue-lit restaurant, there was a splash. Following the sound to its source we saw a solitary swimmer glide out, breaking the silver lines.

"Oh, yes—let's go swimming," Caroline said, tipping her toe in the water as it swirled up the shingle and foamed at our feet. "How can we not go swimming? Go get some towels—go on—it'll be cold when we get out."

She knew, of course, that I could not swim at night, but I didn't mind. I was grateful to dip again into a lighted place, to appear useful, and obligingly I went back up the path. It was as I was returning across the porch, towels in hand, that the matron of the house accosted me, and with her basic English and a sprinkling of International Sign Language made it clear that the water was shark infested—that no one swam. When I explained that someone was already swimming, she first denied the possibility, and then hurried down beside me to where Caroline waited; yet when we tried to show her this rogue swimmer, no amount of searching could turn anyone up among the waves. In the end, to her emphatic pleas that we not go into the water, we gave her our word and the towels.

Only then, appeased, did she leave us to stare at the vast and seemingly useless Pacific.

We lingered at the edge of the surf, both I think still looking for the swimmer, until Caroline, remarking the lights down the beach, said, "Oh, who cares—let's get a drink."

Despite this strange interlude, I felt more and more at home in the night. When one's eyes adjusted, it was nearly bright on that strip of sand. The ground was warm from the day, and there was a phosphorescence, we discovered, in the water: As Caroline threaded the edge of the surf, the droplets sprayed sparks, breaking waves mapped electricity. I moved my fingers in the shallows, and they left a wake of soft fire. At one point, a small dog came out from the underbrush and trotted beside us, smiling up at me until he found a spot and began earnestly digging (for crabs, we were later told). When we came upon the dark shape of a pile of clothes, it looked like another dog, sleeping in the sand.

"There, just like we told her," Caroline said, vindicated yet beyond truly caring; still, there was no person to be seen, and realizing that she no longer wanted to swim—a little wedge of terror had been inserted into the sea—we continued along toward the lights, the ocean rolling beside us in its dream.

The glow turned out to emanate, as suspected, from a *turista* bar and restaurant, set up from the water—a sweeping, semicircular porch that like everything in the town offered views of the bay and island. By the door, a Caribe band with a sleepy front man mouthed pop songs. We ate whole, roasted fish and drank lager beer, staring alternately at the view and our fellow diners. There were only a dozen others there, Germans mostly, by the sound of things. Perhaps twenty minutes after us a tall, skinny fellow with oversized, tinted glasses came in and sat alone at a nearby table. He had a large, raw face, and a slab of a jaw that rested in a grin. It was him, naturally, that we began to talk about.

"He's a nihilist—a German nihilist," I said when I'd caught a good look at him. My humor was returning. The night without made me giddy.

"On vacation?" she said with a laugh.

"Do you expect the nihilists of all people to work all the time?" I retorted. His clothes were dark and tight on him, giving him the leanness of caricature, but more than this he simply had an intensity: Five minutes went by, ten minutes, and no one came around to the table where he sat in profile to us, looking at the water and repelling humanity.

When I pointed this out in defense of my initial theory, Caroline said, "Well, he doesn't look unhappy, does he?"

"No, he's positively grinning."

"He makes a terrible nihilist. You wish they'd bring him a drink, though," she said. "He's gotten all showered and combed his hair and they won't even serve him. It's rotten."

I agreed. He had a dapper quality. Perhaps he was a "dance nihilist." At any rate, I reasoned, why shouldn't a nihilist pay attention to the finer points of hygiene? I could see Caroline wanted to send the gentleman a drink—she probably would have, too, the waiter having come by our table again—when I noticed something else and clasped her hand:

"Sweetie—it's not just his hair. *Look at him.* His clothes —everything about him is damp"—for if the light hit him right, anyone could see his jeans and T-shirt were tight because they were plastered to his skin—

"As if he put them on after swimming!" exclaimed young Nancy Drew. She was extremely pleased, and celebrated by ordering another round.

At this point the band began one of those Swedish gibberish songs Caroline loves. She frequently refers to me as a musical dinosaur, but that didn't stop her from trying to pull me up "on the floor." Another couple—two German women, actually—had paved the way, legitimizing her demands, and the band responded with a grudging rise in tempo.

"Oh, come on," she said, tugging on my arm. I laughed her off, and after a bit she sat back down and finished her drink; she wasn't giving up, though, and I knew as she drank more, she would become increasingly tenacious, that with the next song she'd repeat the whole procedure, which she did, caterwauling "come *on*"—at which point we were both silenced by the sudden appearance beside us of the nihilist.

"I'd like to dance," he said, "if there are no objections," his goggly eyes sweeping over us as he grinned. He was as tall as I, gangly and older, we saw now, his voice quiet and not at all German; besides a disconcerting stare, he really was in no way objectionable.

"Please," I replied, releasing my wife's rictus grip.

I expected, I admit, acts of Frankensteinian grace; I was disappointed to find a few minutes later that European as he was—or wasn't (I'd immediately reverted to thinking of him as the *German Nihilist*)—he'd had the requisite disco training they all receive on the Mediterranean shore. Caroline, however, was happy, and I was happy for her.

When my wife returned to the table after a few minutes, he came along, and drawing up a seat, joined us.

120

"He *was* the one," Caroline said excitedly, turning to him. "He was the *swimmer.*"

"I noticed you both at the beach tonight," he said. "Why didn't you come in?"

"The lady at the hotel told us the sea is shark infested," she explained. "She nearly had a fit when she caught Milty going out with towels."

"Exactly — of course," said our new friend, lighting a cigarette and offering around a pack of terrible Mexican smokes. He smiled, if possible, a little more. I wondered if it was simply the loud music that was raising our facial expressions as well as voices to the level of pantomime. Yet he had, as I mentioned, a remarkable stare, like a person who'd been hungry or insane at some time in his life. He said, "They're all crazy here. It's what I like about these people — they're just crazy," shaking his head and breaking into a great grin again as if this were the most amusing thing.

"How long have you been here?" Caroline asked.

"Two months nearly. I was lost —"

"But that's how we found it," she laughed.

"I know," he replied. "I saw you both arrive." To our looks of surprise, he said, "There's a café across the street from the station, and I was watching when the bus came. There are never tourists on that bus, I told myself when I saw you for the first time. What were you doing on that bus? I wondered — it was the bus *I* came here on."

He turned the mangled stare of his glasses upon me, seeming to await my reaction.

"I can't believe there are any tourists at all. There's nowhere to stay."

"You're at Angela's," he said, surprising us once again. "Most people rent a room, from a family. Boys meet the buses and take people to the families—but *your* bus," he resumed, his entire tone changing as he said so, "*no one* takes that bus. There were no kids, of course, for a bus like that." And he laughed again. "Angela's is a good place, though—a nice place."

I had a funny feeling, then, and if I hesitated to ask the question, I think it was because I was already sure that I knew the answer.

"You should have a job with the Tourist Board. What was it you said your name was?"

"Paul," he replied.

We often acquire company while traveling, and I've noticed that Caroline is happiest with someone to talk to besides myself—man or woman, it doesn't matter. Not that Caroline was the only one to benefit from Paul's company over the next few days: He was, if anything, useful. He'd been around; he knew people. He knew the owners of the restaurant we'd eaten in, for example, and often came there, just as we'd found him, to sit. There was a café in town where he spent his days doing little more than watching the buses roll in and out of the station, watching the sky tremble above the island. He liked us, too. I think he simply liked that we'd turned up on the same bus that he had, and once this disposition took hold, it deepened of its own accord.

At first I found his friendliness, aside from this coincidence, inexplicable, because he didn't demonstrate much liking for anyone else. While he turned out to speak semifluent Spanish, he never struck up a conversation with tourists or locals, never thanked anyone, and if invited to do something, never agreed unless it was of clear benefit to himself.

"He's found *us*," Caroline explained, preening. "Why should our friend need anyone else?" — though we both understood this was disingenuous.

And still, people seemed to like Paul — they *wanted* to like Paul, or at least make a point of extending their goodwill in a way he seemed unwilling to reciprocate. It was not, as we at first believed, that we'd landed among a tribe of innocents: The locals were pleasant, but they didn't offer us this solicitude, for example; or it was only toward the end of the first week that we, too, became the recipients of this cordiality, by which time we understood that they extended themselves to us because of Paul.

None of this, I should emphasize, posed any sort of problem; it was merely fuel for speculation. We decided between ourselves that he'd been a psychoanalytic student, until he'd dropped out to pursue the forbidden art of mesmerism. It was in this spirit that I asked him at one point what he *did* do, having never been told.

"I was — I am — an architect," he replied, adjusting his glasses self-consciously. "Naturally, I've begun to hate buildings. I needed to escape architecture. I needed to go somewhere where people didn't think about their buildings."

At the moment this seemed reasonable. It is, I think, a feature of travel that one tends to accept other people and their propositions of self roughly as they come. Part of the consolation of excursions, after all, is representation, and as a participant, one is duty-bound to in some sense reciprocally accept those representations of others. Nonetheless, I said, "Don't you think there are places with less architecture? It *is* a village, after all."

"Exactly," he replied, pleased, taking off his glasses to reveal eyes that were madly crossed. "I hadn't thought about that until I was already here, so fixated do you become as an architect—but then a mere road is architecture. It is as if in the very act of walking we induce architecture. So I've begun," he told me, "thinking about the island." It was the first time he mentioned the island to me.

I myself began thinking, too: I noticed that even when Paul wasn't with us, people still spoke to us of him. At first it seemed remarkable that by tacit public agreement we'd been so grouped, but there was little use objecting. It was the tone of solicitude that most struck me when I began to listen, for people returned day after day to their inquiries and remarks about him with a belittling affection not dissimilar from his own suggestions that everyone there was crazy. They'd obviously decided as much about Paul, and among their various typologies it was clear at last that it was this that made him likable.

I asked him about it, once, when we were sitting outside the café by the bus station/post office. He had just returned to the subject of the island, which he believed he could swim to in little more than two hours, remarking, "I'm an excellent swimmer." He was not, however, confident he would have the strength to return.

"An excellent swimmer," he repeated, "but practical. I'm a practical man. I'm an architect, of course—it is, you might tell me, an impractical field; there is no money in it I'm constantly being told — but if I had no practical sense, I would have become a painter."

I had not revealed to him that I ran a gallery that showed painting, exclusively, and not believing this was the time, I said, "I think the villagers believe you're crazy rather than practical. Are you entirely certain there are no sharks in the bay?"

He smiled and nodded his large head. "That's what I mean — that's it, exactly. What they don't understand is that there *are* sharks in *many* bays. The question should instead be, Are the sharks in *this* bay *dangerous?*"

"What kind of question is that?" Caroline asked. *Jaws* had emptied the nation's beaches the previous summer. She'd been filling out postcards, and was now, if I wasn't mistaken, applying to them stamps with little images of nurse sharks.

"No," I said, "I see what Paul's saying. You don't believe these are the sorts of sharks that pose a danger to people."

"Exactly," he said. He'd drunk a lot of coffee and seemed unusually agitated. "It's all projection. We think, even these very nice people here — these crazy people — think, 'If I was this animal, I would surely attack people. If I had pointy teeth'" — his teeth were merely yellow, but he bared them anyway — "'and lived in the sea, and was as big as a man . . .'"

"Yes," I agreed, "I suppose I would, too."

"But that's us, Milton. There are three kinds of people: people who are afraid of sharks, people who believe they *are* sharks, and people who believe they have to rescue other people from sharks. But there is no animal like *us.* You see, you're like *me,* Milton," he concluded, as if I'd proven his point. "You just don't like people."

Caroline laughed, and then picked up and went across the street to mail her postcards.

"Don't get me wrong," he said when we were alone, "I only say so because I'm an architect. I've never liked people — even now, when I hate buildings as much as I do. I like *you,* though — it's why I can tell you."

"Why do you like me, Paul?" I asked after a moment, egged on to ask a question Caroline and I had often batted around in private.

"Because you're like a building," he said without hesitation.

"I thought you didn't like buildings either," I said.

"I at least understand buildings," he replied, and we both laughed. I imagined myself as a structure, poor little Caroline the woman who occupied me. It's true that among the generally slight Mexican population I often felt like a feature of the landscape. They simply flowed around me in the streets, as if I didn't exist. In the road, beside us, a group of boys ran by, kicking up dust, chasing something that ran on the ground — an insect or lizard or rodent, or something imaginary.

"What kind of building am I, then?" I asked, though I understood almost immediately that I'd followed Paul farther than I should along this chain of mind. He drew deeply from his cigarette and examined me. There was something cold in his face — even his grin seemed incapable of broadcasting genuine emotion.

"You're a motel," he said, his coldness suddenly less than benign. He laughed again, probably expecting me to do the same, but I only sat back and reached for my soda. When he'd returned to merely smiling, he took another drag from his cigarette.

"What happened just there?" he asked. "We were doing so well."

"What do you mean?" I said, a little irritably.

"We were talking, having a nice time, doing very well — but now things aren't so good."

"I really don't understand. Things are fine, Paul," I told him.

For a moment he looked at me, no longer smiling, and then that great, toothy grin spread across his face. "Oh yes," he said, "you understand. That's what I like about you — we understand each other, don't you think? Because everything was fine, but then things became not so good" — making a nervous, tilting gesture with one hand, something frightening in his voice — "and soon I can see we'll begin to fight . . ."

"Paul," I repeated, feeling in what he said a certainty that unchecked meant we *would* begin to fight, "I don't know what you're talking about" — though of course I did. It just didn't matter whether he was right or wrong — I wasn't going to have this conversation. I was relieved to see Caroline crossing the street up the block, coming toward us, and I waved, breaking his concentration.

Not surprisingly, something changed in our relationship after this. Caroline noticed that we'd cooled, Paul and I, but it was the sort of shift difficult to explain. I told her it was nothing — that I was tired of Paul, which was the case. For his part, Paul continued to seek us out, but now he did so with a purpose in mind: He wanted to talk about the island.

"I'm going to do it," he told us. "I have to go back to the States soon, to work — but I'm going to swim to the island first. I've been swimming out, farther and farther. I was half-way last night," he said proudly, "and I wondered if I should swim all the way, but then I was afraid I wouldn't have the energy to swim back, and I would be stuck."

It was evening, and the three of us were standing on the shore, looking at the island. There wasn't much to it: a long, high hill, brown with patches of dry green; a thicket of palms to one side, surrounded by a skirt of sand.

"I'm practical," he emphasized. "There might be water on the island, but there might not. I couldn't risk swimming all the way there, becoming exhausted, and having to spend the night, without shelter, possibly without water."

The journey across a shark-infested bay struck me as danger enough that his scruples should have been amusing; yet I wasn't amused, for I began to see where this was leading: He was trying to convince us of something. A few minutes later he added:

"It's very hard to find a fisherman who will take me to the island. They're all afraid. They are afraid of the water, of the island, of everything," he said. "Not that I want to be taken — it's important that I arrive on the island with nothing, as free of architecture as possible. But even when I ask if they will just come and *meet me on the island* to bring me back, they tell me all their nonsense about rocks and sharks — but it's all *nonsense*," he cried again, struggling to keep down his voice. "And I know that, because as soon as I offered enough money, I found someone to do it."

"Now, Paul —" Caroline began.

"Wait," he said. "I know — you don't think it's a good idea. But I have a plan. The idea is to be practical," he reminded us. "I'm going to be *practical*. These men are afraid for me because they are afraid for themselves—they'd probably get skinned alive by the *policía* if anything were to happen to a *turista* they were connected with. I can't trust them—they'll try to wriggle out as soon as I pay them. So Milton is going to hold the money and come with the men in the boat, to make sure they do what they say they will."

"Me?" I laughed, taken off guard, suspicious as I was. "I feel the same way Caroline does—I don't like the whole idea." And in truth, besides the danger involved for Paul, I'd begun to see him as a hazard. I had no intention of getting into a boat or tromping around on this island in his company; however, I tried to treat the subject lightly. He let me explain everything I was going to explain—everything, of course, but my concerns about his own shortcomings. And then, when I was through, he replied:

"I thought of all that. I thought about it, and I've anticipated your concerns, because you have to come. I'm going to go whether or not you agree, and so I know you'll come in the end. You won't be able to stand the idea of me going by myself, the danger you'd subject me to—and I would do the same for you. That's why I know in the end you'll agree."

And though we argued with him, Caroline and I, and although by now I thoroughly disliked Paul—by the time this conversation wound down I was convinced of every misgiving—he was, of course, entirely right.

Two days later I came out at dawn to meet the boat. It was a little, beat-up aluminum shell with a bad motor, captained by a man and his son who were waiting by the water.

"I speak *French*," I explained to the father near the beginning of the journey, faced with a confounding question and bitterly regretting Caroline's absence. After that, we smiled at one another, periodically gestured, and then fell silent in every way. We idled along near Paul for three hours as he swam and floated, swam and floated.

The boat was packed with water, some first-aid items, dry clothes, and beer. The men drank the beer and talked quietly together, shaking their heads as they watched this person they considered a fool struggling along beside them.

It was before eight when we set out, Paul prudently wanting to arrive on the island before the sun had reached its zenith. While I was at first anxious and uncomfortable in the prow, cringing to stay clear of what seemed ever-present pools and puddles in the battered bottom, as I settled in it actually became a pleasant morning. Besides the fact there was a current near the island that made the swimming more arduous, and hence longer than Paul had anticipated, even the fishermen eventually conceded that the sharks were uninterested in him. For an hour, when we saw their fins at a distance, the old man would stand up and shout to Paul in a toothless, agitated Spanish; after that he became reconciled to Paul and the animals' indifference to one another.

Our arrival on the island was similarly without fanfare. The victorious swimmer gasped, smiling and delirious, on the shore. He'd taped his glasses to his head, and in his black swim trunks and the modified headgear he looked like an aquatic monster-man in a low-budget film. He drank the water I brought to him and told me about what was, in fact, a fantastically boring event for anyone but himself. All the same, hearing actual happiness inflect his voice, I found for the first time in a week that I liked him again.

At last he sat up and began to look around at this place that had been his great obsession — I would say without rancor that this obsession substantially predated our arrival in the town, that perhaps all he'd ever seen in us was the means of making this journey.

"It's exactly as I imagined," he murmured, his face the face of another man now that his smile, at the onset of genuine pleasure, had abandoned him. Yet there was nothing to see where we'd beached; and after Paul put on a shirt and hat to ward off the sun, we left the men on the boat and began walking around. I think Paul hoped to find some feature of the land, some culmination in his odyssey away from architecture; he reflected on precisely those longings at last, and said to me, as to one who'd accompanied him in his thoughts: "But there I go — just like an architect. It's *not* about that. It's not about anything . . ." In the wake of which remarks he kept turning to look down the slope at the wide blue gulf separating us from the mainland. The sight seemed to fill him with strength. It took us more than an hour to climb the scrabbly hillside, during which time he maintained an anticipatory silence, his mouth, through which he breathed heavily, working over various elusive expressions.

"The possibilities are nearly oppressive," I recall him saying once, having glanced back again at the bay. "Do you think that possibility, then, is the opposite of architecture?" I was afraid he was becoming delirious, and made him drink more water.

Rounding a ridge of the hill to gain a panorama of the

Pacific, however, instead of the hoped-for marvel of solitude — of who-knows-what inversion of presence he believed might be contained on this roadless speck — we discovered, concealed along a shallow cove, glistening with red tile roofs and solar panels, a large marina and resort.

For a moment Paul stared. He took out his cigarettes and lit up, ogling the cabanas and pleasure boats with pure fascination, as if on cutting open his arm he'd discovered a colony of ants living inside.

"I'm sorry," I said.

Seemingly in response, he let out something like a howl.

Eyes still upon the scene, he staggered down, myself at his heels, certain he was going to tumble from the slope upon the nearer buildings. In the end, after prevailing upon him to pull himself together, spying several men in security jackets riding a golf cart toward where we stood, I half-dragged him over the crest of the hill and back to the boat.

We found the fishermen tinkering with the engine, which had developed a leak and dribbled gas into the hull. It smelled terrible, and though we were both quite hungry and exhausted, we ate nothing, I due to nausea, Paul through what I took for despondency. Instead we opened beers. Paul glared at the island as we waited for the men to finish making their repairs. He was still breathing hard, speechless, which I would have found welcome if I hadn't felt unwell and wanted distraction. When the men at last started the boat and edged it away from shore, Paul suddenly bawled out the same horrible howl — only this time one couldn't help but feel there was some self-parody intended: He ran the scream down to its last rattle, then burst out coughing and laughing, much to everyone's relief.

"I hate these people," he said to me—about which people, exactly, I wasn't sure, nor did I ask. I excused myself for a moment, and turning over on my stomach, wretched a long, ugly strand over the side into the wake, watching the foam swirl and melt.

The sun was lowering. When I looked back at the horizon, beyond the receding island, the light bounced off the ocean as if from a vast sheet of metal. Turning around, I could see the mainland shore, a bunker of shimmering sand, the dark blotch of sage and yucca working up the valleys. I was relieved it was done, that we were returning. If only everything didn't reek of gas. The men couldn't figure out what was wrong, and poured fuel from a spare can into a funnel affixed to the engine, nursing the boat along. They must be nervous, I thought, focusing near at hand on Paul's wavering figure. He had a cigarette in his mouth. I stared in disbelief as he struck a match, hearing the sudden cries of *"Señor, señor!"* as the boatmen froze at the back of the little craft, their hands held out as if to calm time.

"Paul?" I said, my voice, which I hadn't used in a while, sounding very small. I wasn't sure he would even look up.

"Oh, shit," he replied, glancing at everyone; and then he laughed again and whipped the match overboard. We watched it slip into the wrestling water, and he sank back opposite me on the gunwale. Our two guides lingered in their fright before they returned to whatever they were doing. They looked miserable, and I felt bad for them, but Paul's laughter was infectious, and I'd drunk too much waiting for them to get under way.

"Shit," I said, "is *exactly* right"—lying back in the hollow of the hull in a coil of rope, starting up briefly to remove a homemade anchor like a meat hook that gouged into my kidneys. "How do you say 'shit' in Spanish, Paul?"

"Mierda," he replied, the unlit cigarette trembling where it stuck to his lower lip.

"Mierda!" I called to the two men. The father, at the tiller, gave me a sick smile, but his son didn't look up from bailing. Frustration clenched the muscles of his shoulders. "Ah, whatever," I said, turning back. "Joke 'em if they can't take a fuck."

Paul, however, didn't hear me, because he was bent down low in the hull, trying to keep out of the wind, another lit match held trembling to his cigarette.

"Paul," I repeated. "Hey, Paul" — the laugh balanced on the edge of my voice, as the two men started in again with *"Señor, señor . . ."*

Paul looked up. The cigarette was lit. The red coal swelled and the match tip hung for a moment in yellow flame. Then his eyes turned toward me beneath the reflected light in his glasses — a look so becalmed, so full of comprehension as to seem disdainful — as, like a film run backward, a torrent of fire rose from the cocktail of gasoline and water around his ankles and climbed onto his hands and the collar of his shirt.

Silently he scrambled to his feet, staggering down the boat, waving his hands about his face as if awaiting the arrival of actual pain. With outstretched arms, the father and son drove him away from the gas can and engine. I took shelter in the gunwale, lifting my feet clear of the mixture of water and floating flame that he sloshed through. He then returned to the screaming men at the back of the boat, a walking fire. His mouth, I saw beneath the rippling yellow screen, was open, as if he was laughing or grinning, though in reality I could hear nothing above the barrage of Spanish. Yet it did eventually occur to me that they were shouting about water, and I grasped, watching him stagger this way and that, that he should of course just leap into the sea. I said as much — I joined in the cacophony; but it was like shouting at a force of nature. The boat rocked and tipped before righting itself. The men, sensing what was to come, grew quiet. Something had to be done, and one can't, after all, just punch a burning man. Rising carefully, when he next teetered toward me, I hefted the crude anchor in my hand and struck his head with a well-turned blow. Silent, he staggered back, hooked his knees over the gunwale, and plunged over the side.

It was ten minutes later, bailing out the last of the burning gas, that the old man spotted Paul's glasses, shriveled in the bottom of the hull. He handed them to me, and for a few seconds I held them as he squinted across our little raft. I think he believed I might put them on.

Arriving at the town well after dark, I found Caroline at the Felicidad, half-asleep in bed.

"How'd it go?" she murmured with closed eyes. "Did he make it? I was so worried about you, but then I got sleepy . . ."

"It went all right," I told her, sitting and running my hand over the sheets, her legs. "Better than anyone expected, in fact. I don't think he knew what he was looking for until he found it — and then, what *is* the opposite of architecture, anyway?"

"So what did it look like?" she mumbled.

"Oh — you kind of had to see it."

I thought she was asleep again, but after a moment, in a faint voice, she said: "How's Paul? Is he downstairs?"

"Paul? Paul's gone. He had to get the night bus back, remember? He had to return to his firm, the poor man. I suppose it's for the best, though. I saw him off.

"He said," I added, rising and beginning to undress, "to say good-bye."

I T WAS EARLY when I went out to find Thales again. For the better part of yesterday, following my expedition with the old man to find a bulb, I'd dickered with the sewing machine, disappointed at the quality of my stitches — disappointed with the entire feel of things. Admitting at last that I'd concentrated on a simple task to the point where I'd complicated it in my own mind, I then spent most of the night making notes on the last few weeks. Only after exhausting myself at the typewriter, faced with the odious chore of reapproaching the Featherweight (I've cobbled together thus far *two strips of cloth* torn from one of the suits bought at Archie's), and truly feeling, I think for the first time, the loneliness of this place — only having gotten myself in such a state did I decide to go out and see Thales.

I'd marked his turquoise pickup parked by the road and made my way through the weeds to his door; yet as I stood in the threshold of the tiny house, hollering quietly, it seemed in fact that everyone was out, until I heard a faint reply from the back room and recalled that Emily would likely be there.

I found her reclining on a daybed, in a corner upon which the window curtains had been half drawn. Emily is Eileen's grandmother—the woman who as a child supposedly met Singer; a woman, as I think I've mentioned, of spectacular age, and blind. She is, if not paralyzed by her years, no longer given to motion, save the slightest dispositions of the face; her features maintain a placid content that leads me to believe she has moved beyond thoughts of convenience or inconvenience; and in general, as her comments to me indicated, she's moved beyond most analytic thought entirely:

"Milton, is that you?" her soft voice whispered as I stood in the doorway. When I replied that it was, she asked in amazement, "How did you get out here all by yourself?"

"I'm staying at the motel—didn't they tell you? Has everyone gone out?"

"But that's marvelous," she said, ignoring my question. "You must have Charles with you."

"No . . . he's coming in a few days," I told the wizened face, her hair a loosed cloud upon the pillow, thick and lustrous; were it not white, it could easily be mistaken for the hair of a much younger woman. I came a bit farther into the room as my eyes adjusted.

"Marvelous," she repeated. "You must feel quite at home, then."

I wondered if I'd overstepped some invisible civil boundary. I'd been to the house with Charles a dozen times during our stay a couple of weeks ago and thought nothing of making an appearance today; but had I ever, come to think of it, been alone in the back room before? Was this a more private portion of the house? My concerns, however, were allayed:

"It goes to prove there *are* still things the old can learn from the young. If I could move, I declare I would get up and join you — one would think you weren't blind at all."

For a moment I didn't follow. I smiled when I did. "Emily, *you're* blind. I'm not blind."

The faintest beginning of a smile was returned to me.

"You're joshing . . . but when did this happen?" she asked.

"It's never been any other way."

"I have to admit," she mused when my words had time to sink in, "it's the most sensible explanation. But imagine — I wonder where I could have gotten such an idea from . . ."

An embarrassed pause followed. Although the room was dim, I picked out now the details of small flowers printed on the nightgown she wore, of her bare feet, also young-looking, peeking from beneath the hem of her dress on the daybed.

"Has everyone gone out?" I repeated gently.

"Oh, yes — just silly me," she said, adding, "When you spend your days as I'm want, you do dwell on some silly things. Do you know, by the way, if Charles's friend has arrived yet?"

This is how it always is. For a moment you're on solid ground, in a recognizable territory, yet if you glance away for even an instant, it seems she's drifted off on the ice floe of a misunderstanding or bit of nothing overheard and misappropriated.

"*I* am Charles's friend," I reminded her.

"Of course you are, dear, but the other fellow," she began, and then the doubt was seeded in her voice. She grew quiet, the smile once more tipping her face. "I don't know what's the matter with me today. I guess he didn't mention the other fellow to you."

"No, Emily . . . it must have slipped his mind."

She was staring at me with her large, dead eyes as I spoke—they're like frozen lakes in her netted and eroded face. Then, unmistakably, she winked.

"Look," I said, uncomfortable and feeling that she wasn't, perhaps, at her best, "when they come back, would you just tell them I stopped by—to say hello?"

"Certainly, dear. Most certainly." The moment stretched. Sensing I wanted to go, she volunteered, "Try not to worry about me, Mr. Menger—you have to understand, when you reach a certain age, your mind turns into a bit of a labyrinth. Come another time, though, if you can. Please do. It's *always* a pleasure."

It had been a long night in the dive across from The Long Valley Motor Inn (little red roofs? window boxes? troop of roses?), and we wound up drunk, and not surprisingly, the following day began as if someone were prying open the door to brutality. I'd left behind a parched dream in which I was living with Jane Garnet in my home in New Jersey. There was a regularity, even a blandness, to our life together; yet I was uneasy, thinking that Caroline would return. I wandered the rooms, listening for the sound of her car, seeking from various windows a view of the drive. In my dream, Caroline was out somewhere in the defunct Pontiac—with its bad brakes it sounded like a gigantic cicada. I kept thinking I caught the edge of it, blooming in the distance. I was upstairs, in the master bedroom, listening for the car, and listening to Jane moving around the ground floor. I had no sense of how to break it off with this woman in leopard print, but faced with the necessity, gazing out at where the yard gives way to bracken and pine, looking into summer, it broke over me that I loved Jane. In the dream I wasn't merely fascinated by her, I felt a thrill I'd never known before to simply hear her voice — a feeling that I feared to name as such because of what it would mean in my life. Some terrible *other* voice, however, was calling, and opening my eyes, I found Charles standing over me.

"What's the matter with you? Where are we?" I croaked, wincing at the bead-board walls and the door he'd left open to appalling quantities of light. "We'll take a sick day. Can't we take a sick day?"

I closed my eyes again. I was awful with hangover, but the feeling I'd had in the dream remained, an impression of color against my lids, even if I felt nothing like love for Jane in waking life. It was the *color*, though. Anything could have been that color, it occurred to me, but it was the most beautiful color, and for a long time I tried to return and to grasp again what, exactly, it had been. Charles said nothing, only switched on the television, sat down, and lit up. I rolled back beneath the covers into an acrid lagoon, the beautiful hue fading. "Oh, that was a mistake," I moaned after a while.

"I let things slide as long as I could," he replied. "There's nothing I can do, though . . . we have this meeting. I can't believe that nonsense I told you last night," he added when a little time had passed. "I was drunk, you know — plain drunk."

My mind fumbled back to the conversation we'd had in the bar, and I remembered suddenly the excursion we'd taken into phobias . . . a phobia he claimed for himself, or that I'd become certain belonged to him: a fear of coincidence. And while it's true that we'd both been plastered by evening's end, I could reassemble, head in the dark, that the night had been young, and ourselves decidedly sober, when we'd begun that conversation.

"Don't make me remember," I said, closing my eyes.

For a while the room was silent except for the drone of the television. I believed he might have gone away, and fell back asleep. When he changed channels I awoke with a start. There were tiny, squeaky voices singing — chipmunks.

"I feel," he said to the haggard face I raised, "I haven't been fair to you, Milty."

"You could begin," I suggested, "by going away" — but it wasn't to be. After a while, seeing he had no intention of leaving or turning off the cartoons, I crawled into the shower; only then did he go out for coffee. Under the water I again closed my eyes. The sound of heels on the parquet — that was all there'd been of her in the dream, and yet it contained all of love, like a death. Like the details of the dead leaving us, more quickly than we can imagine, a weeping away, until they remain only as a sense, and not the sense *of* something.

What had he just said, though? I thought, cringing in the cold water — *I haven't been fair to you*? It was so little to be told, yet even in such a stupor, it contained years. Every word, years. Even tonight, to have Charles in this room, and to compel him to speak as Dante the damned — but you can never ask so much. And what could he have said, then, that would have changed what I believed? Save perhaps "I was mistaken — I mistook you for another man." Don't we *want* to be mistaken for better men?

I haven't been fair to you — still, while there was some *truth* to it (this motel business, to begin with, was criminal), the words blended with Jane's *all kinds of things* until I had nothing but water that smelled of sulfur and a towel the size of a bandana. I climbed into my pants as if I were mounting a horse. I was standing in the middle of the room, on that margin between the bed and the vanity-area carpets, when he returned, coffees in hand.

"Maybe I should explain," he continued from where he'd left off. "You see, I've been wondering to myself, lately, what exactly you're doing here."

I couldn't help but notice this was a question, not an explanation.

"I came down to give *you* a hand, Charles—"

"Yes, of course—I'm not trying to be ungrateful," he assured me, filling the vanity area with smoke. "I just wondered what you'd be doing . . . if you weren't here."

Outside, I rested on the hood of the car. A grasshopper flew from the wiper blades and vanished into the weeds beside the lot. The clouds were low and articulate. For a moment it appeared that there was a sick man suspended in the sky. I wasn't thinking about what Charles had just said. I began, instead, trying to recall what he'd told me the night before, about coincidence. As had always been the case with Charles—his tireless obsession with any topic he'd gotten hold of, an incredible egotism—I'd found myself at last half-agreeing with him. Shutting my eyes, I remembered a fragment from further on in the evening, when I'd protested tiredly that there needn't *be* any repercussions to a coincidence:

"But there *are* repercussions," he'd replied, becoming excited again. "How can you believe there are no repercussions? We only pretend there aren't, when there have to be, if you understand that they're truer—the coincidences are truer than everything else. A coincidence doesn't even have to be true to be 'truer.' It's better. Once, twice, you can struggle against coincidence with whatever *facts,* but in time, in *time,*" he'd maintained as I stared at the moving block of his mouth, "a coincidence wears everything down. It is more true than truth. It becomes the figure on the ground, Milton—you see?"

There *was* a part of me that understood and agreed, though it was perhaps also the part of me that was drunk. It was from this reverie, lowering myself into the car, that I glanced at him and remembered he'd just said something.

"What I'd be doing, if I wasn't here?" I repeated. "I'd be at the gallery by now—or no, better, I'd be asleep . . ."

He'd chosen this moment to ask a question whose answer actually required my best efforts, that only yesterday I'd *wanted* him to ask. It was entwined with everything I needed to say, but phrased by another human being and not my own cogitations, the question embarrassed.

"You're right—I'm being an ass," Charles apologized. "I should have waited until we had something to eat. After what you said last night, though . . . I was too soused to respond, and you know how it is—you imagine things about people's lives—*I* imagined things . . ." And suddenly, having no idea what he was talking about, I was very much awake.

"I got a letter from Caroline a few weeks back," he continued. "I meant to tell you, I was going to last night, but I knew I'd screw it up . . . so I've screwed it up." He rubbed his hand on the vinyl seat. "Milty—I knew when I called you . . . when I asked you to come down here, I knew you might want to get certain things off your chest"—all of which I barely heard, racking my brain to recall what I might have said in the wee

144

hours, how I might have veered from his maniacal babble about coincidence, in self-defense, practically, and told him any detail about myself and the disintegration of my marriage. "There's a lot I should've mentioned," he added. "It's just everything was such a mess." And my thoughts went out, once again, to what he'd told me on the phone:

Do you mind coming down to help me straighten things out? When of course I'd come to think of myself as someone who could only mangle the world. It seemed I'd been unable to tell him this except in a sort of sleep.

"Everything was such a mess," he repeated; yet surprisingly, I felt quite good. *Something is happening,* I kept telling myself. *It's happening now.*

"I remember very little about last night," I replied, amazed at my own calm. "I gather I told you Caroline and I are finished — though I take it that was already in her letter. What else," I asked after a moment, "did she say?"

"She said she wanted to make sure you didn't misrepresent her. It was silly — I could have told her she had nothing to fear, that you wouldn't even mention it. Much more like you not to mention it at all, in fact — which you didn't. But she said she wanted me to know," he rambled, "that the two of you had nothing in common."

"Isn't it amazing how some people have that power, Charles — to be correct? To be factually correct, morally correct? *She was probably right about fucking everything,*" I shouted into the red amphitheater of the car. Still, I continued to feel strangely free of anger: "Sorry — I haven't talked about this. Barely with myself, even."

"Did she leave you for someone else?" he asked.

"No. She left me for nothing." After which we were quiet.

I was thinking of my wife's hand—her handwriting: There's something hopeful in the look of her lines, little soldiers carried from childhood with so little service. They group themselves for thank-yous, invitations, and postcards—and now, it seemed, for letters. Charles and Caroline share a love of the postcard, I thought, and I marveled that I bore him no ill will. If anything, I was relieved, as if some good I'd done had been repaid with a freedom I'd been unaware I lacked; when I glanced over at Charles, though, he looked exhausted. Burdened with these things, he'd likely been unable to sleep. I suggested a nap. He pretended at first this wasn't even desirable, yet soon gave in, murmuring instructions, telling me to wake him when we came to Ellenville. I heard everything, filled with a strange elation.

I thought, then, of Charles's mother, whom I'd met only twice, although she lived in the same town as the one in which I grew up. My impressions had been of a withdrawn, even depressed woman; but what I was thinking of in the car was the change that came over her features—ordinarily expressive of nothing save existential patience—when her son entered the room.

It was during a holiday weekend that I'd first visited Charles's childhood home. Mrs. Trembleman sat with folded hands in the living room, recuperating from an unnamed illness. She was watchful but unengaged, even with her husband—a pleasant but blurrily drawn man of slight build and inclination, a machinist for the Company. There was a parade huddled like a gray cloud on the television, and I sat down beside them, unaware and unwarned of the oblivion to which I was consigning myself. By a sort of twenty-questions process with Mr. Trembleman, I at last arrived at the topic of the *Hindenburg* airship, which Charles's father, as a young German, had been present in person to watch go down in flames on its final field. He'd retained an indelible interest in the event that he brought to parades and their aerial mascots. At no point during the conversation did Mrs. Trembleman even glance at me, let alone speak. And then Charles, hunting about the house for a book he needed at school, came downstairs, or in from the garage where he stashed his paintings. I remember the sense, watching Mrs. Trembleman's face, that she'd been ruined by Charles. She behaved in his absence as if she'd grown addicted to an intelligence that was nowhere else to be found. When he walked into the room, her face turned to him like a flower toward the sun; and when he left, she wasn't downcast so much as reassured. If the house had been larger, she would, I suppose, have withdrawn to a distant chamber. As it was, she grew quiet. She gave no explanation, and oddly enough the matter required none — we all, it went without saying, admired her son.

I hadn't known Charles very long — this was shortly after he'd won the Hatfield Prize from the University, and everyone on campus seemed to be talking about his work. Those people, like myself, who'd known Charles beforehand, however slenderly (and everyone suddenly seemed to), took a proprietary pleasure in him, and I'd looked forward with the same fascination we bring to biography to meeting his parents. Nothing could have disappointed me: However I found them, I see now, they could only increase the fascination I felt for my new friend. By contrast or congruence, they could only contribute.

I'm not sure why I thought then of Charles's mother. It may have been the sight of him, curled childishly against the car door; or perhaps that I recalled her name was Ellen, and was drawn to her memory by the name of the town I was to look for. It would be, as I would have told Charles, one of so many minute and meaningless coincidences.

Hours must have passed, though, before I was startled back into a consciousness of the present. We were on a narrow road, overhung with new foliage; I'd been musing about Ellen Trembleman, and then about the town of my birth, which, like my father and Charles's mother, had lain for years in a sort of illness, when directly before the car a deer bolted from a lattice of brush. I braked and swung into the other lane, passing the startled creature where it quivered beside the yellow line. A few seconds later I looked back. There it stood, still thin with winter, frozen as a lawn ornament in the dapple of the canopy. It watched me until the gentle curve of the road brought us out of sight of one another. Only then, emerging into open lands again, did I realize the sky had begun to dim, the sun to sink low—and it was with this that I began to wonder if I hadn't missed a turn in the road. Glancing at Charles, awakened by the careening of the car, I saw that it was so.

"Where are we?" he asked, staring around in amazement, looking at his watch. "You never stopped—"

"There was no Ellenville," I protested, though I, too, was surprised to discover that I'd driven for more than four hours in my reverie.

"We—I don't even know where this is. We passed Ellenville ages ago."

The countryside surrounding us was a fresh and monocrop

green, and we both looked about, seeking a sign, anything. I could see Charles was struggling to master a growing anxiety as we entered a town of some sort, a few homes set back from the road, inklings of municipality.

The town—I still don't know its name—lay upon a hill, and as we climbed, the sun slouched ever lower into the fields, so that as we crested the hilltop it seemed as if all around the hill and town a sea of gold had inundated the lowlands of Georgia. We passed through streets endless with evening, boled by dark and ancient oaks. There was a high, white church all shut up, a gazebo turning colors in a public park. It was very quiet. It reminded me of a place I'd been before, but in the moment I didn't know where—or it was like a photograph of this same place, but a place of which I had only ever seen another photograph, a place whose picture had been taken at two distant times.

I don't remember what I was saying to Charles, then, as we drove around that corner behind a hardware store and an empty lot, riding over the open tracks of a rusted rail crossing. We were looking for a gas station or a convenience store where we could ask the shortest way to Ellenville. I do remember the little houses of the street opening up on either side of us like a book. Sometimes an event shines its light in all memory around itself; but just as often, as now, it leaves a crater of upheaval and darkness at its margins disproportionate to the duration of the moment. It happened so quickly.

I imagine I was going to try to explain this feeling of pictures that had come over me; though perhaps I was going to ask Charles about the last paintings I recall him making—little geometries of the city of Elizabeth—and what had become of them. I turned my head to discover whether my curiosity was appreciated, and instead discovered that his expression was one of horror. I didn't see the child on the bicycle until I turned back and found her teetering before the car, face composed more of surprise than fright, and then we felt the impact and heard the bright clatter of metal and the sound of something soft against the hood.

Why, I've since read in the papers, the editorials, didn't I stop?

But I did stop — I did.

She was not, as most people imagine who've only watched accidents on television, swept under the car. My foot spasmed on the brake, and she was knocked from the face of the grille, the wheels crushing the bicycle. I stood for a moment in the road, you see, looking at her lying by the green swath of a yard. One of the spoked wheels — the one uncrushed — was still spinning, but she was motionless, while the evening seemed to rush in and grow perceptibly darker around her. And then there was blood on her arm, and at the side of her head, like a mistake upon the golden hair and the yellow dress. It all opened up as I stood there, that spreading darkness — every moment deepening and swallowing up anything that had come before. The entire street seemed to sink and condense into the moment as I looked down upon the girl on the verge, all the houses staring onto the road, at me beside the car, and her either alive or dead. I expected people to pour from those doorways, I expected the yards to fill with commotion; but if anything, the street became more silent.

I looked up from where I'd crouched and saw Charles, his face a disbelief; and then, from the far end of our long block, I discerned a car coming toward us. I remember thinking that for the driver of the car, none of this had happened yet — it was all in a future that, at that moment, only Charles and I had seen, like one of those black stars that implode in space, gathering mass from their neighbors, growing inescapable as they pull down other stars into their darkness. And without giving any more thought to what I was doing, I climbed back into the front seat. I grinned horribly, I think, at the unknown driver when we passed each other; he flashed his brights at me. As I rounded the next corner, beginning to drive faster and faster, I saw his car slow beside the shape folded on the roadside. Understanding then, I turned on my lights.

And after that, it was like losing consciousness. I didn't know, but I was apparently talking for most of the time, to no one but myself, although when we gained a major road twenty minutes out of town, and Charles asked me what I was talking about, I had to admit I was talking about nothing at all.

"Why didn't you stop?" he asked.

"I did," I said feebly. "My God, did you see her?" My God, how fast I was going!

I could still feel the town behind us, an unfurling menace. Even as I was slowing down, realizing that the worst thing I could do was speed my way into the arms of the law, it seemed that what had just transpired was less something I'd done than something done *to* me. I wondered if, behind any of those windows, there had been a pair of eyes.

"Why did you keep driving?" he said, but it was no longer a question composed of shock. It was simply a question.

"Why didn't you say anything?" I replied, not really wanting to have this conversation. "Why didn't you say anything then, when it mattered?"

The moon had come out. On either side of the road, leaves

tipped beneath the weight of moonlight like boughs bearing snow; and snow suddenly seemed a thing I might never see again, that possessed reserves of gentleness I'd never taken notice of before this night. I regretted bitterly coming to the South, and I thought of Elizabeth — the little Elizabeth of my youth — and it came to me, as things often do past the point of use, that it was of Elizabeth that the town had reminded me. Town of my disaster. I think it was an hour later — I had no idea where I was going — when Charles finally said to me, "We might as well stop here for the night. You shouldn't be driving."

We were passing through a commercial strip. Everything breathed detention, and I couldn't focus on the big white and red signs thrown out at the road.

"Anywhere in particular?" I asked. He shook his head. He was as lost as I was. We passed a police station, and I drove on, another mile. "What about there," I suggested of a renovated fifties-style place.

For a moment he didn't answer, and then he motioned across the road to its unreconstructed counterpart. "Here, stop here," he said of the two-story cinderbox with a sort of Tudor theme. It was called the Dutch Treat, which I half recalled was a metaphor for a dirty trick. In the moment, it was more than I could take.

"I'm not staying there," I said in a low voice. When he neither responded nor in any way signaled that he'd even heard me, I continued:

"If this is a matter of habit and superstition, anyplace here is as good as the next — you've been to none of them. If it's a matter of money, I'm happy to pay the difference. I'm happy to pay for the whole fucking thing. I am unable to imagine what else on earth could motivate you to unerringly choose the worst flea-ridden establishments night after night, but I *cannot* continue to abide by this idiotic logic!"

My voice had crescendoed by the time I'd finished; whatever socialization and bizarre theorizing had, up to this point, prevented me from speaking my mind on the subject, the disaster made matters of etiquette evaporate. Charles stared silently out his window.

"Why can't we stay there?" I said of a Motel 6. "Or there—what about there?" of a Radisson, up ahead where the strip unraveled and the town came to an end.

He was silent, and then murmured, "We can stay anyplace you like."

I laughed out loud. "*Thank* you," I roared, veering into the Radisson parking lot (never had I been so happy to find a Radisson)—"Thank you"—as its light of disinfected efficiency bore through the Southern night, and we gazed into the glassed lobby with its micro-chandelier and its carpeting and furniture themed in acceptable browns and golds.

I cut the engine. In a quieter voice I said, "I need you to go in and sign the paperwork—do you think you can do that?" I felt full of electricity and the visible wheals of past lies. There was no way I was speaking to another human being in my present state.

He moved his fingers slightly in his bandages. "Sure," he said. "I'll get them to fill everything out." Putting on his jacket, he got up and stumped into the front office.

When he was gone, I stood by the car, looking at the grille, which had been dented a little in the collision. I felt better, having said what I'd said. I reached down and grasped the wands of metal to bend them back in line, and scalding my fingers, found something lodged between the chrome bars. Reaching gingerly within, I withdrew the rubber grip — translucent, milky, flecked with glitter — of a bicycle handlebar. When Charles came back out, he saw what I was looking at and suggested I pull in closer to the shrubbery. We didn't say another word that night.

And what *would* there have been to say, anyway? That I should have done things differently? That I'd made mistakes? There is nothing I could have done *at that point* that might have helped. I could only aid an impersonal law, and hurt myself — which all sounds poor, I know. It is too simple, though, to imagine from the safety of a chair, or another life.

I have one thing more to offer in my defense: I considered for the first time, as I lay down less than an hour later, supperless and alone in my little blue-walled room washed in the steel of air conditioning — perhaps the last such room I might lock from the inside — that there was something not merely eccentric but wrong with my traveling companion. I'm not trying to avoid my culpability in the accident, yet even *then* he could have placed a call from the phone by his bedside. He might have blamed it all on me — I was, after all, behind the wheel; but it would have touched him, his life — this Singer business. He'd have to appear in court. There'd be questions. Perhaps the company name might be mentioned in some unfavorable light. It might have *stopped* him. There he was, though, driving around with his bandages in this benighted land — he didn't, it was clear, want to be stopped.

As I lay upon the tops of the covers like a fugitive — the room, I noted with sorrow, smelled like an ashtray — I wondered if whatever had kept him quiet when I drove off and left the girl there originated in something as crude as the fear he'd lose his job. Not that the question could lead anywhere — whatever it was would keep — but his job was the thing I imagined. His silence certainly didn't originate in loyalty to me, and his job, I realized, was what I most knew of him. I'd never had a *job;* still, I was aware that people slip into all sorts of moral error at the bidding of their jobs. They begin to make choices. And it's no small thing, but it is also a small thing. It crossed my mind.

Going a step farther, I can say I recognized that night in Charles something of myself. I'd had some new apprehension of him in the bar the previous evening, and it was still confused — difficult to tell from the adrenal rush that was only now ebbing, leaving me exhausted — but I'd begun to perceive in this man I'd always regarded from a distance as one regards a mountain, as one can only regard, with a little awe, those things so unlike oneself, a resemblance to me that I couldn't yet put into words.

I knew that we'd both noticed this, and I also knew that from here on I would be a little bit stronger than I had been, and he would be — he already was — a little weaker. I can't remember when I finally slept.

THE NEXT MORNING, Charles woke me at 7:30. A few minutes later I'd taken a booth in the "Jubilee" room while he phoned Ellenville to reschedule the meeting we'd driven past in our flight — "a little radiator trouble. Back road — yes — took ages to flag someone down. Ages." Afterward he sat across from me, newspaper held open between us. Requests to pass condiments indicated he wasn't surly or particularly out of sorts, just quiet. He smoked, pushing aside his food, folding the local gazette at last around the quarto of a particular page. He said, "She's ten."

I had, I suppose, after an hour of enforced tranquility, assumed that this was to be our disguise: that we were going to forget about it. And why, I'd reasoned, glancing about at the few people in the room, strangers engaged in their own newspapers, *should* anyone pay us any attention? After all, it was nearly as if nothing had happened. So it shocked me a little to hear Charles say even those two words out loud, innocuous as they were in themselves.

"Her name is Margaret Duffey," he went on, offering me the folded paper until I took it. "There's a picture of her, if you want to look."

"Is she still alive?" I asked.

"It appears she is. She hasn't woken up yet, though."

The waitress came and went with another round of coffee.

"Does it say anything about us?" I asked.

"Read it. It says they're 'pursuing leads.'" I looked at the grainy photo of a girl in pigtails, grinning for what was likely a class picture. I would, I told myself, read the words later.

"Where are we going today?" I asked.

"Back to Ellenville," he said. "It's just south of Macon."

For the rest of breakfast we said little; and by the time we'd got on the road, we'd ceased speaking altogether. I wondered if he was angry with me for what had happened, or for what I'd told him in the aftermath about his motels. Caring little to begin either conversation, I let my eyes linger on the land rolling by.

It was beautiful as the world can only be in the wake of disaster. The sky was pitilessly soft and wide, held in place with tiny clouds, and we moved through a story-land of signage for "Crystal Cave" and "Echo Canyon," the reminders that we were approaching "Bat City," the morose hoardings for "The Land that Time Forgot" and "Lost Battle Cave." After several hours, however, I realized that part of this perfection I'd discovered lay in the fact that we were traversing the same countryside we'd driven in a blind fright the night before. Quite likely we'd passed these billboards or their Janus companions while fleeing through the dark; now, in the vacuum of speech and the penetrating beauty of the day, the words "Lost Battle Cave," particularly, began to work on me, like the lyric from a forgotten song.

We backtracked to a road (ELLENVILLE, 67MI) I'd been too shattered to see and he too shattered to direct me to in the night. I tried to focus my thoughts solely on the land, the "aesthetic" and the "Kennelness" for which Charles had already reproached me, but the pleasures I'd at first rediscovered in the details of our journey had begun slipping almost as soon as I understood that we were circling rather than escaping the town that reminded me of Elizabeth. There was a terrible tension in the Impala, too; something that only thickened, so that if, in the beginning, I was content to say nothing, after a time any interaction became unimaginable, fraught with whatever imprecations my companion had no doubt spent his silence loading the air. I could only contemplate with dread our approaching sales call.

Aqua and white diamonds patterning the façade and a large red and white banner chanting SALE! SALE! SALE! promised more of the glad-handing and nostalgia-talk that now could only seem ghastly. The silence that gripped the car had robbed me even of the foresight to ask to remain behind, until it was too late and we stood staring through the Sew Fine's plate-glass door at the decorative features of a Singer salesgirl. It was with relief that I discovered the shop to be cast in a mirroring melancholy, an atmosphere within which our own mood might pass unobserved, and whose origin became clear as soon as we found the manager in his office. Behind a glass wall, within a lowering haze of smoke, he watched us proceed through the hall of shiny machines.

"Charles — Charley my boy, thanks. Thanks for coming," he murmured, rising, seemingly unaware that we were a day late. The salesgirl who'd accompanied us hovered beside his large, red face, the waxy and youthfully black pompadour. Margaret Duffey's picture lay folded in the headlines on his desk beside a tray of dead soldiers. The manager's hands worried at the back of his neck and he murmured, "Did you all read the papers? Did you *see* this? It's a shame is all . . . I have a granddaughter." Charles placed his hand on the sleeve of the man's plaid blazer. The manager laid his own upon the salesgirl's wrist. At his touch, she drifted off to join her peers, and in the distance they slipped around the showroom, all except one, who stood in the windows at the front of the store, a silhouette whittled by light. They wore blue and white skirt suits. They moved carefully, in silence. It was, I reflected, like a finishing school for airline stewardesses.

"It's not really surprising," the manager added, taking my hand now but failing to give his name, "what with the abmorality of the world today."

"The what?" I asked.

"*Ab-mor-ality*," he repeated. Charles glanced a warning at me to make no grammatical ventures. The manager took a handkerchief from his breast pocket and wiped his face. "We're just little people, here . . . we live in such a little place. And you think you know *everyone*, and that there are *limits*" —he turned his hot eyes upon me, majestic with dyed brows. "I'm sorry," he said, looking at Charles again. "It's discouraging. I am discouraged."

A long silence followed. I felt that Charles was preparing to say something, allowing the moment to gather weight before he began—which he eventually did, concurring:

"I've found, myself, that everything just turns out to be more difficult than I could have believed." There was an undercurrent to these words too close to our situation, yet the men merely nodded their heads, and then the manager sank down at his desk, flexing forward in his suit, hands at his chest. I thought he might be praying; he turned out to be finding his cigarettes. Charles gestured for me to extend him a light.

"But who would do something like that?" the manager asked, groping in the air, cigarette wedged between his second and third fingers. "Just leave her there. It's the *leaving her there* I can't understand. I know the Duffeys. When the Killdeer jumped its bank, I sandbagged with Mr. Duffey and his son, Ed . . ." And then, once more, he lapsed into silence.

"We can only hope they catch them," Charles said after a while, "whoever it is."

"Oh," the manager affirmed, looking up quickly, "we will." He placed the burning cigarette in his mouth, his hair shining beneath the overheads as he stared again across the floor of his domain. "We're just little people," he repeated, "aren't we, Charley? But a man like that — even animals can tell when one of their own is sick. A man like that is dying. Isn't he? He's a dead man, Charley. We'll find him all right."

They were ghastly words for ghastly men, and we waited until the manager drew a breath and said, "It's too hot in here. Let's go. Let's get some air."

As it turned out, what he intended was to leave his office and emerge into the expanse of the store, where we almost immediately found ourselves, as we had at the Modern, standing before a table upon which sat a sleek, new-model plastic Singer. The manager ran his hand along the back of the machine as one might a beloved horse (he was, as were all of the managers I met, a nonsewer), and then bellowed softly. The salesgirl who'd stood in the windows approached.

"Show us something, Jenny my beauty," he said, wiping his brow with a handkerchief, retiring backward into a chair beside a presumably inferior machine. "Sew for us today."

She wasn't by any stretch what I would have called a beauty—she had small eyes that beat nervously at us before she sat down and spread a wide, close-mouthed grin—but she had elegant hands and irreproachable carriage. She turned the machine on, and the sleek, blue body hummed into life. The manager lit another cigarette and bowed forward, jaw crushed into his palm, watching her. The girl blushed and reached into the cabinet beneath the machine to draw out a bolt of yellow cloth, at which he sat back, then hunched forward again. Placing the fabric under the presser foot, she began to sew; and into this moment of focus, Charles spoke.

It occurs to me that during the unbearable silence of the car, during that time I'd assumed Charles had been elaborating an awful chain of accusations, he'd been doing nothing of the sort. He had—he must have—been instead plotting out what to say in this room, to these people in doubt and turmoil. It was easy to see his relationship with the Singer Sewing Company as the "job" I'd contemplated the night before—residing outside my friend, and to which he made procrustean accommodations. Only there, at the Sew Fine, did I first conceive that during his quiet moments I was generally the furthest thing from his mind; that he was frequently meditating upon one thing alone. Those words from the previous morning returned: *I haven't been fair to you, Milty.* And an inkling of how this could be stole sadly over me.

"It's almost impossible not to find parallels," Charles told us, clearing his throat. "She's ten, little Margaret Duffey — or so I've read. *His* mother left him when he was ten. She left on foot, and he never saw her again."

"That's right," the manager concurred after a moment. "She divorced his elderly father and left Oswego, New York. She left eight children, of which Isaac was the youngest. One wonders, sometimes, where she went. One sees her walking . . ." and he made a vague motion with his cigarette. I realized they were, of course, speaking of Singer. Seeing in my face the first pang of those sorrows I've just described above, the manager (for he was a good man, and not, as I, a good man by fits), misunderstanding, patted me on the back.

"Can you imagine," Charles said, "the man who *created* the showroom — that spacious, elegantly appointed retail space, more like a church" — the manager nodded modestly — "and stocked those rooms only with sewing machines, dozens of identical sewing machines, and beautiful young women" — Jenny blushed deeply — "striding the floors, working the black machines with their manicured hands and the gentle rock of the treadle, so that anyone could see how easy it was? The same man who gave women one of the first great labor-saving devices, who changed women's lives forever as if he had personally visited each and taken on some part of their labors — he was motherless. And yet," Charles added, "and yet, he filled his life with women: He married five, several simultaneously. He had six mistresses. He fathered twenty-eight children among his five wives, all of whom claimed, and believed, he was legally married to them and to them alone."

"If I'm not mistaken," the manager volunteered, as my sadness gave way to confusion, "he legally married only two."

"But even so," Charles pointed out, "it was a family like a mansion with its thirty-nine members, nearly impossible for a single mind to keep track of. Except that he was a practical man: Until he moved to Europe, leaving his American wives and children behind, he had been able to grasp the whole thing, to avoid the otherwise unavoidable mistakes, by calling all of his first four wives *Mary*. True, circumstance assisted him — Mary Eastwood Walters Merritt, Mary Ann Sponsler, Mary McGonical — but even Catherine *Maria* Haley became Mary. He was, as I've explained to Milton, a man who understood the power of coincidence. He wasn't above harnessing that power."

Charles paused, his eyes resting upon mine before returning to the stricken manager. I was stunned — and not, initially, even by Singer's behavior. Only a moment before, I'd believed I was to hear a sermon, or at least a conversation, about sorrow and grief, abandonment and loss, and instead we were in bed with an industrial octopus. But then again, I conceded, having stared at Charles until he finally turned back to me, weren't sorrow and grief exactly what we were speaking of?

In the ensuing silence, the sound of the sewing machine filled the world. I had a sense of the machine's needle moving faster and faster, like a train acquiring speed on a descent. For a moment Jenny stopped, raising what might have been the plan for a jellyfish, and then, lowering her eyes, placed the yellow cloth back beneath the presser foot and continued on her inscrutable way. We were each, I imagined, more than anything wondering what it was she might be creating, when Charles again spoke up:

163

"He fled the scandal of his enormous family in New York, and settled in Paris. He later fled Paris to escape the Franco-Prussian War, settling in England, where he built a mansion that he named 'The Wigwam.' But he was quite old by then—he died before its completion; and it was in this way that The Wigwam became, instead of a home for himself and his fifth and final wife, an American Women's War Hospital during the First World War."

Charles smiled at the manager. It was a smile of co-mission, of true friendship, and one I rarely recall Charles bestowing upon me. The manager leaned forward in his seat, chin on his hand as if harkening to the music of the machine. He murmured:

"His final, lawfully wedded wife would be the model for the Statue of Liberty, but he was dead by then, the poor man."

Before us, Jenny now lifted her foot from the treadle, and the conversation melted away. I didn't understand the sleight of hand that had carried us from the girl I'd struck down the previous evening to "poor" Isaac Singer, but there we were, together beneath the flickering lights, watching Jenny give birth to some new thing. She slid from beneath the needle a garment that unfolded and unfurled and turned out to be, when she rose and held it before us, a girl's dress—yellow, short-sleeved, ruffled at the neck and hem.

"That's beautiful, Jenny," Charles said, as they passed it among themselves.

"But why did you make *this*?" I asked, lost again, fingers closing about the small, soft dream, until I understood that of course, of course—but it was the yellowness. It was all I could see. And then the manager said:

"Actually, it's the only thing she knows how to make," allowing his cigarette to fall to the floor, where he crushed it out, not unkindly, beneath his heel.

As I shepherded us down a darkening highway that evening, I shuddered at the libidinous charge that had once more attached itself to interactions alien to, even seeming to preclude, such a current. Worse, it was no longer in the salesgirls or the machines that this charge lay; it had invaded the subject of Singer himself, bedded, so to speak, in the very history of the man. Already uneasy, I found Charles's company oppressive, and after a short time, determined to seek a private refuge for my thoughts, I suggested we stop for the night at the Alpen Haus, whose hoardings pester drivers on Route 271 until they believe they've crossed the border into Switzerland. It struck me as a fine compromise of country-inn pretension and ski-lodge comfort (ALPINE LIVING BELOW THE MASON DIXON the sign trumpeted from a thicket of redbud); Charles, however, pointing out a welcome sign for a wedding party, insinuating that we might find the Alpen Haus crawling with haymakers, asked if we shouldn't, being fugitives, instead stay across the road in the *Happy* Motel. The name seemed at best wistful, at worst cruel ("They make good coffee," he informed me; and, "They're actually just as expensive as the Alpen Haus"—the cheek of the man!), but I was exhausted, and in the end magnanimously turned into the desolate parking lot, commenting only, "At least we won't have trouble finding separate rooms."

He said nothing in reply, and I let the day go at that. Eyes cast up above my bed at a "painting" of two hunters saluting a garish mountain sunset, I shuddered at the expanse of time that lay before us.

And what if I were to simply abandon this doomed outing? I wondered as I sank toward sleep, climbing down amongst the thoughts of the afternoon, those sunken doorways to familiar dystopias, the partially excavated and fancifully reconstructed ruins of my past. I found myself upon my back in some snow-capped retreat, upon a vast and plush bearskin rug, a warm and prickly rush of sensation, an intricate fire roaring in the hearth and throwing its glow upon naked Jane, rocking above me in pornographic detail. The light moved around on her skin like film, the sepia story of something I could nearly read, until I grasped that it was heat — heat alone coursing across her breasts and arms — and I was suddenly wide awake again, and knew that what had seemed in the moment to be a conscious, if obsessive, activity had in fact been long out of my control.

I'd opened my eyes in near darkness, as one sometimes does, to the sense of having just entered a fresh silence: It was quiet, yet there was an echo I remained alert to catch when I would otherwise have again closed them. The illumination of the half-open bathroom door showed the room unchanged, but the air felt unexpectedly rich and moist. And there *was* a sound: Sitting up farther and feeling for the light on the nightstand, I became aware of a sound like water, like a river in the dark.

At first I could detect nothing unusual — just this muted commotion. Pulling on my pants, I poked my head outside and looked up and down the veranda. The doors to some of the rooms were open, as if to admit the night air; I noticed

Charles's door ajar. When I walked over and pushed the door wide, my companion's bed was turned back and empty. I heard voices behind me; then, at a distance, and turning, I began to see that something was wrong with the light that broke over the parking lot. Holding my hands against the glow, I discerned perhaps forty people at the far end of the lot, backs to me, gazing across the road at a fire truck—it was that, surely, which had clanged into my dreams and awakened me when it lapsed into silence. The red engine, pulsing gently with lights, was dispensing its hoses before the Alpen Haus, and the Alpen Haus was on fire.

A single feeling took hold of me in that instant: simply, *At last.* At last for the smoke pouring from the second floor, black against the building, pink against the night. At last for the yellow streamers hurling themselves up the whitewashed walls and timberwork, like vines upon the trellis of the second-floor veranda. It is true what they say about fires: They are jewels—and there is a garden in a fire as there is a garden in a jewel. The crowd had given the fire its whole attention, and I joined them, noticing as I drew closer the many people wearing pajamas or other bedclothes, come to take refuge from the burning building. There was something like reverence in the air, and perhaps because it was my first waking fire, or perhaps because the people gathered at the curb didn't actually *live* in the motel, and their terror had already ceded to fascination, it reminded me of my dream.

I felt a desire to cheer, as I'd often cheered in sleep. For while I didn't understand as much until that moment, I'd been waiting ever since I arrived in the South for a fire. As my odyssey went awry, I saw now that only fire could make perfect again, and it had struck as if the dumb world could write a message upon a flame—striking not to destroy, but to *show* me. Admittedly, I was overexcited. I still had an erection. Yet there was this: In a few minutes, I thought, I'll find Charles; and when I do, we'll be able to speak again. We will talk about the fire.

I stood at first near the back of the mesmerized crowd, a skyline of light-limned heads and shoulders; glancing around, however, I discovered Charles's profile to my right, and I went to his side. His face bespoke his concern.

"Is it him?" I asked.

A woman in a gigantic yellow nightie—really, just a dark blot until that moment—leaned toward me. "Of course it's him," she hissed, eyes full of tears. "It's a fire, isn't it? It's a motel . . ." This had, of course, been my reasoning, but it sounded a little thick put so simply. "Jesus," she added, clutching her arms about herself as several local cops, faces bright as holidays, crossed the street and began taking down names.

A car exploded in the lot out front of the burning motel. The firemen trained their drizzle upon it, then retrained their nozzles on the building; increasingly, though, things appeared to be over. There were flecks of ash in the air like the thought of snow. The crowd began to disperse, and we walked together, Charles and I, back to our rooms.

"That was where I wanted to stay," I said, recalling my suggestion.

"We were lucky," Charles murmured. He was shaking. Even back beneath the veranda, he couldn't take his eyes from the plume trailing in the stars.

"The fire," I told him, "was just like the fire in my dream"—drawn once more by the recollection, until I considered that it no doubt sounded crass to frame a public trauma within my own fantasies.

"Your nightmare?"

"Yes. I have it all the time — or at least it seems that way, lately: about watching a fire back in Elizabeth."

"Elizabeth," he repeated, turning from the remains of the blaze, the cloud of smoke and steam rising in a column. "What was it you said you dreamed?" he asked.

And so it was that I told him of the girl with the hoop, and the old man that the child meets on the dark street, and the wonderful fire he brings the child to see, that they all, we all, watch in a trance. The telling seemed to calm him as it calmed me; it was *my* dream, and in telling it, I see now, I found for the first time in days that I knew exactly what to say.

"I never understand that it's a nightmare until the end," I explained when I'd finished, feeling that perhaps this aspect had grown unclear. "Even when I look back on it, I don't find the dream frightening, in itself."

"My worst nightmares don't frighten me," Charles replied, "they make me sad"; and then he fell silent, watching the squad cars shepherd people to other shelters. I thought he was trying to make an end to the conversation, and was about to say good night, when he added, "He was right, you know."

"Who was right?"

"The old fellow who put you, or the boy, on his shoulders. I can remember those fires from when I was a kid, like the one in your dream. They'd have them every year in Elizabeth, just like that. Singer would throw them, if you can 'throw' a fire — a big public display where they'd burn down something fifty men had spent all of a long Sunday building. Everyone would come with food and blankets and we'd sit out, into the night, and watch as they lit the fire. Then we'd watch as the fire department arrived like a parade to put it out. The fifties"—he shrugged, rubbing his face and leaving a spot of soot; I offered my handkerchief. "It was like fireworks for the children. And it was always a little sad, too. There's something heroic in a dying fire. It is like any other dying thing—you want to help it."

"I wasn't really sorry to see the fire, tonight," I agreed, surprised at the feeling in his voice. "There was even something wonderful"—but catching sight of his hands again, I broke off.

"Are you all right?" I asked.

"It's just different. Once you've been in a fire, it's different."

We returned to watching the aftermath, and I said, "Strange—I don't think I ever went to any of those picnics. At least not that I recall. It wasn't the sort of thing we would have done, my family—we weren't, you know, folksy"—breaking off again, sensing he'd said all he wanted to say.

Charles took his cigarettes out. The last police vehicles had crossed the road. Only a faint pulse of red touched the dark veranda where we stood outside my room.

"Emily once told me she'd been taught as a child that when you died, you'd find yourself together with every person you'd ever known. All at once, all for no other reason than to see you. It wasn't terrible for her—it was the most wonderful thing she could imagine, I think, having been reared way out in the country. To die in your sleep, and awaken to a room full of people, and never a stranger.

"You must be sorry you came here," he suggested after a moment.

"It wasn't," I admitted, "what I imagined."

"No, I can't believe it could be," he said. "I suppose you've wondered why I don't just go home with all ... *this* going on. I'd be wondering myself. I don't know if it makes any difference to be told, but we're in trouble" — a smile breaking across his face and then vanishing into the corners of his eyes. "Yes" — his eyes leaping at mine — "in that way, too" — wiping his face with the bandaged hand that held the cigarette — "but the Company is what I mean. The Company's in trouble."

"Are they going under?" I asked, both more and less surprised, already sure of the answer. The night before, my suspicions would have seen in his confession a confirmation of my worst intuitions about his obligations to the "company," but these suspicions seemed simplistic now; after the last hour, after this afternoon, my thoughts were for his well-being.

"It amounts to the same thing," Charles acknowledged. "They've been talking about selling the sewing machine division, to the Chinese I think."

"The 'sewing machine division'? What else is there?"

"They make all kinds of crap now — aerospace equipment, computers. It's not like a person, Milty. It's just a name — you can replace everything about it, as long as the name's the same." For a moment we were quiet. He was a painter who'd abandoned painting to work for a sewing machine company that was abandoning sewing machines.

"What would you do, then?" I asked.

He shook his head.

When Charles left, and I returned to the disorder of my bedding, I revolved in my mind what he'd said; but the more I did, the less I made of it. It seemed, for example, unlikely the Chinese would cease to make sewing machines, yet did he mean they'd bring in their own management? Was he simply incensed that this most American of companies, becoming a foreign entity, would lose its identity? At any rate, if he *already* maintained that the Singer Sewing Company had so little identity, what, I again mused, was he *doing*? Knowing nothing of the business, I couldn't decide whether his fears might be merited by circumstance; and continuing to ponder, I also realized his confession entirely failed to explain why he didn't just go home — I'd felt so satisfied a few minutes before in that respect, if nothing else; but as I coldly examined what he'd related, it was difficult to believe he meant by some quixotic example to "save" a sewing empire. I supposed, next, that this wasn't his point, that he was speaking of things on a whole other level . . . but I was getting farther away from any conclusions on the subject — and from the subject itself. I'd have to ask. I'd have to sleep.

And in this way I was eventually able to altogether abandon Singer and its troubles; which was how I recalled, during a momentary aside in the progress of sleeplessness, the kernel of what had drawn my eye again and again to the signage for Lost Battle Cave. Already my nights were eroding — I suppose it should be no surprise, but I had no "system" as of yet, and the hours of insomnia that formed the prelude to my dreams were spent rummaging through the days, trying to stay clear of the accident, the afterimage of the girl's face before the car. When I again came upon the billboards for the cave in my picture-book memory, I knew this time, immediately —

For it was *Alsby Kennel,* risen in this land of his imaginings: painter, politician, utopian — but especially the latter two, for if I wasn't mistaken, it was he who'd coined the cave's name. The idea stood out, an apparition in the cluttered shed of my mind. I thought of Harvey's mythical painting with a twinge of interest: Subsequent to watching Atlanta burn, in the breakdown of the Civil War, hadn't Kennel, believing that the South must fall but that he might in the breach (and it was madness alone that oiled such speculation) secede from all sides, declared himself a general? And hadn't he, leading his regimen of local irregulars, holed up in a cave near the family plantation, in the Georgia foothills? I had no books with me, and the specifics were slippery with the years, but hadn't that been the cave — "Lost Battle" — I pondered, staring at the phosphorescent arms of my travel clock?

Yet if the intuition began perfectly, like a vision, as with everything that night, my vision made less and less sense when I pawed over the remembered facts; for as I understood things to lie, there had actually been no battle at all during this abysmal culmination of Kennel's brief military ambitions.

What then, exactly, had occurred? To the best of my recollection, having declared his independence, and within a matter of days received word through some intelligence that an entire Union division was marching upon his tiny sovereign nation, Kennel and those loyal to him had "dug in" to the limestone cave complex that underlay the neighboring hills. Their decampment would prove an ordeal of cold mud, and instead of the "honesty of battle" (a phrase to which Kennel made frequent recourse by what accounts we have), there had followed a long winter, famine, and this act of defiance underground. It is unclear whether rumors of the Union division had ever been more than rumors, but what is known with a fair degree of certainty (virtually everything we know of Kennel's private life during the latter years has been culled from the diary of Lieutenant Bibbins, formerly and afterward his manservant) is that come spring, half alive, chastened, the survivors emerged and returned to their homes and fields to find their insurrection virtually unnoted in the chaos and misery of the Southern defeat. Demoralized and fearing recriminations, Kennel is presumed to have suppressed all record of his bid for sovereignty, destroying his own journals and ordering Bibbins, who in this one particular fortunately disobeyed Kennel, to do the same. Strangely, unlike most of his fellow plantation owners, Kennel never asked the Union government for pardon but, ridden increasingly by paranoia and bitterness, emigrated.

I had, down the years, often pondered this catastrophic turn in the great man's career—it seemed, as much as if not more than historical truth, to illustrate a psychological truth: that the moments perhaps most expressive of a person, even of a people, happen largely in the dark. But perhaps, I mused in my bed, there were other "Lost Battle" caves; or perhaps this was the cave, yet hopelessly elaborated by memory, named in a purely metaphorical frame of mind—and again I craved my books, locked in my library hundreds of miles away in the arms of a Jersey winter. At last, gifted with the near shore of sleep, I determined that in the morning I should ask Charles. Recent posturing to the contrary, hadn't a fascination with Kennel been one of the few things we'd honestly shared? And even if we could determine nothing with any certainty between the two of us, wouldn't he, with the crumbling of his recent industrial illusions, at least welcome the distraction?

· · ·

These were my final words to myself on the subject that night, like a balm on a fevered mind. In the morning, however, my inquiries into the matter were preempted by the stupefying fact that our gas tank *had been siphoned*. Comprehension stole over us as the engine sputtered in the parking lot, and while Charles visibly fumed, something in his manner showed that he was pleased to have his outlandish claims borne out. As he gloated and stood guard, I was given the unenviable task of sucking gasoline into the plastic line from a nearby Seville.

Not satisfied, he spent the remainder of our getaway lecturing, explaining that although I no doubt wouldn't believe him, it was typical that the siphoner would strike during the confusion of a confused night. He wasn't even *surprised,* he said as I rolled down the window to spit, imagining some kissing cousin to the Arsonist skulking amongst the vehicles while I'd lain consumed with my speculations about Kennel. Clearly this wasn't the best moment to engage his attention, both of us in a foul mood, but reminded by this last train of thought, I brought up my notions regarding the cave as we departed from a service station several towns over.

Charles regarded my questions with none of the curiosity the subject had seemed, on the threshold of sleep, sure to command; still, I wasn't put off. An hour later we stopped for lunch. I flipped through sugar packets decorated with the stern and collectable portraits of Civil War generals, and he started in on his postcards. To the sound of scribbling I reapproached the matter of Kennel and this cave, but he neither agreed nor disagreed with my recollections — he simply couldn't be roused.

I returned to my minuscule gallery, disheartened; and then, toward the bottom of the caddy of twenty-some paper packets I found a reproduction of Kennel's well-known portrait of the Savior of the Union—the one in which Sherman's hand extends blindly into his breast pocket beneath a wreath of medals, for what thing? The general's mouth slips to the side with the thought of it. Charles glanced up and saw what I was looking at; and despite his reticence only a few minutes before, he said, "It was Kennel who famously, if somewhat cattily, remarked, 'Sherman didn't really defeat the South—he just singed it'"—taking the sugar packet from my hand for a moment. He smiled. "The picture contains all the disdain of the creator for the destroyer. How a man can render emotion—hate, but even love itself—with color is surely one of the great mysteries." He was right: Kennel visibly hated Sherman, although he not infrequently painted portraits of men he despised. He was even said to have enjoyed such work. The painting, perhaps even more for being reproduced in this Lilliputian format, seemed to capture Kennel's vision of Sherman as a janitor, a slovenly locust of a man inexplicably marked by God to humble a great land.

Charles returned to his cards, and I was left to wonder if he was deliberately trying to provoke me; whatever thought had sparked this little outburst, though, left nothing in its wake. Having come this far, I made an executive decision: We didn't, I found, referring to our schedule, have anyplace to be until the following day; and as nothing I might do would impede his commission by the Singer Sewing Company, rather than spend our time brooding in whatever motel rooms, wouldn't it be better, I suggested, to have an outing? Given our at least onetime love for Kennel, mightn't it even be fitting to make this pilgrimage, for old times' sake?

I made a great many points. I let the questions hang in the air; and getting on the road, finding the highway strewn with billboards for the Cave, it so yawned in our path, figuratively speaking, that at a certain point a deliberate act of evasion would have been required to turn aside from the exit sign that announced in small white letters: LOST BATTLE CAVE—"ONE OF THE SEVEN WONDERS OF OUR TRUE REPUBLIC."

"I see," were his only words as we left the highway.

The town into which we drove seemed composed of the outbuildings from a mining operation. Hard against the road, the colorful Lost Battle hoardings portraying objects such as cannons, waterfalls, and bats were the largest structures, the churches, of the town. Yet the buildings thinned out around us, and still we drove. We entered a boggy wood, and then a ravine in some rumpled hummocks, drawn onward by signs sporting fresh icons, until after half an hour, in the distant declivity between two knobs of stone, we made out the wooden palisade of a Civil War fortification.

Perhaps a dozen automobiles lazed in the parking lot. Outside the car, a warm day awaited; the surrounding hills stilled the air and enshadowed the scenic overlook where a freckled boy crouched, bearing refreshments.

I led the way down a flight of railroad ties to the imposing fortress. Birds hugged the lips of the hills, and the trees clustered in their budding foliage like old war veterans, kindling to memories of finery. The refreshment boy dallied upon a grassy slope, a shepherd, stooping now and then to grasp the rocks and pebbles he cast at the precocious creatures of the forest.

"You're *sure* you want to do this?" Charles said, scowling at the stockade — as we drew near, more obviously a plywood façade erected around a ticket booth. A solitary woman dressed in a Confederate costume and eating from a Styrofoam plate examined us from behind the ticket window. "This is a *cave*," Charles reminded me. "It's *dark* inside."

"The cave is illuminated, is it not?" I asked the woman at the booth.

"Is it what?" she replied.

"There are lights in your cave?"

She nodded suspiciously.

"I would think, if anything," I said to Charles, "that this gives you some indication of how important this is to me, my willingness to venture into a dark cave." I then returned my attention to the cocked face of the ticket lady.

"Is this," I asked, "the Lost Battle Cave Alsby Kennel took refuge in at the end of the Civil War?"

"General Kennel?" she asked. "Never heard of him. Have you read the literature?"

"Was there ever," I said, changing tactics, "an actual battle fought in this cave?"

"Every weekday, and twice on Saturdays and Sundays," she replied. There was a sleepy pause, like a sunspot. "Do you want the battle? There's a battle at 2:30."

I consulted my watch: It was thirty minutes away.

"We'll take the battle," I decided, though I still couldn't understand what historical relevance a battle might have. I bought two tickets for Charles and myself with additional, colorful "Lost Battle" passes. It seemed a pity, whatever this place might turn out to be, to have made such an effort to get here only to miss the "Battle" itself, and I told Charles as much. The same woman then came out from behind the booth and met us at the turnstile.

"Follow the arrows and watch your heads," she warned of the reinforced masonry mouth, perhaps a dozen feet high.

I must admit that I felt some apprehensions as I was to descend. The dark in caves, it's true, is not like other darks: A cave is not a hole, it is a flower put out by darkness. One brings light into a cave as an astronaut brings oxygen into space, and a man with a fear of the dark can't help but be aware of what it would mean for this light to go out. Cold and damp wafted at our hair. I thought of the grave. Still, there were bulbs strung along the ceiling, and on either side ropes and large green arrows painted on the wall guided the visitor down. Consulting a badly reproduced map of the cave complex given us with our tickets, we marched into the secret earth until we noticed a slackening in the breeze and a leveling-off of the path. Making a final, brisk turn, the tunnel opened up.

My first impressions were truly those of awe, for we'd entered a chamber every bit as vast as promised in the literature on the reverse of the map, but my admiration was given too hastily: Glancing at Charles, I marked an unmistakable coolness in his demeanor, and it dawned on me that the magnificent curtains of prismatic stone, supernaturally bright and fresh as coral beneath the sea, were in fact contrived through batteries of colored lights bolted to the roof of the cave.

"Stunning," Charles remarked; yet clutching my hopes

and remembering this was less a journey of geology than history, I continued into the cavern, toward a circular hole in the floor down which a thread of water glimmered from the upper reach of the dome. I recalled Bibbins's mention of the existence of a river or creek in the cave, flowing even during that cold winter, and gazed fondly down the hole into which the water streamed — a perfect and straight filament visible for quite some way, as if it bore within itself the light from the room; although here, too, what could have been a delicacy acquired an aggressive scarlet cast from lamps attached to the surrounding rails. My delight had faltered.

And then, glancing about, I noticed Charles had disappeared. The room contained only one adult, accompanying some Scouts. They were gathered around one of the many plaques placed at the periphery of the space, and presuming I might find information offering further directions or pertaining to the history of Lost Battle Cave, I now ventured up to one of these postings. I was staring at a diagram cast in bronze of bedding planes and water seepage. Subsurface structure was rendered in surface texture. The next plaque depicted further millennial ramifications of the cave system. Hoping more pertinent information might lie elsewhere in this complex, I chose a tunnel near to where Charles had been standing when I last saw him and proceeded, stopping beside each new plaque as if beside bread crumbs in a forest.

I passed through two rooms in this way, meandering up and down boardwalks in a passage that deposited me finally in what was labeled the "Lesser Cavern" on my map — a high, plain room the size of a basketball court, its rail delineating a hard-packed, navigable space from a warren of chutes that fell away on all sides. There was a single other occupant — a slender woman in a gray skirt suit, standing before one of a handful of further plaques. She seemed familiar. I positioned myself at the plaque beside hers (she was reading about water-bearing limestone formations in central Florida) and cast a glance along the rails. Our eyes met.

"Jane," I said in surprise.

"Subduction," she replied, "leads to orogeny."

"Beg your pardon?" I said.

"It's an old geologist's saw. What are you doing in this hole, Mr. Menger?"

"I don't know," I replied. "I was hoping" — but discerning that any reference to Kennel would necessitate a long-winded digression, I opted for "I would actually just like to find Charles."

"And you looked in a cave . . . Did you get tickets for the Battle?" she asked.

Feeling we weren't building a conversation so much as a rubble of sentences, I said, "What are *you* doing here?"

"Milton, my questions are hopelessly better than yours," she told me. "But if you must know, I'm following you both. You left without so much as a good-bye."

I laughed. "You followed us?" She stared at me quite earnestly, though, or in a way that seemed earnest. "It's impossible —"

"Impossible is so categorical." And to my continued smile, "Charles is a creature of habit. He's not exactly difficult to keep track of; you on the other hand" — and she wagged her finger at me — "Milton, you've been making things complicated."

The thought of the events of the past forty-eight hours

made me pale, but the idea that she might mean the accident was ridiculous. A more specific objection to her claim sprang to mind:

"This is the last place on earth Charles wanted to come."

"Is that what he told you."

I studied her face. She was, in my brother's words, a beautiful girl with a flat tire: I didn't believe her, and she saw as much.

"Oh *come on,* Milty — do you really think Charles has never been here before? Haven't you noticed how he behaves when you take him anywhere new? He's a wreck."

Once again, I was struck by how well they knew each other, but I still didn't believe her. And then we were distracted from our exchange by a booming announcement over the until-then-unobserved PA system, commanding in a crusty and I suppose Civil War tone of voice: *"All visitors please return to the Great Cavern. Militiamen, take your stations. The Battle of Lost Battle Cave will begin in five minutes. All visitors please return to the Great Cavern. Those visitors without tickets to the Battle will be assisted to the exit ramp. Thank you."*

"My husband was always telling me things like that," Jane informed me: *"Return to the Great Cavern."*

"Shouldn't we, though?" I said, alarmed, already feeling out of my element. At the addled sound of my own words, I hastily added, "Jane — why *are* you following us?"

She petted me on the arm. "I can never tell if you're serious: *Shouldn't we, though?"* she mimicked. *"Jane — why are you following us? As if you're either very smart, or exceptionally — really, remarkably — dim."* A sparkle entered her eye. "So which is it, Milton? I mean, between friends, why do *you* think I'm following you? It's important, you see — I'm a *rational* girl who needs her motivations. I might even be able to stop following you if someone would just please tell me what exactly *is* my motivation."

I was staring at her, deciding whether to just walk away — and if I did, whether it would do any good, or whether she would simply rattle on in pursuit (which was ludicrous, the idea that she was following us at all) — but then what if I were to kiss her? Was that what this was all about, really? Her face so close to mine, her mouth a little open, exceedingly kissable — when there was a distinct *click,* and everything, every corner of my universe, went black. My hands flew out, and grasping around, took hold of the rails beside which we stood.

"Of course," she said, "the lights have to go — they *were* a bit much, weren't they?" Perhaps she noted my sudden and deep intake of breath. "Are you all right, Mr. Menger?"

I waited, hoping light would return. Finally, I said, "Actually, no. Not at all — I'm afraid of the dark."

"Nyctophobia? How sad for you!" There was a booming sound, and in the distance a martial symphony began. A moment later one of her well-manicured hands had grasped my arm just above the elbow. "Pretend you've been asked to close your eyes because some fabulous surprise awaits you."

I had an inkling of what she meant, though I couldn't help jumping convulsively when one of her other hands — she seemed to have so many of them — landed upon my hip.

"Do you dance, Milton?" she said, clasping me. I staggered against her and she whispered, "Steady there. I'll lead."

Gently, she took my hand and placed it against the small of her back. In darkness, to this terrible music like friction, we made several revolutions of what may be described as a waltz. I might as well have fallen from a window with her in my arms, so far from my thoughts had the possibilities of the moment withdrawn.

"Well," she said, "are you enjoying yourself a bit more now?"

"No," I confessed. "I think we should try to find the others."

"*The others.*" She sighed. Her breath was wintergreen against the side of my face. She'd backed my legs into the rail. A small, lightly clothed breast nuzzled my arm.

"I can't remember what we were talking about anymore." She breathed in my ear. "It's like everything went dark. But you know, I like you, Milton. You're not very practical, but I like you. What is it you do, anyway, when you're not following Charles around?"

"Do?" I said, falling through this unending night.

"Your job, Milton. You're no dancer . . ."

"I don't have a job. I have a gallery . . . I collect paintings . . ."

My hopes were fading for some return of light. Worsening matters, just as quickly as it began the music now ceased, to be replaced by indecipherable announcements in some distant region of the cave. In such an underground darkness a feeling inevitably comes over me I can only describe as suffocation. As if I could fall in any direction and at the same time every ounce of surrounding space is preparing to break in upon my quivering life — as if every direction contained both a precipice and an infinite, converging mass. I recall feeling her face beneath the palm of my hand, and then I ran several paces along the rail before being paralyzed anew by the fear I might collide with some fresh and unforeseen menace. Stalactite.

Stalagmite. My hands went up to protect my head. My breath came in heaves.

"I *can* hear you, Milton," she said. "If you want to make a game out of this, that's your business—" Her voice drew nearer, and still gasping in terror, I lunged away from the safety of the rail into the void. "And I see you *do* want to make this into a game."

"Look, why don't we talk about it later, when it isn't quite so dark," I suggested. I heard her rustling, a hard laugh, and touching her hair with an exploratory sweep, I dodged farther out into the room. It was awful, being away from the rail—like paddling into deep water from which I doubted I might ever swim ashore. I had no sense of proportion.

As if reading my mind, she said, "You're taking this all out of proportion. I can tell you're attracted to me."

"And I am," I admitted. "It's just very dark in here."

"Yes, isn't it wonderful? I'd think even a man with nyctophobia would have to admit this is a *lovely* dark. But hang on," she said; and although I'd barely heard these last words, my entire attention was focused upon her the next instant, for there was a flash and a thin flame appeared before her face, less than ten feet away. It lit almost nothing beyond the triangle of her mouth, nose, and eyes, yet my heart leapt.

"You have a light," I gasped.

"Milton, I smoke. Shouldn't everyone? It's you we were talking about, though—you're our mystery man," she said, her smile dimpling yellow, the long flame perched on the tip of her lighter. I moved toward her, drawn by what was, after all, more than light—it was a bubble of air, of space, a place to breathe.

"You do seem a bit friendlier now," she remarked.

"What? Yes, sorry. You have no idea—to have some light—"

"You can understand I've wondered about you. Have you wondered about me?"

"You have no idea," I began again, quite close, my hands rising involuntarily toward the flame. When she was within reach, however, the lighter snapped shut and we were once more thrown into darkness.

"What are you doing?" I cried, swiping at emptiness.

"That's what I've been trying to ask *you*, but you're as bad with the light as without. You're paying attention to all the wrong things."

"What should I be doing?" I whispered, realizing she'd moved away, feeling distance explode around me.

There was a pause. It sounded unmistakably irritated to the ears of a frightened man. Feeble as I felt, I wasn't beyond understanding why. "I'm going to make this easy for you," she said at last. "I'm going to begin by taking a few things off."

"What? What do you mean?"

"That's right—forget the light—you'll have to use your imagination. Follow me here: We're going to start . . . well, we'll start at the top, with this," she continued, and I heard a nearby rumpling of cloth. "Shall I throw them at you—would that make it better?"

"Can't we just have the light back?" I replied miserably.

"*Forget about the light already.* If it makes you feel better, no throwing. We'll just take *this* off now"—there was a zipper sound, and a moment later—"and this"—followed by a brief silence. "You might give me a little support, Milton. It's cold in a cave, and it's hard to do buttons, as you might have noticed, in the cold — not to mention the dark."

I lowered myself to where the ground, at least, seemed to promise no hostilities.

"There's not much left," she announced after a suitable time. "I just have to roll these down, like so. And then of course there are these" — a brisk snap — "eyes on the prize, Milty. Shall I leave my heels on? Do you like that sort of thing? This might as well go, too, if we're going to be serious . . ."

"This really isn't necessary," I murmured again, at the point of breaking into prayer. "Did I mention to you that I'm afraid of the dark?"

"I see you're sticking with it, too. Which is good — fear is sexy, Milton. I like a man who's not afraid to share his fears. These are fearful times, after all, and it's fearfully difficult to be civil during wartime. But I'd like to be civil with you, Milton. Let's pretend that I'm General Kennel, and you're what's-his-name — Corporal Bibbins . . ."

I think I groaned. It was my own sociohistorical nightmare.

"There you go. Or the other way around, if you like. What *are* you doing?"

"I'm sitting down. I need to sit down."

"Good. Excellent. It's a start. Now" — her voice drawing near, so that I was forced to escape crabwise to another chamber of the darkness — "where was I? Oh, yes — you'd just destroyed my fortifications," she said as the music suddenly reappeared and swelled to some awful call to arms. "So now vanquish me, Milton," she whispered, closing in through absolute space. "Vanquish me —"

But as I clung to these words, in the tumult of cymbal clashes, there was a rushing — I covered my head again — and then silence. The music ceased. In the distance, a pebble tumbled and knocked down and down.

"Jane?" I said, both relieved and freshly frightened. "Ms. Garnet?"

I waited several minutes. *She's fallen in a hole,* I thought.

For a long time I crouched, my relief emptying out grain by grain into the familiar fright, but also sadness. In the vacuum of humanity, the dark seemed to pick away at me, as if I were a rock on a shore, eaten hour by hour by the sea. My dissolution in that prehistoric night lasted for what felt an eternity — unbearably long, although I suppose composed in reality of less than five minutes — before there was a thunderous boom over the PA, and a tremulous red glow flickered down the tunnel by which I'd found my way to the Lesser Cavern. Hurriedly glancing around, discovering by this illumination neither Jane nor her garments, I grasped the rail a few feet away and scuttled toward the Great Cavern, where I could now hear a series of smaller explosions taking place.

It was, I understood by this time, the Battle re-creation getting under way, yet my heart hammered with each powder shot that came from ahead, down a smoky corridor painted in yellow light. Emerging into the Great Cavern at last, I was relieved to find the smoke accumulated by the ceiling, the Battle laid out plain to the naked eye. Men were strewn on the floor in their blue and beige uniforms, gasping out their lives. From declivities in the rocks fiery pulses emanated. In vain, though, I searched for fellow visitors, and wanting more than ever to find Charles, assuming that somewhere, at the heart of this exposition, there must be other onlookers, I knelt beside a Confederate soldier—a boy of perhaps fifteen with a spectacular chest wound—and said, "Where is General Kennel?"

He gazed up at me, beads of sweat starting on his face. "In Munitions Cavern, sir," he breathed through scarcely moving lips.

Unfolding my map, I wasn't surprised to find "Munitions Cavern" located precisely where the two sides seemed, by the volume of gunfire, to be locked in stalemate. During a lull in the shooting I selected a cave mouth corresponding to one in the literature and crept down a tunnel awash, like the previous passage, in colored smoke. I stepped over the dead, and walked in a stoop so as not to strike my head on the irregular ceiling, at last emerging into a space about half the size of Lesser Cavern, broken up by wooden crates and stone formations. Beyond a brace of boxes I espied the Scouts, and, with a sigh of relief, Charles.

The counselor gave me a glassy smile, and my friend, checking his watch, came and stood nearby. Together we watched the Confederate troops—or Kennel's troops, depending on how you looked at this—keeping up their gunplay. There were, I noted, several well-decorated men back beyond a massy outcrop of stone, conferring and gesticulating.

"Is he," I asked a Scout, singling out an older, bearded gentleman with a pinched and anxious face and a mass of ribbons on his arm, "General Kennel?" The child nodded wordlessly, eyes riveted to the scene. Kennel was conferring with a man I gathered was Bibbins. There was a note of strain in their voices, but affection, too. Eventually Bibbins darted off on some errand, and there was an explosion, fresh colored smoke, and a young man ran past shouting, "There's a breach! A breach!"

I turned for a moment from the scene. Charles and I winced at one another.

"What happened to you?" he asked in a low shout.

"They switched the lights off," I shouted back. "I thought I was going to die—"

One of the Boy Scouts shushed us, even as the noise grew frightful. Kennel's orderly handed him gun after gun and men fell around them on all sides. For an instant there was a lull, during which I thought Charles and I might rekindle our conversation; but taking a rifle and pistol in his hands, the general suddenly leapt up for a countercharge, weapons blazing with those of his loyal men. It was hopeless, in every way. Charles suppressed a yawn; Kennel staggered and collapsed in a hail of returned gunfire, and amidst the final explosions, the kids cheered.

I looked again at my friend, his eyes lightly on this vignette of violence. He knew as well as I that the general had died years before his time. And yet it wasn't so much a true as a shared history I craved. History—where you are whatever it is that you mean to me. Might we recognize one another in such a history? Or would we, either way, choose to pass in the dark?

"Jane—" I started to say, drowned in a continuous, childish applause. "*Jane,*" I nearly persevered; but then, to his look of incomprehension, I merely added: "Let's get out of here."

Ten minutes later, climbing into the car beside me, as my hearing returned from a shell of fog, he said, "Now do you see why I was less than thrilled by your suggestion?"

He punched in the lighter, and stared at the tip of his cigarette for a moment. "It doesn't matter what they promise — they'll promise you the earth. The reality, though — the reality always falls short" — rolling down the window and looking along the gulch at the ticket booth, where Union and Confederate soldiers now milled together, knocking back beers.

T HIS MORNING, after the rain had rotted away in the night and the whole earth was like the inside of a church, I went out to see if I wouldn't run into Thales in the fields. Nearly an hour passed, and at last, noticing his car was gone, and recalling that today is Sunday, and perhaps Eileen had dragged them both to "The Methodists" as she claims to do from time to time, I retired to the room, thinking I might instead make progress on my sewing.

Somewhat before this, before it was even light, I'd decided that the best method to practice my stitches would be to *make* something. It may seem an obvious conclusion, but I'd arrived at it for the first time as I sat in the calyx of the Singerlight, writing. I'd been thinking of the salesgirls in the showrooms, and how they would always give us some article before we left. I'm wearing a vest right now made the morning following my adventure in the cave, when we paid a call to the Sew Right. We were down in coastal Alabama where everything was green, winterless. The rain lay like a comb in the grass. The vest, like the shirt, was obviously made to fit a man Charles's size, but worn open, as it is now, it gives me a strapping quality Thales was the first to remark.

I could in time, I believe, make such a thing — or a simplified version. Rather than try to assemble some garment from scratch, however, as those far more proficient ladies, I elected to disassemble for the purpose of reconstruction the suit Thales brought by a few days ago — Charles's suit. I know: It's scarcely mine to play with, but then *elected* is, in truth, a wistful choice of words, for this deconstruction was accomplished in a frenzy of frustration. It's hard to explain, and it was very late, but I felt something, some little object — a stone, a bit of nothing — inside a pocket. And when it wasn't in the pocket, it seemed to be in the lining. It was like a chase, like a thought on the tip of the tongue. It became simply a case of having once begun employing the "ripper," being unable to stop until the suit was reduced to an elemental state. In the ensuing silence, I was filled with a sudden certainty that someone had been listening or watching during the entire eruption, though of course it was only me there, alone. I can't imagine — I can't imagine what I'd been thinking.

Calmed in the wake of this fit, I laid the pieces out on my bed, struck by how unlikely they appeared, pulled apart at the seams and revealed to contain all manner of curves where before I'd perceived only straight lines. It doesn't in any way resemble the suit that once graced my friend, except in color — blue, his suits are always blue — for beyond even the oddity of the pieces themselves, there is simply too much material. Quite the opposite of, but somehow congruent to, how it feels to look upon the body of a dead man, a person familiar in life: the dead, contrary to our cinematic fears, being smaller than the living. They are like our children.

He must have worn the suit when I first, and he last, came here, to the Idyll. We'd driven straight from the showroom the three hours to the motel. Charles was, I recall, at pains to point out during the ride that this was a social call.

"Does that," I asked, "mean that we'll be staying at their home?"

"No—we'll be staying *in the motel*," he said, seeming a trifle hurt. "There are three of them in the house—it's too crowded. No one ever comes to the motel, anyway—it's really more of a guesthouse"—by which I understood that I was to be treated to yet another evening of dilapidated accommodation. I was about to say as much, but when I glanced over, he'd again found an article about the girl, who by the headline remained in a twilight state.

There was something deeply irritating in the way he sat, one leg cocked over the other, reading with his well-groomed face the details of a past life. I envied his lack of responsibility; and sitting beside him, I admit wishing that I'd simply killed Margaret Duffey. The desire was, of course, only a fresh despair, and I spoke nothing of the sort, but no matter which way Charles held his paper, whatever fold he offered taunted me with her name.

It was dusk as we pulled into the Idyll's empty lot and took our rooms—I the very room in which I sit this morning, typing. In my darkened mood, the motel struck me as abandoned (no one came to meet us, and standing by the shower not long afterward, I noted the inordinate time it took for water to rise strangling through the pipes). Between the sheets, however, all this faded, for the day ended as it began: in thoughts of Jane. *All kinds of things,* she'd said. It came over me, however peculiar such a remark may sound, that here was a person I could talk to. I needed so much to talk to someone. I imagined that we met again, on some better-lit occasion, and that I told her about myself . . . about my debacle with Caroline, about the accident. She laughed at me — even in my dreams she laughed — but I didn't mind. I wondered where she was; and I wondered whether I'd really escaped her in the cave, or she me. Removed from the terrifying dark by the light beneath the half-closed bathroom door, I wondered what any of that humiliating interlude had been about.

For I still hadn't mentioned our encounter to Charles: nothing of meeting her, or of her inscrutable claim, let alone of what followed. I was embarrassed, but I also found it didn't matter that I didn't believe her: I suppose I saw us as alike in being ridiculous and exotic creatures in this place, strangers here — and strangely vulnerable. I felt her hands again, and it seemed to me, lying in the Idyll that night, that they hadn't been cruel, but creaturely. Had it only been this that she was trying to say?

I awoke the next morning with the curtains open, as I'd left them, and the sun on my face. For a moment I couldn't remember where I was, or when; but then I recalled Charles, and went outside. I'd slept late — I hadn't slept so late or well in a while. His door was closed, and judging from the rumblings in the interior of the room, he was still asleep. I looked across the road, the painterly strokes of barest green upon the black earth. Over the warm asphalt, the fields and the distant tree line crinkled and swam. A pickup hurtled past, and the world settled, silent and swollen.

I'd just kicked up my feet for a nap under the veranda when he came out, dressed in his usual regalia. He stretched and patted his face, extended a curt good morning and glance of commission, then headed across the lot and behind the motel, following a path I've now taken many times through a patch of wintered-over ragweed. We passed a rotting outhouse, its shadow swarming with gnats; a rusted heap of farm equipment; a narrow trench perhaps ten feet long, staked with string as if part of an archaeological dig; and at last I perceived, ahead, a little house set within a mangy bank of privet and the shade of two willows. I chuckled aloud, understanding what sort of people could build in good conscience the accommodations to which my friend was accustomed. Such a person might certainly be found residing in this single story of clapboard and tar paper, a monument to decrepitude presided over by a childlike ego: tin roof cocked on top; grand front door flanked by narrow white-painted columns, badly weathered, and approached over a wooden step set on two cinder blocks, grafted onto a structure so small that not even the inclusion of two screened porches set like wings either side of the entry could trick the eye into imagining there might be more than three or four rooms in the whole pile. The effect was so forlorn that I was genuinely surprised when a cheerful shout emerged from the darkened interior of the porch on the left, and a moment later, from the right, came the half-affronted sound of an older, feminine voice:

"Mr. Trembleman . . . ," to which Charles responded only, "That's right, Ma."

I continued in his wake, and had given up trying to make anything of the gloom contained within the screening, when the voice resumed with "And hel-lo *there*" — as a woman in a pale, high-necked dress wavered into view and came toward the screen with smiling concentration.

"You don't know him, Eileen," Charles cautioned, but he didn't stop or even turn to introduce me, and instead walked directly to the front door and let himself in. I followed in time to catch sight of him turning out of a room that seemed to be the parlor, little wider than I can span with outstretched hands, and cluttered as if the whole of it were a desk at which innumerable things had been manufactured to various states of incompletion. He passed through a door on the left, and when I pursued him, I found myself on one of the porches, staring out at the yard through which we'd come. He held out a hand to a small man in his fifties who did not rise to greet us. "This is Thales," he said. "Thales Grubber. Thales, I'd like you to meet my friend and associate, Milton Menger."

We've already seen a bit of Thales in these pages, but my first impression was of a mild old fellow, gazing at us attentively if inscrutably from beneath a boyish and oily forelock. He was perched in an armchair and wore an orange hunting jacket and flannel shirt whose collar had been nibbled to nothing.

"What'd you do to yourself?" he said to Charles, gripping my hand and mushing his mouth in a frown. Almost immediately, from the other porch, came Eileen's voice:

"What did he do to himself, Dad?"

"Well, he's got his hands all in bandages," Thales replied, still not letting go of me. His eyes hovered on mine, and then he said in nearly a whisper: "I built this house."

"Pardon?" I replied.

"I *built* this house. When I wasn't even twenty I built it."

Had he watched my face as we walked up the path? Was he challenging me to say something against his peculiar home? Or was he simply pleased with his own handiwork? After a moment, he released me.

"Don't just stand there," he said, looking at Charles now, "set down" — indicating a rickety swing that dominated the tiny room.

"I don't know if you've made a note of this," he added as we sat, folding the lock of gray-blond hair from his forehead, "but among early hominids, standing originally arose as an act of aggression. When, you might ask yourself, have you ever felt menaced by a man on his knees — even a seated man? Though of course it's largely habit now, our risings and standings, think about it: how we are all, on account of this habit, in a continual state of aggression, one against the other. It makes the contests of the world entirely comprehensible, when you consider such a thing in such a light.

"Mr. Menger," he said, turning to me, "to what do we owe the pleasure of your company on our humble lands?"

"I'm helping Charles on his rounds, while his hand heals," I explained.

"And what about that hand?"

"I was hurt in one of those motel fires, up by Memphis," Charles said. Thales continued to watch him. "Haven't you heard about the fires? I called from the hospital — you put Emily on the phone."

"Was that *you*, then? Eileen, I owe you a dollar," he hollered across the way. "I've got to say, Charles, you didn't sound like yourself at all."

"They gave me the run of the pharmacy for a few days," Charles acknowledged.

"Just a couple nights ago," I volunteered, "there was a fire in the motel across from us." From within the house, I heard Eileen cry, "Oh my!"

Thales only said, "Mr. Menger, I don't watch much daytime television."

There was now a distant tappitting, like Morse code, growing clearer until Eileen appeared in the doorway bearing two cups of tea in trembling saucers. She was a striking woman, bird-thin and with a haughtiness accentuated by a high wool of hair. She wore a faded but fitted dress with a small, blue brooch on its field of smaller blue traceries. I'd thought she might stay and sit with us, but she retreated almost immediately to the other porch. When she was gone, he continued:

"The more I read in science and history, Mr. Menger, the clearer it becomes that the world is entirely composed of people trying to kill one another. It amazes me, the violence that is nearly contained in each of us." Thales took a sip of tea. "You must find it humid down here."

"I imagine," I replied, lost to his train of thought, "it's something in the summer."

"It *can* be. Though if a man regulates himself and his diet, it's possible to *absorb* most of the humidity. I've read of men in the Indian subcontinent, for example, who were able to thrive for substantial periods underwater."

"Thales," Charles began, "is —"

"A *discoverer*," Thales said, at which there was a hubbub

of voices from Eileen's porch. I determined at this point that a fifth, hitherto invisible, person was involved in this conversation, but had to wait several minutes more for the murmurings to begin again across the way. In a lighter, even cheerful tone, Eileen now called out:

"Charles — Emily wonders whether Mr. Menger and yourself would care to visit."

If Thales's porch was a bare and unkempt space, I'd had an inkling of Eileen's preferences from her brief appearance, which was borne out as soon as we turned from the clutter of the parlor and into the "female member" — Thales's term — where she awaited, very upright in a padded but armless chair. Beside her was a little table decorated with milk-glass objects; the single unscreened wall adjoining the house hung with matchbook still lifes. Beneath these ran a baroque chaise I did not at first realize was occupied. I started when I became aware of the wizened face regarding us from above the top of a folded blanket. Thinking it was a large doll, I leaned closer.

"My grandmother is quite blind, Mr. Menger," Eileen explained.

The woman — it was Emily, of course — smiled at me.

"Aren't we the Southern Gothic, dear?" she said in her soft voice.

"Oh *really* — I should find us a refuge." Eileen grimaced and turned to us. "What with your fires, and the rampant siphoning scourge — isn't that the case, Charles? A bit of a refuge in such a world." But before he could answer, the phone rang and she started up.

"Charles," Emily said as soon as they were alone; and then, when he went over, to my surprise she said in a small voice, "Let me touch your face, Charley."

I watched my friend kneel, and taking the very old woman's hands in his bandages, run them around his eyes and mouth. I thought I should look away, but I didn't. Her expression changed little — it never changes more than a little — but there came at last a look of satisfaction, even certainty.

As it turned out, the phone call set in motion events that would drive us from the house for most of the day. There'd been, the previous afternoon, an extraordinary request by a neighbor that the motel might be used to make accommodations for a hastily convened wedding. The call confirmed this unusual state of occupancy, and necessitated both Eileen's proposal that Charles and I share a room that night and an unprecedented feat of laundry — something to which our presence, we were told in so many words, could only be a hindrance. Cups in hand, we found ourselves trudging across the stubbled earth, Thales a dozen paces ahead, detector in hand and headphones around his ears.

I was, to tell the truth, relieved: Both the house and the Grubbers were suffocating. But while I glanced at Charles for a wink of acknowledgment he seemed, as in the showrooms, entirely at home with our host's ramblings. Watching Thales sifting dirt in his hand for bits of an old watch, hearing him cry out as he recognized this or that thing dredged up from the clay, I was struck by how circular his mind, and in fact his entire world, was — as if everything he found was something he had at some time lost. Scarcely an object appeared that he couldn't trace to himself or his family. When I asked Charles what Thales might be searching for, he said, "remnants of the Civil War."

Thales told us as much after he stopped to rest, pulling his headset around his neck. He had a pocket full of metallic bits — nuts and bolts from tractors, shell casings, a pair of wireframe spectacles minus the lenses. The old man hunkered and pointed along the gentle roll of farmland still plowed under for winter. "See those lines, running against the grain — there, and there?" — slicing the air with his hand, indicating two large furrows, as if an enormous piece of machinery had come this way long ago.

"That's where the War came through."

We walked on, until we reached a rise on the edge of a little copse. He tore a NO TRESPASSING sign off a tree and folded it for a pointer. "It stopped here, and then it continued, that way" — adjusting his directions — "toward The True South."

The better part of that day was spent touring the land's various "remnants." Like many ancient, unexcavated structures, they were difficult for the untrained eye to pry from the landscape; and even after Thales had spoken up on their behalf, I still hesitated to believe they were part of an era of internecine strife. We saw a series of what looked like brick beehives overgrown with kudzu; a round, grassless area protected by a fieldstone wall; and many examples of those vast drag marks — for, as Thales claimed, the War had come and gone on several occasions, each time reducing the land to cinders.

It was near suppertime when we returned to the motel, bearing pockets and hands full of metal the old man would later organize in his sheds. Our most remarkable find predated the War: a ladies' bicycle — his great-great-aunt's, he believed — tires rotted and chain rusted to a lump. Wedding guests were beginning to appear, and Thales, indicating that my room was the "best" room, suggested Charles move his belongings in with mine.

An afternoon in the myopic world of the Grubbers had left me with a headache, and by the time we walked down to the house, I'd determined to quietly sit things out. Our dinner, however, can be best understood if one grasps that drink made the old man talkative. It was a close night, and some further mention of humidity led him to rummage in one of his sheds and return with a bottle of remarkably old Tennessee whiskey, whose drying powers he extolled. Soon scarcely a topic could arise without drawing from him some broad theory of knowledge or material composition. Made both continuously aware and suspicious of the breadth of his observations, I eventually asked him what and where he'd studied.

"It is a question I'm not infrequently asked," he replied, directing himself to Eileen: "You recall that Dowd fellow that moved in along the road asked the same thing, back when we were looking into his well poisoning." He shook his head at the memory. "I went over, you see, and I showed him where his well was"—becoming visibly amazed as he said this and repeating—"*I showed the man where his own well was.* And so he asked me where I'd been educated and what my degrees were."

Overlooking the implied hostility in Thales's remarks, I asked whether his familiarity with his lands—the way he seemed to already recognize everything he ostensibly found—wasn't impossible to expect from someone who hadn't dedicated his life to sifting his own backyard.

"And yet, Mr. Menger," he replied, "don't most people find what they're looking for?"

I tried to catch Charles's eye. The table was watching with quiet bemusement—all except my friend, who'd become increasingly somber as Thales became more voluble. "Curious choice of words," I said. "I believe I can see why you like it so much down here: It seems everyone finds just what they want; perhaps even your dreams come true."

"Dreams *are* true," the old man corrected. "But wouldn't you agree that people who have difficulty finding what they're looking for are precisely those who *don't know* what they're looking for?" I was reminded of that habit I liked least in Charles: the smugness of the theories he posed and pressed, regardless of any interest but his own.

"One would think you were making a claim for yourself—"

"Mr. Menger, I'm a *discoverer*," he said carelessly.

"—yet nothing you brought home today bears any relation to the Civil War."

Thales poured himself another whiskey. "What," he asked, "*is* the Civil War to you?"

I stared at him, feeling as he pulled back to these further inanities I was simply shoveling words into a trench of subjectivity. I let it go: "Mr. Grubber, I'm a *collector*. It doesn't disturb me that I have no idea what I'm looking for. I wouldn't pretend to . . ." Though for the first time in our conversation, Thales seemed genuinely interested:

"What do you collect?" he said.

Despite myself, I smiled. "Maybe we should stick to the topic of the War," I replied, declining the wavering snout of the bottle; at which Charles, without looking at me, murmured:

"Milton collects things that *other people* discover. I think, in fact, he's always cherished the notion that there's no difference between a collector and a discoverer, yet so much rests on your choice of words—isn't that so?"

All day—for nearly two days—we'd barely spoken to one another; and now he'd reached out of his silence to deal me this *blow*. Even Emily, plied with soup from Eileen's bowl, seemed to pause within her more general pause; I watched it in their eyes. Surely on the ladder of meaning, "discovery" had some precedence over "collection." Still, what was he implying? That Thales was an artist of some sort, like himself? That I was somehow undeniably not?

The next moment they were all talking about other matters, but I sat back in my chair, melting into a darkness containing things I couldn't bear to see. For some minutes, I didn't participate in the conversation or even pretend to listen. Focusing in on my companions, however, I was paralyzed to find Eileen watching me with expectant curiosity:

"Are you feeling yourself, Milton?" she repeated.

"What?—yes, yes . . ."

"Then I take it that sounds *okay* to you," Thales said.

"I suppose it does," I replied after a hollow moment; I was further confused as everyone arose from the table with some purpose in mind to which I'd obviously acceded.

There must be people who do such things all the time —who blink over portions of the life narrative, such that they are left in even simple circumstances with intractable nonsense to decipher, as one finds after going for popcorn in the middle of a film, lost ever after to the reasonings of the screen. Embarrassment kept me from making this observation aloud, and instead, we were all filing out of the house into the yard when I called out, "Eileen — Eileen" — until she, last to leave before me, turned. "Now that you mention it, I *am* feeling out of sorts."

She came back into the doorway.

"I think a rest will do me some good. Perhaps a lie on the porch . . ."

She patted my hand. "Do you need me to stay with you?"

"No, please. I wouldn't keep you."

"All right, then. If you have any wants, ask Emily — she's in her room. I don't believe she sleeps anymore. We'll take care of everything," she added, and then left, closing the door.

A wilderness came over me. Surely, Charles must sense a line, always tacitly acknowledged, had been crossed back there at dinner. But perhaps, I decided after a blind interval of rage, it was better in that light not to further demean myself in some squalid appeal for explanation. I'd sunk down at my place at the table. The room, depopulated, was sharp and formicated with consciousness. Unbidden, the explanations clustered around: the gleams of wishes and things thought lost; the little voices that start in and lure a man from the verge of sleep. I forced them aside and stared doggedly at the ruined plates. *I haven't been fair to you.* I forced them aside.

So I waited, and though I discovered Charles's manner unchanged after they returned from whatever errand, I felt now that *he* might be waiting for a moment alone together. It was my best hope. Explaining that I needed to sleep, I asked him to accompany me, and we made our silent way back to the room, finding the wedding party out front, hunched in a sullen cluster. They nodded to us above their beers, and for the next hour I heard the tremor of their boasts and fears merge and divide like creatures in the night.

And still I waited. I watched Charles brush his teeth, climb into bed, and turn his back to me in this wretched, compounded silence. Certainly, in the wake of the accident, he might have decided our reunion was a terrible mistake. Yet here we were, still driving; and here he was, speaking these poisonous things—made worse by the *way* he'd said what he did, as if he had first to overcome a great boredom. As if, beyond any accumulated regrets and misunderstandings, nothing that had passed between us meant anything. Switching off the light, I lay back upon the covers, fully clothed and far from sleep.

The room was dim despite the flicker of the bathroom light. I hadn't even noticed, at first, that Charles had begun to snore. When, some time later, I glanced across the room, there he was, profile murkily visible, lips writhing gently with each breath. I turned over, stuffing my head beneath the blankets, willing my mind into the clemency of sleep.

My thoughts went out to Caroline, drowsing in whatever bower she'd lain her head. She was, I recalled tenderly, a sleepwalker. On many occasions I'd awoke to find her side of the bed empty, and I would get up knowing I'd discover her standing by a window—always a window—unconscious, but as if looking out. I don't know what drew her to windows. I don't know whether she looked beyond the glass and allowed that night-lit world into her dreams, or if she poured the material of mind out across the dark lawn of our home. If I brought her back to bed, I would sometimes find her up within the hour, auditing the yard from another room.

I was at the trembling edge of sleep, feeling amongst these recollections, but now I became aware of a sound: I could liken it only to the muffled drone of a central vacuum cleaner, so I naturally thought of the *center* of a house — and in the dream I was in *my* house, suddenly, in New Jersey. Full of dull dread, I began searching for the source of this noise — a sort of engine room, I imagined — before, waking with a start, I found myself back in the same motel room in which I lay that night, and in which I now sit, writing. I could hear machinery through the floor, or voices — a violent argument occurring in a space beneath my room. I was kneeling on the carpet, ear to the ground, when I came fully awake, and understood that something in the very *real* world was badly awry.

My father is a sinusitic monster, so I was, as are most, familiar with the outline of my friend's serenade: the wheeze of sawn wood; a blubbery slapping that brought to mind nothing so much as a barnacled shore aquiver with the rubbery rivalries of mating sea lions. As a drowning man discovers the deepest truth of his lungs when they fill with water, I discerned in this circus of seals the high whistle of a kettle; and farther down — at the moment I began to feel a twinge of nausea — an insistent gobbling, like a man eating a bowl of porridge without the use of hands or spoons.

All of which does little justice to the existential struggle in which I found myself, but half awake, locked: because in my already demoralized state, prey to insults both real and imagined, it seemed as if every psychological torture at my friend's disposal had become, tonight, physical, and all his arrogance toward me an assault. I placed the pillow over my head, but it was impossible to escape, and instead I had the impression in the dark room of something palpable, of an antagonism that had taken form as a hole takes form in cloth: a sucking void opening moment to moment, by wider and wider degrees. I'd broken into a cold sweat. I reached for the bedside light but in my excitement knocked it from the nightstand.

Rising and placing my feet upon the carpet, I went to Charles's bed and shook him. I grabbed hold of his arm and shook harder, and when he remained composed, I at first gently and then with increasing hysteria slapped his shoulder, an exposed hand, his cheeks, until at last I was grasping at his face, shouting his name and winding his hair in my fists. The sound, however, was unrelenting—and worse, it seemed to draw strength from my efforts, taking on a querulous, combative tone, a tone even of injury. It was then, glancing up toward a recognition like a migraine, I saw that within my outlandish fears lay a kernel of truth, for some terrible, life-denying power had tainted and bloomed in the heart of the room, his body only a sounding board upon which these motifs played. I could *see* it—or could *not* see, but knew *precisely* where it must lie: It roiled like a darkness within the darkness, *in the very center of the room.* I thought of what my friend had told me about rooms, how each of us has a room into which we fit like a key. And in comprehending as much, in grasping such a demise, I was suddenly drawn across the carpet, past Charles, down the narrow alley between our beds, to the doom at the heart of the room that seemed to be one with my realization.

Feet slipping on the precipitous slope of the nylon nap, I hovered above my end. Much as a man lost at sea, without hope, eventually collapses and drinks from the briny ocean encircling his raft, understanding it will kill him, though luxuriating in the taste of water, I felt above all a desire to simply surrender, sink through the rubbery abyss, and embrace the fantastical night. A moment more I held on, gripping the bed frame for dear life; and then, with a shriek, I flung myself backward toward the bathroom light. I was clawing at the wall, at the tile threshold, beginning to slip one last time down that funnel of carpet toward the yawning center, when something in the bead-board paneling gave way beneath my hand, and I lunged forward and struck my head.

Time, a blank interval, elapsed. I found myself lying upon my side in the dark lobby of the Idyll, one of my legs, as if in the trailing wake of a current, feebly sweeping at a door in the wall I'd never noticed — the same door through which I had, it seemed, in a blind act of self-preservation, just escaped. Cautiously, I sat up, feeling where the carpet had corrugated my face, wondering how long I'd lain unconscious. Hearing beyond the still-open door the echo of recent horrors, I shut it quietly, and climbed into one of the armchairs arranged around the television. Perhaps it was the closing of the door and the subsequent silence, but after several minutes spent collecting myself in the near blackness, I became aware of a presence in the room. Slowly I sat forward and listened.

I have, as I believe I've mentioned on several occasions, a fear of the dark; I am, on the other hand, gifted with a focus — be it auditory or visual, but generally brought to bear on works of art — matched by few. Fears can be misleading, and fully conscious of this, I tried to concentrate on what details I could glean from the lobby. Even with the door sealed, I detected faintly the gurgles of my friend in the guest room I'd just quitted; though after a moment, I was forced to conclude that I was, instead, listening to the digestive vibrations of the office dehumidifier. There was, too, a very thin, high whine, a singing such as is made by a television with the sound turned down. Almost simultaneous with this discovery, I noticed that the TV, which I'd taken in its darkened state to be off, was actually *on*, although muted and with the brightness set to a minimum. Feeling, still, that there was someone besides myself in the room, I tried to determine how I might draw my companion out, but the dim square of light continued to distract me, until I had to concede that upon this almost black screen there were moving images, so faint that I had to peer for several minutes to make out anything other than a sheen coming from the glass.

I heard, then, a snap, saw a flash to my right, and a flared match guttered before Charles's face, not three feet from my own, as he kindled a cigarette.

I made a soundless scream. He paused midpuff to stare at me.

"Couldn't sleep myself," he said, placing the cigarette back in his mouth.

I continued to watch him, which he seemed to take easily enough.

"I suppose you think I've been bad-mannered, lately," he added, "but people say and do all kinds of things they don't mean, late at night."

I wasn't sure this was an apology for what had occurred that evening, yet our entire altercation — could one even call it that? — seemed increasingly unreal; and when I reflected on what he'd just said, it was, of course, true. I replied as much.

For a moment we were silent, and then he mumbled, "The reception is terrible. You need to get yourself a new set of rabbit ears."

I thought he was kidding — this was, after all, beyond the pale of bad reception; but then, for obvious reasons, I began to feel he wasn't talking to me. Looking farther to the right of my friend, I saw, less by the light of the television than by the coal of Charles's cigarette, another man — Thales, in fact — his attention riveted on the incredibly dim TV.

"What are you watching?" I asked, half joking.

"It's an old machine," Thales explained. "It's got a broken receptor —" He seemed to lose his way, and turned to me. "Where were you," he asked, "the first time you realized it doesn't matter whether you have the damn thing plugged in or not?"

I reconsidered the television. Now that my eyes had warmed to the dark, I could see, as Thales had implied, that the TV wasn't plugged into the wall outlet. There was, however, what looked like a news program on. After a moment, I decided it was a documentary. It had to do with the Civil War, but contained footage of jet planes and other things incongruous to the 1860s. Perhaps it was a documentary on the history of warfare. It was hard to make out, and entirely silent. I craned forward in my seat.

"Isn't there any sound?" I asked.

"I don't know," Thales replied. I got up and adjusted what I took to be the volume control.

"Broken. The volume's been broken on this old set ever since I found it," he said. It was fantastic to me that he could discover this inexplicable property of his television and not know whether sound was part of the phenomenon, but he seemed content to leave it at that.

"Do you have another television?" I asked.

He saw now that I was interested in his TV, and was amused. "Yes," he said, "I do—back at the house. Though the sound's broken on that one, too."

Reluctantly, I returned to my seat, and watched a whiskered man in a Confederate uniform address a small crowd.

"What are they saying?" I asked.

"I have often wondered," Thales replied. "Still—I prefer it to the daytime television."

"But there's *one* station," Charles complained.

"Not true. There are two, now. Eileen discovered another about a week ago"; and to demonstrate this, he reached forward and twisted the dial.

"When you say 'daytime television,'" I said, "do you mean that these stations only run at night?"

"An excellent question, but difficult to answer." Thales slowly turned the dial through dark screens, scrutinizing the resultant darknesses, so that one might have thought—as I suppose was actually the case—he was merely fooling with an unplugged television. "I've only seen them at night, yet it's possible there is simply too much ambient light during the day"—still turning—"and like the stars, the stations, while they exist continuously, need the cover of darkness to be visible to the naked eye. I imagine dreams must function in much the same fashion."

Charles leaned in mischievously at this point. "I thought you said *two*."

"There are," Thales insisted as he stopped, and we stared

together at the television until we knew that, as promised, he had found another station. There was an image of a car — an accident. The car lurched to a halt, and then, suddenly, the scene was engulfed in flame.

"It's funny," he mumbled after a bit. "This isn't the same one — it's a different number on the dial. But that's how it goes, doesn't it? When it rains, it pours."

He sat back in his chair, then, and we watched the new channel. "Just as well — other one was Eileen's idea of a station. Cooking shows, trained poodles — that type of programming."

Onscreen was a rolling scene of fields and houses, as if viewed from a train. Then it began to snow, until nothing more could be seen. From this blankness emerged a vast and manicured lawn, across which a dog raced — a collie, such as I had when I was a child. It was somewhere up North, and it sent a pang through me.

"What are we watching?" I asked, finding the subject elusive.

"Hardly matters," Charles said with evident boredom, "does it?"

Still, no one made any move to do otherwise until Charles checked his watch.

"About time, isn't it," Thales said.

"Thales was ready to put money down that you'd sleep right through," my friend joked.

I had no idea what they were talking about, though it occurred to me that I was, perhaps, suffering beneath the ambiguities opened up earlier that evening during my interlude of enraged distraction.

"I didn't realize how tired I'd be," I said, hedging my bets. The men laughed.

"Why don't you sit a while longer," Thales suggested, "while we get the gear together." He then produced from the darkness behind him a thermos, and poured into its lid a cup of coffee that he passed to me. The two rose a moment later and stumped out of the room, into the night, leaving me alone with the strange television.

A marvelous calm had eased away even the natural anxieties I might have felt over the darkness and the occupations in which I'd evidently agreed to engage. I'd grown quite used to the TV, and after a moment got up and flipped between the channels. On the first station now was a program on various objects that resembled nothing so much as the crossbreeding of products already familiar to me: I was shown a radio with slots in its face for making toast; a frying pan with a flashlight built into the handle, drawing its power (rather ingeniously, I thought) from the heating element on a stove. After a while, I decided to return to the second channel; though I never arrived, for along the way, going counterclockwise on the dial, I found yet another. This also didn't appear to be Eileen's station. In fact, it resembled the channel discovered earlier — perhaps a syndicated program was playing on several bands. Whatever the program was, I saw with renewed interest it was now focused on the recent spate of motel fires. There were a series of what I took to be reenactments: I watched the curtains of a room go up in a blaze; a can of gasoline trailed a glistening arc through the dark; someone was rolling in the grass, a fallen pillar of flame. Still, without sound, it was difficult to determine what conclusions were drawn, and I glanced around the room for something else with which to occupy myself.

My eyes had adjusted more than I could have believed to the poverty of light. Spread on a table between my seat and the seat where Charles had slouched was the paper he'd bought the day before on our drive over to the Idyll. I must have squinted at the page for a while before the electrical glow and the minuscule increase in radiance from the window — for it was growing light — showed me the first, the very largest words. It was the name of the paper, and I was surprised to discover Charles had bought a national — the *Washington Post.* And then, my eyes drifting down among the display fonts of the headlines, I saw with quickening interest something about Singer.

Turning the paper over, I noticed below the crease a picture of the gated entrance to a factory — the one in Elizabeth, if I wasn't mistaken — high and black and weathered, and below that, a stream of people — a trickle compared to the city that used to find employment inside those walls, yet several hundred — emerging into sunlight. Some were waving. There was a woman near the front, bent forward, and my first thought was that she was weeping. But then it's *true,* I grasped, my face nearly touching the page, because even before I teased out the caption, I understood: They'd closed the plant. Singer had built it in 1873, and those windows had watched every other Singer factory in America come and go. It was the end; the stroke carried a finality I'd failed to grasp when Charles had confided his concerns that night at the Happy Motel. What remained of the company's retail and industrial sewing operations, I read, would be shut down in the coming weeks, for, in the words of a weary-looking vulture in a suit — the picture box depicted him hunched without the gates in a troika of other weary scavengers — "The Singer Sewing Company has ceased today to be an American concern." The once-great sewing giant would, it appeared, be concentrating its efforts on computer aviation equipment. It was Charles's worst nightmare.

Every word seemed unbelievable to me — perhaps as unbelievable as the slow collapse of Elizabeth had felt to my parents, a thing my father had inveighed against as if it were a calculated process directed toward himself. At that hour, however, there was no way to shed additional light on my discovery. I wondered, sitting back from the newspaper, listening for the return of my companions, what Charles already knew; clearly, it was impossible something of this hadn't been imparted to him in advance of the general public. Hearing the tromp of boots crossing the veranda, I quietly folded the paper back over. Whether I should leave it for him to broach, or try tactfully to enter into these events myself, was a question I would leave to circumstance.

On the TV, as if to echo my thoughts, there was a breaking story about the closing. The picture was fading with the dawn, but I watched the ghostly silhouette of the tower with the sinuous Singer S. A man was speaking to a crowded room — word of this historic event had to be reverberating across the networks — and people, reporters, riddled him with questions. The clamor of the media was strikingly at odds with the spokesman's solemnity; and then, without warning, the man seemed to collapse at the podium. For a moment, pandemonium erupted, and then I stared as fire leapt up and covered the scene. An instant later everything had changed and I was looking at a cavernous industrial space, in which hundreds of sewing machines sat in rows, bent over each one an indistinct figure, making what I do not know.

As footsteps reached the door I hurriedly changed the

channel, and they came in to find me searching among the subtleties of screens for another station.

"Too much light," Thales croaked. "You've lost it." He held, I noticed, a gun in his hand—a rifle of some sort. Charles, I saw, had two more.

"We better get moving," he said, "it's nearly light," of the blue filtering through the slats of the windows.

It turned out, of course, that we were going hunting—*this* had been what I'd missed over dinner. We rattled through the dawn in Thales's red pickup, climbing a logging road through the foothills of what he facetiously referred to as the "Atlas Mountains." Here, the old man explained that much as he'd like to, he was not accompanying us on the hunt itself: From previous observations, he had reason to believe the War had come through this way, and he'd brought his metal detector to test out certain hypotheses. The gun was, in his own words, "a precaution." I'd never been hunting before, and guns are a mystery to me. Standing in a clearing an hour's drive and forty-minute walk into the woods, Charles had me practice on a rusted still full of axe strokes, dragged up from some dell during Prohibition. When I'd sunk a dozen rounds into the iron drum, we agreed to meet Thales back at the truck before dark, and with that, shouldering our rifles and some lunch, we left the old man tinkering with his machine.

We proceeded up a narrow valley and then along a ridge, wading through last year's leaves and the early ground cover of mayapple. The sun seemed to pull at a laggard season. The water in the canteen tasted like steel.

"I didn't know," I said, drawing up beside him, "you liked to hunt."

"I don't, really," Charles replied. "Thales suggested it. But I always need to get out of there, get some air."

I was relieved to hear him say this, not least because I felt for the first time in days he'd set us apart as like-minded persons.

"The thing to understand about Thales," he said to my glance, "is that whether or not you agree with him isn't his measure. After all, what does it matter if he maintains the world is flat, and you know it's round? We're only visitors. *His* world is just as he believes.

"Though sometimes . . . sometimes I think each of us," he continued after a moment, "is such a monster, who can never be defeated on his home ground. It even seems to me a wonderful thing, then — that the machinery of the world might be held, somewhere, in abeyance."

He was, I saw, speaking to what had transpired over dinner, but also, I sensed, alluding to Singer, and an impossible hope: that a place existed where events, even regions of our own lives, might pass over us, where we might sleep and find, awakening, the world unchanged.

"Charles," I asked, "did you know what you were looking for when you came down here?"

"To the South? I don't think so — or at least I have no idea anymore. Why, did you?"

I shrugged, pausing to cross a log fallen over the damp mouth of a stream. "Do you think you'll ever paint again?"

"Milton," he cried, and for an instant I thought he was angry; until he looked back and said, "Milton, really — for the last time: I've thrown all that away. *It's gone.*"

And when I mumbled, "You don't actually mean —" he turned and laughed. "No, *no*. It's just I've come to that point, where I can never go home."

Home — and my thoughts carried me to *my* home. I suppose there are people for whom home lies at the end of every road, and people for whom it lies only behind. I fell into his wake, unsure if I should say something more, hoping that perhaps Charles would speak first, that this was the beginning of some confidence about the Singer Sewing Company, and what we would now do. Instead, however, he drifted into silence, and soon we seemed far from one another again.

As we walked higher up, the green grew so weak it was just a warming of the browns and grays. Reaching a level run on the ridge, we stopped and climbed into the crotch of a massive old tree to await the deer. After an hour, tired of watching the defile that Charles believed contained a track, I fell to examining the worn mechanism of the gun.

"It's quite simple, isn't it?" I said when he noticed what I was doing.

"Very, though of course it was an enormous idea at the time. Guns were the first small appliances to be produced with interchangeable parts, and the first mass-produced machines to enter our homes — not just the homes of the rich, but all sorts, urban and rural." He paused. "The sewing machine was second, after the Colt pistol. Did Harvey," he said, "ever show you that little pistol of his he kept in the glove box?"

"No — he never mentioned it."

"I don't think he used it even once. And then he was shot, with his own gun . . ." The next line of hills lay like bears in the cold light above the valleys. The blue made my eyes water.

"Did you ever have a friend?" Charles said, sighting his rifle up for a moment, into emptiness. "Someone in whose company you didn't become yourself, exactly, but that part of yourself that they most believed in?"

It was as if he'd turned and stared at me, so much did it seem, to my mind at least, that Charles was again speaking about *us*. Yet I suggested, "Isn't that just the way everyone is, to some extent, with everyone?"

The nose of Charles's rifle drifted along the horizon, settling at last upon a shred of the moon, like a wreck at the base of the sky. "Yes — of course. What's funny, though," he continued, "is that if this same friend were to ask you to become this little part, this thing in which you both, apparently, believed, together — what wouldn't you do, to keep hold of the whole rest of your inadmissible life?"

I didn't know where he was leading us, sitting opposite one another as we were, guns in hand. I wasn't even sure which of us might be which in his diagram of friends, and yet I felt he was confessing something: For several breaths, I even wondered if he was asking me to kill him; and the entire trip into the hills, through such a lens, seemed poised to take a most desperate turn, of the sort that belongs locked in dreams. I gazed again at the gun in my hand, then at Charles, who'd turned away. And still, perhaps this wasn't the case at all; or perhaps it was something I wanted that I could read into the shape of a cloud — and I remembered the rage I'd felt only a few hours before. Surely it wouldn't be the first time I'd let such a rage pass, as it were, out of my dreams. Either way, there was a murderous energy in the air. I was silent, and relieved when he continued, of his own accord, on a former track of conversation: "Yes — Harvey and his little Colt. I've always found it strange that mass production would be violent at its inception. Maybe strange isn't the word. You know the story, don't you, of the Winchester widow?"

I shook my head.

"After the Indian Wars, the widow of Oliver Winchester, who'd amassed a fortune manufacturing guns, was haunted by the idea that the spirits of the Indians killed by her husband's rifles would come looking for her. It's said the notion was planted in her head by a fortune-teller, but for whatever reason, it became only more persuasive with time. She lived in California, and was building a grand house back in the late 1800s. The palm reader told her as long as she didn't stop building her house, she'd be safe."

There was a stirring among some boulders where the ridge sloped away into a thicket of saplings. For a few minutes we waited, then slowly his rifle tipped back up.

"And so she never did, all her life. It became like being alive. The house grew through hundreds of rooms, without order, without purpose, with windows onto nothing, stairs to nowhere. It was a compulsion, a physical madness."

"Do you," I said, "believe in ghosts?"

"I believe," he replied, "people can be haunted."

For my part, I came to believe by day's end that while a person could be haunted by deer, a physical deer of the sort one could shoot was a rarer phenomenon. Having taken our posts at a series of fruitless observation points, it was near dark by the time we gave up and made our way back into sight of human habitation. The gun had grown massive in my hand, but so had my sense that I should broach the topic of what I'd seen in the newspaper during the night. There was something hunted in the way Charles hurried through the dusk, a disheartened look in which I read more than misgivings over a failed day of sportsmanship. Compounding matters, we'd become lost during our descent, and only when the light was nearly gone did we arrive at a familiar road. I was preoccupied with such thoughts, eyes only half upon the yard that had come into view — the first outbuildings of some poor farm — when I beheld a beautiful, tall buck, poised in the last low beams of light.

He had, it seemed, scented us, but placed as he was outside the woods, in a clearing beside a sheet-metal toolshed, he'd decided his best gamble was to freeze. Looking closer, I saw then, not ten feet away, a doe, posed like himself in an attitude of attention.

There was a momentary brightening from a road just beyond, and headlights swept that corner of the yard and were gone. The deer stood in a fallow flower bed, silhouettes whose shadows slanted across the lawn and faded at our feet. All the lights were off in the house; there were no cars in the drive. I put my hand on Charles's arm.

He glanced at me, then at where I took aim as I raised the gun to my shoulder.

"What are you doing?" he whispered.

I know there are laws about shooting in populated areas — Charles had warned me as much that morning, when he had an air of experience and confidence; but his words rang false at the end of the day, and an excitement had overtaken me, the same I imagine roils the blood of our nation's hunters every year. Everything became keen — the dense smell of the earth, the final pricks of light. Even the heaviness of the gun became a purpose. I could feel the life of the buck beating like a vein in my neck.

"Take it easy. There's no one here," I said quietly, squeezing the trigger before the animals had a chance to bolt.

The gun roared and streaked the sky with sound. And while I discovered I hadn't aimed true, I had accidentally winged the doe, which seemed to quiver but remained standing, horribly, with a chunk as large as a head torn from her haunch.

There was just enough light to see the pale opening in her brown hide, yet she remained, as did the buck, as if frozen. I'd heard stories about animals, and even men, dead but locked within the last nervous impulse of their bodies, the electric surge of life's ebb spasming like the empty action of waves on a beach.

"Stop it," he said quite loudly as I reloaded, reaching, even, for the gun. "Jesus—would you just look what you're doing!"

My success, however, emboldened me, and the silence that once more enclosed us cemented my conviction that we were as alone in that roadside yard as if we'd been miles deep in the woods. Ignoring him, I stepped away, and again fired upon the buck.

My second shot, thankfully, was an admirable one. Yet as hunting adventures went, this was taking a grim turn. I was alarmed to find that while I'd hit him squarely this time, the impact had blown the creature's head entirely off, and now both animals stood in the dusk, mutilated, but unable to fall. I lowered the gun and stared at it. I recalled the distinction Thales had drawn between the obliterating power of hollow-point rounds and the "cleaner" lower-caliber munitions used during warfare. My difficulties, I suspected, lay somewhere within this divide.

"You *idiot*," Charles said, looking between myself and the carnage. He blinked stupidly for a moment, then murmured, "Let's go. Let's get out of here."

"What do you mean?" I replied, still examining my gun. Perhaps it was a trick rifle. Or perhaps they were trick animals. "What's the matter with them?"

He stared at me for longer than seemed necessary, then walked from the edge of the wood into the yard, right up to the hapless creatures — they gaped a ghastly white where they'd been wounded. Arriving at the buck's side, he began to beat the body with the butt of his rifle — a dull thudding — as pieces, chips, first dark then bright, flew off the animal's back. As I emerged into the clearing he switched his attentions to the doe, breaking her tail off in a shower of debris. I was halfway across the yard when he snapped her body off the legs, leaving stumps of plaster and rebar stuck upright from the ground like saplings; then he stormed around, plowing again into the woods from where we'd just emerged.

I don't know how we found our way that night — I was convinced at times that Charles was deliberately trying to lose me in the outrage of Southern brush. That he was a smaller man than I only seemed to assist him in his race to escape, until I'd ceased to call ahead, concentrating solely upon keeping him in sight. It seemed possible at moments that alone I might never find my way back to the familiar, might wander in Thales's mountains, haunted by plaster demons, forever. Great was my relief when we stumbled on a dirt road with the headlamps of a truck burning patiently for our return. Charles didn't say a word in the car, and I was simply relieved he didn't further humiliate me. Thales, for his part, accepted our silence as a case of the sulks brought on by a failure in the hunting department.

Upon awakening the next day, even before leaving my bed, I began to think of what I might say to my companion, supposing him to have remained in a nettled frame of mind. In the lounge and at the house I searched for the article about the plant closing — at first for a conversational pretext, and then, in bewilderment, for confirmation alone — but the furniture and wastebins were devoid of reading materials, the television hopelessly dysfunctional by daylight.

For I should tell you that as the morning wore on, and Charles remained ominously silent, I began to question the entire preceding twenty-four hours, parts of which *seemed* realistic, but other parts at best unlikely. Had a whole day really passed since that miserable supper? And was it still *this* his mood reflected, if these peculiar events, and the apologies that lay among them, were no more than a dream?

Reluctant to bring up our hunting expedition — fearful of the abuse that might be heaped upon me for what, after all, had seemed the most believable part, and without any means of determining the day or date (and what *had* yesterday been, in any event?), I was at a loss as to how to begin a conversation about the closing of the Elizabeth facilities. Had this event, whose announcement fell within the disputed time, even taken place? Paper, television, hunt — it was as if I'd opened a door, taken a turn down a road into lands that overlapped the provinces of mind. And yet some part of it, I was sure, remained true.

LAST NIGHT I lay listening to the phone ringing, walking the line of rooms; and pushing a heap of candy wrappers from the bed (in spite of the vending machine I've returned in the last week to my college weight), in the resultant silence, I rediscovered the insect eating away the inside of the chair by the sewing machine. I was thinking about the second time I saw Charles's mother, nearly five years ago, not long after I met Caroline, but before I'd introduced her to anyone.

I was with Harvey that night, at P——, ostensibly attending a reunion for which he'd come all the way from Memphis, though in fact there only because I lived half an hour away. We'd stood in the pompous and bannered alumni hall for more than an hour, knocking back drinks and shaking hands, waiting for Charles to appear. I was curious to see no one else, and found my classmates much as I imagined: people who'd died in their own lives. With wives, children, family, and friends, there'd been no one to save what little spark they'd had; or more likely, it was these very well-meaning loved ones who'd snuffed them out. And so with a bad show of goodwill I circulated and exclaimed, asking around, comparing notes until Harvey and I deduced that Charles had replied to nothing, spoken to no one, and obviously had no intention of appearing—which news surprised Lucy Sharp, the class-spirit whip:

"*I* thought if *anyone* was going to be here!" she brayed, wagging a head that retained, impossibly, the same hair she'd had fifteen years before. Everything about her, really, was remarkably unchanged—even the gap between her two front teeth seemed part of a familiar outfit. This was cleared up somewhat when she told us she'd dressed as herself in college.

As to how we convinced her to abandon the evening she'd been phoning and otherwise harassing everyone about for six months and come with us, I have no idea, save that she'd been brightened out of consciousness and responsibility by several trips to the bathroom. Only the largest features of her mental landscape were visible in this whiteout, and within the first few minutes of running into her we knew that she'd been divorced from her husband—"that nonentity"—for a month, and that she'd had an emergency hysterectomy a short time before this, following what sounded like a horrific car accident. One kept expecting the conversation to come to a calamitous end; I involuntarily turned away—and perhaps this is why her face, too, has been brightened away for me on that snowy night. As she stands by the ice swan, under a hill of chestnut hair, all I see is that gap between her teeth in the rearview of the rest of the night. You could, it seems to me now, have pointed her at anything, and she'd organize it. It was Harvey's idea to point her at Charles. She'd dated Charles briefly, back in the day, and said she knew where his house was — I don't think we'd have found it again, otherwise.

It is undoubtedly a trick of the mind, but when I look back on Harvey, my recollections of him are similarly abbreviated by the years: a blue blazer dotted with snow in the night — a blue blazer and a white turtleneck, and he's running through snow toward the car, parked on the grass behind the administration building. People wore blazers back then; I was probably wearing such a thing, myself. It was May, but it had been snowing when we arrived, and as long as it snowed, you felt you might do anything.

Harvey sat beside me like a copilot. There were certain places along the way he wanted to stop. We stopped somewhere that looked like a castle that was really a gas station, and we stopped at a little strip of gray beach with cattails and potted palm trees shivering in front of a Polynesian-themed restaurant. Everything seemed a bit unreal, so deep into spring, the ground grassed but the air flecked like a shaken paperweight. For fifteen minutes we stood on the edge of a gulch, behind a suburban neighborhood, where Harvey insisted on shouting to the other side. He was undisturbed when what we'd taken to be an echo turned out to belong to someone else, shouting back.

I'd believed that with a little luck I would do all right by myself on our mission of discovery. Only when we got off the highway did I realize that while I'd imagined a voyage of nostalgia into my childhood, it was the streets in a most general form that I recalled. I remembered my hometown as one remembers algebra, and I was surprised by the almost total lack of those specific details I assumed would light my way: They were not, it seemed, details of this place at all. Fortunately, Lucy was happy to do the directing.

"You just wait until we get there," she whispered, navigating the dilapidated downtown. "I have a surprise!"

"You do not," gaped Harvey, who loved surprises.

Wordlessly she bit her lip and nodded.

The hour had grown late for unannounced house calls — my watch said 9:00 — but I think we believed that the nature of our mission would guarantee a warm welcome; and so we penetrated into that neighborhood "across the tracks" from where I'd grown up. We meandered among nameless avenues of row houses, the snow doing its gentle housework about the town, softening the decay, the displeasure of detail. I had no idea where we were when she banged on the back of my seat — "That's it! This is it! Here! Here!" — and we parked in front of a little attached two-story place with a Virgin Mary birdbath in its sink of a yard. Colorless in the falling snow, I didn't remember it; still, I recognized Mr. Trembleman when he came to the door. He seemed troubled, but he recalled something in Lucy's face, and shook her hand.

"What brings you kids out on a night like this?" he asked.

"We came to see Charles," Lucy, our interpretive chipmunk, piped as he allowed us into the living room. Mrs. Trembleman, seated on a green satin chair, looked up at the sound of her son's name, eyes mantled in insomniac darkness.

"Hi, Mrs. Trembleman," Harvey volunteered. Her smile radiated mistrust.

"We came to see Charles," Lucy repeated.

"Of course you did," Mrs. Trembleman replied. I don't

think I'd heard her speak before; unlike Mr. Trembleman, she had a strong, hale voice. It was like waking up. It was a wall. "He cleared out a long time ago. No surprise."

This had been a distinct possibility—it was, after all, a great long shot that our friend might be found living at home or even visiting if he wasn't already at the reunion—but in his mother's voice there was something that told us there would be no consolation prize. As if to emphasize as much, she turned off the television. If she'd asked us to leave, no less of a pall could have been cast over the room.

"Where is he?" Lucy asked in a punctured tone.

Mrs. Trembleman shrugged. Her husband, who stood at our elbows and seemed blistered by his wife's remarks, had the task of pleasantries:

"We got a letter from him the other day. Says he's taken a job in the South"—though looking back, I'm not sure whether Mr. Trembleman failed to mention Singer because it was innocuous to him or because the leaf had fallen too close to the tree.

"A card," Mrs. Trembleman corrected, "with a picture of a motel on it."

We should have left then, but I think I'd formed in my mind some mistaken notions about Ellen Trembleman, among them that our disdain for those around us—hers perhaps more honest than mine—gave us some secret rapport. My eyes had held her face for the last few minutes, waiting for the reciprocal glance. I think I believed that if I spoke it would be different; and I was, in a way, correct.

"I guess it *is* no surprise," I chimed in, "that he'd clear out"—regretting borrowing the words even as I said them.

"I just keep thinking I'll hear from him, that he's done something" — I was going to say *remarkable*, but she didn't allow me to finish:

"Why should *you* hear from him?" she said in an even tone.

"I mean in the papers," I backtracked, although this wasn't at all what I'd meant. She raised a hand at her husband, preemptively.

"I should like you, Mr. Menger," she said after a moment. I was surprised she remembered my name, and hesitated, believing this was the beginning of a communication, but then I understood it wasn't.

She had a large, what would be called "handsome" head — a bit too manly, like a more massive version of Charles's. She was just sitting there in the armchair I'd found her in fifteen years before. Her husband placed himself between us. She seemed prepared to ask some terrible question of me — a question that to answer incorrectly would be to die. After a pause, she murmured quietly, "You have nothing more to say," which might have been a question, but so might the last thing she'd said. I began to speak, and then I stood. I was thirty-five years old. Until we left the house, I dreaded that she would say or ask something more; and so we allowed Mr. Trembleman to show us out.

"It's a beautiful night," he offered through the screen door. "Thanks for coming by. I'll tell him. I'll tell Charles when I see him," he said, although we all knew by then that he'd never have the chance. "Drive safe, you hear?"

We went back and sat in the car. "That was the pits," Lucy mumbled. For my part, I sensed that my companions understood that some small outrage had just been committed, and that it had been perpetrated against *me*. All around the car the snow stood in the air. It seemed no longer to rise or fall. The ground was black and unspeakably hard.

"How do we get back to the highway?" I asked, starting the engine.

"We can't *leave* now," Lucy said. "We *can't*," she repeated a moment later as I put the car in gear. She was implacable: "I still have to tell you my surprise," she whispered, at which Harvey turned gamely around and she said, "It's my *birthday!*"

"You're kidding," he played along. "For real?"

"For real for real." It was like having weights lowered on my head.

"What the hell are you doing out here on your birthday?" he said.

She seemed a bit thrown by this, but then murmured, "I want to go to the track."

I ignored her.

"I want to go to the dog track," she said in a louder voice.

"We're not going to a dog track," I told her as I wheeled down gray and empty streets through the snow, wanting to ask for further directions, afraid she'd withhold them.

"But it's my birthday," she repeated.

"What, are you *three*?" I said.

"Oh come on," Harvey guffed from his soft heart, "it's her *birthday*."

"It's my fucking birthday, too," I said, "and I say we go home."

Lucy's head shot over the front seat. "It is?"

"What's the matter with you?" I cried, but the horror in my voice couldn't hold, and I laughed despite myself, and Harvey laughed, and then everyone was amused and I could see we were going to the track, wherever that was. The moment lay like gold, and was gone.

"You know, the more I get to know you, the less I like you," Harvey told me when the laughter had died, and Lucy appealed, "But *really* . . ."

I was still laughing, yet it was spoiled. We pulled over at a liquor store like a cage and I made him get out for something to take to the track.

"I thought you said you lived here," Lucy said after we were alone.

"A long time ago, on the other side of town. I went to boarding school—" And then, to bury the moment: "So . . . why are we going to the track, besides that it's your birthday?"

"I don't know. I wanted to go for years—when I was with Charles I wanted to, but *he* wouldn't take me. He wouldn't go to casinos, either. *Joan* got him to"—she'd been best friends with Joan Peebles, and they went out with Charles serially for a while—"but just once, even her."

"Well," I said, thinking I'd cheer her up, "if he was going to get twenty—"

"—people to lift him up to her third-floor window so he could propose?"

"Right, sorry." I winced. "Seemed like a long time ago."

"It was. I'm just saying, were *you* one of those people?"—offering me a stick of gum.

I shook my head. "You sound like you're saying it isn't true."

"I'm *saying* it was just different going out with him is all. Were you guys close?"

"I don't know." I began to explain, but I saw I'd given my answer. She carefully unwrapped her gum and folded it into her mouth.

"You're rich, aren't you?" she asked after a moment. It was a surprisingly shy question, and I smiled.

At this point Harvey got back in the car. We could hear someone calling out to him as he closed the door — a couple of guys coming across the adjoining lot, hooded and urgent. One of them threw a bottle as we pulled back into the street, and it shattered beneath the undercarriage.

"It's mean out there," he said cheerily.

The track looked abandoned, but the tiny sound of the announcer crept over the walls and into the car park, and we went inside the cement stadium through an enclosure like a bus station, filled with bus-station people. We placed bets based on the names we liked — Lame Fellow, Black Cloud, Charley's Folly — and while the regulars stayed behind glass, huddled as if against some deeper cold, we went out into the flurries to lean on the rails and watch the dogs flinch around, wiry and heaving with heat.

"It's just like I imagined it," Lucy said, scrunching her shoulders in pleasure. "Or" — catching my amused glance — "*we're* just like I imagined us. I mean, I always thought I'd go all dressed up like this. And look" — for there we were, in our reunion suits.

"It's your birthday present," I told her. "I kind of assumed you'd been to a dog track before"—both shaking our heads in unison. No one, she repeated, had ever wanted to go with her. When I asked if she was bad luck, I was sorry she just looked away.

Harvey, though—Harvey was in his element. He placed three bets for our every one, slipping into the clubhouse, then returning to us to drink from the pints he'd bought at the liquor store. He did all right, too. He placed bets for Lucy and won her fifty dollars. We watched him enviously as he threaded in and out of the bright box. Excited, unshaven faces followed his patent leather shoes across the floor. Alone among men the color of cigarettes, I remembered what Harvey was like at school. I marveled at how easily he walked among them. Outside, flashing through the distance, hovering hot and uncoiled before our eyes for an instant, the dogs seemed like the lives of the men in the glassed hall. I thought about what Harvey had said about liking me less and less, and it rankled all over, and I tried to make this person beside me at the rail like me. Once, when he went in after giving her a handful of money, we kissed, and she asked if I was with anyone, and I lied.

We stayed until Harvey had lost most of what he'd made, and then we piled back into my car. Lucy was hungry, so we drove into town and stopped at a diner, and it was there—we were all drunk by this time—that she confessed that it really *wasn't* her birthday.

"But wait, wait"—she grabbed at our hands; she *had* always wanted to go to the track. Harvey found this very funny; he seemed more and more alive as the night wore on. Piling back into the car, he wanted to stop again for liquor, though we were already lost. The idea of getting directions at the liquor store amused everyone but me. Instead we stopped at a gas station. The town had grown larger than I or Lucy remembered. We got directions to the highway, but became lost again. We stopped at another gas station. Lucy bought a map of the city and gave impossible instructions from the back as Harvey brandished the last of his winnings. There was a bar he knew, a bartender somewhere — "Yes, yes!" she exclaimed. Improbably, she remembered that Charles had taken her there, once, too. I heard the map revolve in the backseat. They were arguing over the name. It wasn't the same place at all. It was a conversation too misshapen to even be an argument. I told them to shut up, but no one was listening. Harvey was laughing a lot. We all were.

We were in another part of town I didn't know. Guys at an intersection watched us, hunched in their parkas. In the distance, down side streets, I made out the pale hulk of the highway lifting above the roofs. The ruckus in the car was deafening. I told Harvey that he could stop and get something for the road, but that it was late — too late for this place he wanted to find . . . and so I slowed halfway down a dark block, and that's where I left him. He was, as I said, drunk. He didn't notice at first that there was no liquor store.

For a while he ran beside the car — longer than I thought he could. His face looked very white. And then we turned a corner and were alone. It had begun snowing again — slow, soft flakes like islands. Lucy was a bit hysterical when she realized I wasn't planning to stop.

"It's my birthday," she kept saying. "It's my birthday."

And I — well, forget about me. I said, "All right, *all right,* take it easy," even though it wasn't true anymore. We were still lost, or continued to be lost. We went around and around streets that looked in the dark like they were made out of earth, snow draped in the air like a house closed up long ago. The snow was a state of mind. I don't think it touched anything. Once, just before I turned the car down the street that would actually take us across a bridge and into somewhere else, onto a ramp and out, we saw Harvey again, running. He was a ways down the block, without his jacket. He slipped and leapt on the icy ground, a moth chased through the dark. Behind me, I heard the girl sit up. I heard her breath catch. It was a nightmare.

"Forget about him," I warned the still silent back of the car, a huddle of darkness in the rearview. In my mind she was somehow inflicting this upon us. "Go to sleep," I warned, making a turn down some brightened avenue, with the wheels vaulting the bridge and the world swinging up and down behind us.

In a motel in Ocean City later that night, I made her kneel naked on the map of Elizabeth. It's likely my inability to remember more than her face in the rearview is one of language's mnemonic tricks, or a lingual trick of memory. At the time it seemed to me I was punishing her; but looking back, it just doesn't seem that way anymore.

I AWOKE THIS MORNING from the dream again—
the dream of fire—to find I'd left a window open in
my room. My mind had taken its cues from the snap of pages
blown to the floor, and I'd returned, as if reminded of one face
by another. I've been thinking, as I write, about how time and
fire come together on a page—how paper yellows, browns at
the edges, and finally erodes inward to memory. I am, I think at
times, simply trying to reverse that process.

Following the night that may or may not have been, we
left the Idyll early. It was 9:00 before we stopped for gas, and
when I asked Charles if he wanted anything from inside, expecting that while I pumped he'd get out as he always did for
a paper, this time he just muttered "No, thanks"—as if it were
the most ordinary thing in the world.

At the register I tried to catch a glimpse of the news, but
I had no one ahead of me on line, little time to browse. And
wasn't it, I thought, unlikely the papers would hold out some
sign for me now, days after the fact? The plant closing was a

little thing in the mind of the nation, a soft disaster, however magnified in the night. Climbing back into the car, I saw by the set of his eyes that it was, at any rate, pointless by then to try to draw my companion out: Whatever his feelings about myself or his notions of the news, he'd begun to sink his thoughts into the showroom. He would be devising his sermon.

A Stitch in Time is the lone survivor in the gutted downtown of a small city whose name I've since forgotten. It was late in the afternoon when we arrived, and the sky burned very hot, but very far away — the day reminded me, in the moment, of Carthage so long ago. It dazzled the eyes and smoldered on a dark jacket. By the time we'd gotten inside, Charles had broken into a sweat, and we both looked wrinkled and unwell. The manager magnified our discomfort when he greeted us as if he didn't realize who we were.

"Where's Donnelly?" Charles asked, staring back with equal bewilderment at this man in a yellow shirt and pimples. One of the salesgirls, recognizing Charles, put down a magazine and came forward.

"He's gone," she said. "Mr. Donnelly is gone. Mr. Anderson is here now" — turning to the manager. "Mr. Anderson, this is Mr. Trembleman. Mr. Trembleman is a Singer man."

"Oh, dear," Mr. Anderson replied, extending his hand to Charles. "I hadn't expected you."

As may be imagined, having spent the morning and preceding day convinced my companion was guarding a secret, I listened carefully to Anderson's words: From the first, it struck me that his demeanor toward us was that of an underling toward a crumbling giant. The girls were instructed to be quiet. Lynette, who'd introduced us, brought out a pot of ash-gray coffee, and we sat around our beverages in a quadrangle, drawing up chairs to where she took her place at the familiar Singer.

"I understand Donnelly had been here a good while," Anderson said.

"The Donnellys," Charles answered, "began as area agents before the Civil War—they became free agents around 1900, and Donnelly Jr. took over from his father during the forties."

There was a brief pause; then Anderson said, "Those were the days, weren't they, Mr. Trembleman?"

Was there a trace of irony, of something unkind, in the question? It seemed in its tenor to ally us with the departed, and there was in that pink and nubbled face with its hair of indeterminate color a quality that must have seemed the antithesis of what sewing meant to my friend. I decided a moment later, however, that I'd been mistaken about Anderson, for I think he, too, felt for Charles when he added: "Sew us something, Lynny. Sew us anything you like." The light shimmered in the windows of the store, caught like an animal against the glass. She took out a bolt of baby blue and turned on the machine.

The noise of the sewing machine is, I've since thought, like that first music: the sound of blood rushing in the walls of our originary room. They say, in fact, that it is quite loud in the place we come from—80 to 90 decibels. And while it is only the sound of a pump, of a cunningly made machine in which life and love were long confused, perhaps they were not confused at all: There is for each of us in that primal din a great love. I'd become lost among such beautiful things and was surprised when Charles finally replied to a question long rendered rhetorical:

"It's as if we've all grown smaller, isn't it, Mr. Anderson? But we're men of our time, you might say" — perhaps realizing that if we'd arrived as priests, he was addressing the heathen. "He *was* a large man, over six feet — exceptional for his day. He must have been striking to his peers, and must have known as much: For years he'd struggled as an actor in a traveling troupe — a career of dubious morality in the nineteenth century, though requiring, I think you'll grant, a certain degree of self-reflection. He struggled across the country in this company, and then, when he admitted to himself that his success would be mediocre at best, he abandoned acting and struggled as an amateur inventor. He struggled with everything. He was illiterate, or practically so, and we have only other people's recollections to help us see him. I think," Charles opined, bandaged hands draped over his knees, "he must have wrestled with himself in a constant and agonized way."

My friend paused. "How old are you, Mr. Anderson?"

"Twenty-nine," the manager replied.

Charles shook his head. "He struggled for the better part of his life between the threads of different careers and ideas, and it wasn't until he was forty years old — as old as we are," he said to me, "that he began to make what we'd call a living from his most famous invention, the sewing machine."

Mr. Anderson glanced at Lynette, but her eyes were fixed upon Charles while her hands, as if owned by another mind, squirreled about the singing needle.

"He wasn't a moral man," Charles continued. "He was habitually profane. His business partner's wife would not allow him into her house, even when they'd all grown rich together. He became, through his own misbehavior, an outcast from the wealthy New York society in which he lived. He was to them the New Man—larger than life, of hideous appetite. He could never sublimate his passions into marble: He didn't build museums, he built machines and children. And he was violent: On one occasion, when one of his wives confronted him after discovering Isaac driving up and down Fifth Avenue in public with another woman—one of his *other* 'wives'—he first choked her into unconsciousness, and then, when their daughter tried to intervene, choked *her* into unconsciousness, too. Eventually, as a result of multiplying marriages and affairs and the accompanying legal suits and bad press, he fled the country to take up residence in France and England."

Mr. Anderson sat slowly back as Charles talked—and without a comrade, without a fellow soldier in the Great War, he simply went on and on. A week before, I think I would have tried to stop him; today, I did nothing. I know some genuine sadness touched the manager. Only after more than an hour had passed did he interrupt to ask if Charles had spoken with Ms. Garnet. A puzzled silence ensued.

"But she's Singer, too, isn't she?" Mr. Anderson insisted, glancing at Lynette and then Charles. "I mean, I thought she was *it*. I thought . . ."

"She's with the Central South," Charles replied, at which Lynette muttered, "I *told* you."

Mr. Anderson blushed—it was clearly a mess. I saw the thoughts wheel behind Charles's eyes: for if Jane had been there, she'd surely come to find out about us; and then of course one had to wonder where else she'd been, checking up on our progress. I gazed at Charles—he was talking again.

The manager, chastened, sank further into his seat, casting out tangled smiles into the river of my friend's words.

Afterward, we sat mute in the car. I was simply amazed something so ridiculous could be *true* — that Jane *was* following us. I was trying to read the meaning of this on Charles's face, when he snarled, "What? What can you possibly say for yourself? I had to hear it from *Anderson* — from that human paperweight they hired to replace Donnelly, because *you* didn't tell me." And to my look of surprise: "Well, you didn't. I saw you, you know — I saw you together in the cave."

If I'd begun the day in bewilderment, suffered through self-loathing and bemusement, I'd stumbled at last upon amazement; for here I was, being chastised for *leaving something out* of my disclosures to Charles. In hindsight, I should have taken him up on this directly, but in the moment I was so flabbergasted to be caught on the horns of actual evidence, exactly the material I lacked concerning his own omissions, that I lost my footing and defended myself:

"It was nothing! I didn't think it was important!" I stammered — yet it was a lie, and we both knew as much.

"She's following us, isn't she? Why else would she have been there, at the showroom . . ."

"I knew you'd get all bent out of shape — *that's* why I didn't say anything. And even if it *was* what she said, how was I to know —"

"She *is,* then — she's following us," he gasped, incensed. "Aren't you supposed to be *helping* me?"

"How was I supposed to know?" I repeated, before, bringing my voice down, I parried: "Anyway, how can she be following us? There's a whole country—"

"It's the *Southern Territory*—"

"Then there's the *whole South*—"

"And," he said in a quiet and shaken voice, "she knows me." The silence that followed was wildly elaborate.

"Charles . . . what exactly *is* Jane to you?"

He grimaced. "She used to be—technically, she still is—my wife."

It was the answer to a question I didn't know I'd asked. I was so relieved—tickled, even—I chuckled. "I suppose this is about alimony . . ."

He gave me a black stare. "It was a mistake. I was young, and she's hypnotic, isn't she? Isn't she?" he repeated. "I think she hypnotized you, Milty"—but it was over.

"How long," I asked coolly, "did this go on?"

"Four years, more or less," he grumbled.

"Charles, a mistake is a night, or a month, a year, maybe—"

"Don't be an idiot," he said. "Some mistakes last longer than it takes to drive to the next town. What did she tell you? What did she *say*?"

"We talked for five minutes," I told him, my humor ebbing. "After the lights went out, I have no idea what happened to her. She seemed a little crazy."

"Crazy," he repeated. "What if I told you she wants to *kill us*?"

"Please—it was *underground*. I was paralyzed with fear. *Emily* could have killed me—"

"All right, all right—what if I told you she's trying to kill *me*?"

I had pulled the car into a rest area—a Civil War memorial battlefield. I'd sobered up, but I needed a moment to wipe my eyes. Letting the engine idle, we looked out at the lawns with their obscure geometries of trenches—the drag marks, I realized, that Thales had identified. Charles rolled down his window and lit a cigarette.

"Why would she do something like that?" I said, finding his behavior a touch hysterical—delusional, for he replied earnestly:

"She's still in love with me . . ."

"Of course she is," I soothed. "And here I was thinking she was after your territory"—going so far as to hint as I got back on the road: "What *is* she doing in your territory anyway? Doesn't she have a job? Don't both of you still have jobs . . ."

His eyes were kind, honest, even as he avoided the question: "We have to *do something*, Milty." And whatever the truth turned out to be regarding Singer, the answer was obvious: "We have to go somewhere else, somewhere she wouldn't expect."

So it was that we slouched onto an old post road that drawled across Mississippi into the failing sun. There is an infrequently reproduced Kennel in the Tate's collection, of the seemingly deserted slave quarters of his own Georgia plantation at dusk. The light dazzles upon the fields. One would be surprised, one feels, to come upon any living thing in such a world, as if people have gone back into the ground, the animals risen into the sky, and we're left with mineral and light. I don't think we passed a single car, only a tractor limping along; and having selected a route unknown even to Charles, I was becoming afraid night would overtake us in the middle of nowhere, when we came to a breakdown of trailers, aluminum houses, and fast-food restaurants at an intersection with a larger road.

It was dark as we parked at the Southern Lights. We'd said little to each other since our exchange at the rest stop, and then, after checking in, we were only too grateful to escape one another's company and retire to our rooms. I lay in bed, sleepless, the oddity of my companion's revelation having by then driven from my mind an entire week's apparitions and fears. Yet how sad his announcement seemed, now I was alone. There sunk into me the knowledge that whatever I believed Jane and I had understood about one another that day in the cave, it paled against what she and Charles at one time shared. For all I knew, she still *did* love him. Escaping loneliness, I'd come South to find myself wandering among ghosts — people I couldn't grasp, whose pleasures and tortures were a mystery to me, though they all, round about, seemed to hold tight to each other.

I suppose it's natural that in writing about loneliness I should find myself a bit depressed. Coming to this evening, the day lost, I lay in bed as dusk saturated the room, falling in and out of sleep. Awakening in the dark, there is always that moment when the room is any room and no room at all. Sometimes it's just a shiver, this feeling; and there are also times when one must choose slowly what is what, picking substance from shade, as if choosing one's life anew. Though there are, finally, those times when even the light doesn't seem a waking light, and you doubt your own mind. It is something I now imagine

I'll always think of when I wake in whatever room, that *every-room,* before dawn. I'll listen for the faraway crackle and roar of that river underground. I'll watch for the ripple — that abysmal ripple of fire.

For what awoke me that night at the Southern Lights was warmth: The fire alarm had failed, and my body ridiculously explained away the heat with the suggestion that I *was* in the South, after all. I pushed back the covers, then the sheets, until at last I lay sweating upon a stripped bed, my half sleep filled with a clamor, a rumbling roar. Someone, it seemed to me, was pounding on my door. Someone — Caroline? — went to go see; but finding her gone a long time, finding myself alone among the pillows, I got up. By then the noise had moved on — all except the roaring.

The room was brighter than expected, and I believed at first that it was dawn. I was thirsty. Something exploded far away as I ran the tap for a glass of water, and nothing came out the faucet. Listening to the sounds that enveloped the room, feeling the heat had become oppressive, I turned from the sink just as the light in the bathroom flickered out. I was standing in that place where the washing alcove meets the carpet when by the window-glow I saw smoke trickling up the bottom of the door: a waterfall run upside down. It unfolded itself against the ceiling, pooling in a ring. I reached up and touched the pool. It was hot, oily. *I am dreaming,* I told myself — *I'm dreaming Charles's dreams.* I put on my pants, went to the door, and walked out, into a rolling bank of dream-smoke. And falling against a railing, as if through a break in the gray and shuddering wall, I glimpsed at last the ancient fear of fire.

It's been said that all fears are doors or windows with lesser or greater views of the same object, yet it had always been dark when I stood before my fear. Fire is old, but darkness is older, and fire seems nearly kin to us, to think thoughts as one with us. One *understands* fire. It moves, and your dreams come true. You are animals in the forest together. I can only imagine what it must be to wander from room to room, without escape, knowing that the fire will outlive you.

I was, as I said, outside, but the smoke had sagged off of the burning roof, and it was into this I'd emerged, running aground upon the wrought-iron rail around the veranda, holding my breath as I filled up with fright. The draft from the open door *did* open a way, though, as when the clouds part around the moon, and I saw by the dancing flames the rail in my hands, beyond this a dirt flower bed, and beyond that the rear parking lot containing a handful of people who spied me at the same moment and waved energetically. As the smoke closed in again, I vaulted toward this mirage and blundered into the waiting night.

It says a great deal about how rapidly everything took place that, despite the seize of panic I'd felt seconds before, my first instinct was to turn around and go back into my room for my suitcase — I was dressed in only an undershirt and pants. Seeing my chance in another tear in the smoke I even started, but a young Pakistani woman, the daughter of the manager, grabbed my arm in her small hand. She let go only when I turned to her and she could see that the madness had left my eyes. I began then to look at the fire.

There are fires that burn for days, weeks, even months; and of course there are fires as old as, and much older than, the earth. But as I looked into the fire, it occurred to me that fires are not young or old in our time, but in the time of the things they consume. They run through their entire lives — provided they're allowed — with whatever they have. An ancient fire lies at the faded tip of a match or a cigarette quenching in an ash-tray. Not to say it was an incomprehensible time, for it occurred to me, looking farther into the fire, that when we speak of *living* somewhere as opposed to visiting, *that* time, too, doesn't pertain to familiar, clockwork times, but to a time apart. I thought of the places I'd *lived* in my life. Are six months, for example, sufficient to have said *I lived here*? A year? Or is it to be claimed that time is in this case qualitative — that one man's year is not the same as the next's? In which case one is left with the obverse of the question: How long may someone be somewhere and remain a tourist, a stranger? May one go on forever? And certainly, if one could go on forever, what better place to go on as an eternal stranger than a motel?

As we learned later from radio broadcasts, the fire had be-gun somewhere in the central section of the Southern Lights and grown, prevailing with the winds, to bridge the roof of the eastern wing. It was still young as I stood in the parking lot, and it twisted and turned like a creature deciding. Being whatever it would consume, nothing flammable can be truly strange to a fire. It reared a dozen feet tall, a sort of second floor, and when the wind came up, it poured itself down over the veranda, so that little bushes in the back lot, conceiving, ignited. When it opened a room, or found a dry, straight heart in the wood of a rotted beam, it grew. It left anywhere it had ever been reluctantly. I watched the fire edge its way across the asphalt shingles. Smoke billowed over the lot into a sliver of woods beyond which gleamed a Burger Barn sign like barroom neon. From the opposite side of the blaze came the familiar racket of emergency vehicles on the main road, and my thoughts suddenly lit upon Charles, absent among the people standing in the back. I began walking around, seeking him.

As it turned out, it didn't take long: I nearly tripped over my friend where he lay against the door of a van, breathing raggedly, legs splayed on the ground. Like a fool, he'd taken the time to get fully dressed, and it had nearly cost him his life. He looked ashen. The ambulances and fire engines were pulled up nearby, and he'd evidently made it this far toward them, though now he couldn't be convinced to take my arm and hobble the last fifty yards. When I volunteered to go bring someone over, thinking he might be too injured to make it the rest of the way, he whispered:

"I saw her, Milty" — then broke into a coughing fit.

"What are you talking about?" I asked as he nodded wordlessly. "Jane?" And glancing where he indicated, I crouched back behind the van, too, because *yes* — there she was in her car, a green El Dorado, the driver's-side door open, one heeled foot thrown out as she smoked a cigarette and watched the scene. Even amidst the confusion of lights and people I'd spotted her immediately. The hem of her skirt shimmered above the running board. A fireman had approached her to offer "assistance," and they chatted pleasantly until he lumbered back toward the burning building, and I again ducked out of sight.

"We'll go to the police," I said with deliberate calm of the cruisers barricading the entrance. "Throw your arm over my shoulder. We'll walk over and tell them the whole story, everything, whether she sees us or not. What can she do?"—though as I said this, looking at Charles with his bandaged hands ("Another fire, officer—a different one—this is my third, actually"), and then considered myself, driver of a car that only last week had run down a little girl (and who *had* been watching from those yellow windows?), I fell silent. I imagined the conversation that would follow: Jane exclaiming "But I *was* a guest at the motel"—making eyes at the law, the registry charred; the remarkably worldly constable drawling, "Area agent you say. Haint the Singer Sewing Company *closed down* its 'Merican operations?" Checks would be run, questions whose significance couldn't in the moment be fathomed would be asked and the hasty answers recorded like a net to be drawn tight at the last—for whether we were merely caught in coincidences, they *were* more true than truth, I grasped, Charles's words flooding back to me. But I saw that he already understood.

"Help me to the car," he whispered.

We crept to the rear of the motel, keeping the burning building between ourselves and our nemesis. Most of the other cars had already been driven out of the smoke and flames, and we found the Impala nearly alone, snug against the blaze. I was afraid of everyone by now, petrified as the engine gasped in the heat and caught. I ran the wipers over the sooty glass, sweating in the furnace waves that beat against the hood. Throwing it into reverse, we slid across the ash-flecked pavement, Charles looking behind us while I rolled my window down to see, parting people with the coals of our taillights.

"Keep going," he said, "keep going," as we rolled on, backward, toward a wall of trees cast like a mask by the firelight, until I saw a dirt drive curving into the woods, and I backed into this, lurching a rutted arc into the rear lot of the Burger Barn and the hulking shadow of its Dumpsters. I shut the engine and we stared through the bare trees at the flames.

Everything was red and gold. Jane would be waiting, watching it all burn, and believing, no doubt, that we were trapped inside. I recalled our encounter in the cave, and shuddered to think of her hands reaching for me in the dark. I marveled at how unerringly she'd reached through the whole night of the South to find us.

"You see, Milton," Charles said after a time, "there are things you learn when you've been someplace before" — erupting into yet another coughing fit.

In light of his condition and the narrowness of his escape, his joke surprised me. My own terror receded breath by breath, and he sputtered himself into silence. The words rested lightly in the air before I thought about what he'd actually said, and picked them up:

"Wasn't the whole idea," I asked, "to choose somewhere you'd never been?"

"Milty—"

"But that was what we agreed, so she couldn't find you—"

"She can always find me—"

"But that's because you always stay in the same damn motels. We were going to go someplace new—"

"I thought it *was* new. I couldn't remember—only she could possibly remember—"

"You could have *killed us!*" I shouted; yet realizing he'd simply become lost in his own head, my outrage was already combined with helplessness, and I said more calmly, "I don't know where we are, Charles. I don't think I've ever understood what we're doing. And lately . . . I've begun to wonder if you have any idea, either."

He was coughing again. It was a wretched sound—a hospital sound. And as I waited so I could ask him point-blank about Singer, about whether we were doing anything at all anymore other than fleeing from firetrap to firetrap through the thawing South, I looked through the dark tangle of branches at the flaming motel and thought of what he'd said about a dying fire.

"I'm sorry," he gasped at last, barely aloud.

I was still watching the fire through the window, conscious only dimly at first of the silence in the car. The silence was the ground upon which we breathed our breaths—his quick, mine by this time calmed; upon which the distant whoosh of the inferno and the firemen with their metallic racket and radio equipment played. But it was increasingly the silence *itself*, raw and fresh from the coughing, by no means shapeless, to which I was drawn.

I turned a little toward the windshield to give my ear better perspective on this space in which neither of us seemed willing for the moment to speak, but where, once I'd cleared away the clutter of surrounding noise, even breathing, the infinitesimal sounds a body makes when at rest—the thrum and whine of blood in the ears and the sound of one's own pulse and digestion—I had to concede there was still *content;* and it was to this, with a sensation of vertigo not unlike what I experience in the dark, I now attuned myself.

The entire process was one I would later unpack while devising my technique for sleep. I didn't want to look at Charles. To do so would be to fall into the error I always made with him, for he has the face of a good man — the face, it struck me, of those leading men from movies we've so learned to trust. Instead I listened very carefully to this silence; and as I listened, I began to hear that he was doing something in that quiet, without moving, without any discernible activity whatsoever, between his gradually slowing breaths.

What are you doing? I wanted to ask, but held off — and it was fortunate, because a moment later, listening yet more deeply, I comprehended what it was. The realization was like touching someone's face in the dark. It contained a physical certainty. I felt, given enough time, that I might actually come to know everything about Charles in this way, sitting in the car, but I didn't know how much time we had, and the first thing I'd grasped, before I became aware of anything deeper, was that he *wanted* me to ask him about Singer, what we were doing here, and why Jane was chasing us. *This was what he wanted.*

And of course it was the most natural thing in the world to ask these questions; to turn to my friend and ask — as simply and earnestly as one might ask a friend who had *not been entirely fair* to him — that he lay these matters open. Were we not in this together? Was my life not in his hands as much as his in mine? Was it not clear certain information had been deliberately withheld up until this point?

He would tell me, too, exactly what I asked for — if I asked, he would tell me everything I wanted to know. Whatever it was, he'd answer. But I began to see that just as this certainty was the first tangible sense to emerge from the silence, it was just as certain that if I asked now, if I did as he wanted, anything more would be foreclosed: He would answer my questions, I would get on a plane, he on a bus; there'd be apologies, explanations, heartfelt words—yet I would ask only what I already knew to ask, and he would answer only that much. *I would find exactly what I was looking for.* The more carefully I listened, the clearer it became that Charles had in fact thought this all out—expected that we'd arrive at such-and-such a place, that there would be a fire, perhaps several fires, and that having come this far, in despair of going on, I would ask my question and he would *tell me,* because he'd thought it through this far and *he wanted me to catch him here.* This was the place, as far as he was concerned, to end; beyond which I would refuse, he presumed, to continue in ignorance. Yet to catch someone in the place he wishes to be caught is a trap within a trap; and more, which he himself hadn't considered, whatever lay beyond this point was something of which he was *equally ignorant,* so that if I'd always run behind him, now nearer, now farther away (*there are things you learn if you've been someplace before*), if I didn't ask, we would continue into the darkness together.

I cannot, and I've never been able to, separate my admiration for Charles from a desire to best him. And I'm aware that this isn't what we're supposed to do—this isn't what some imagine it is to *help.* But I believe I *was* helping him in what followed—and I'd reply that to do otherwise than I did that night would only be to force him back into failure. You meet people all the time whose lives lie beached on a shore above them, as if hurled there by a terrific storm the likes of which they will never see again. No—I was going to leap in and grasp the drowning man like a brother, and we were going to sink together into a stranger night and dark.

"Forget about it," I said. "It's done—the worst is done. It may even be for the best if she thinks we're dead. All I ask is that *I* choose the next place we stay."

"But how will you . . . ?" he whispered.

"Isn't it obvious? It's the simplest thing in the world, Charles. We'll stay at another Radisson if we have to."

For a moment he was bewildered—a real gift is a bewildering, often terrible thing. Then he chuckled. Life contains so few real gifts, I had to wait for this rasping, grating chuckle to know whether he'd understood:

"Milty, I'd been to that Radisson before . . ."

"What are you talking about? You *hate* those places—"

"But it was different with Jane," he said. "She *only* liked places like that."

For an instant I couldn't tell if he was serious. There was something pained in his expression, something desperate, but it passed, and with that I saw he'd accepted: We'd play this out to the last. He hunched forward in a fresh spasm of coughing. There was a can of soda in the back I found and gave to him. Feeling cold now that we'd sat for a while, I was pleased to discover one of the jackets I'd bought at Archie's draped over the seat, and I put it on. The fire at the Southern Lights dwarfed the motel when I last looked, a yellow column flowing a little to one side, the glow pressed to the clouds.

Only the following day did I become aware of how much the night's machinations had run on adrenaline. Not to say that by morning I'd come to doubt my realizations, but that the night had required reserves of strength and awareness impossibly distant at the arrival of dawn. We must have seemed like men crawled from their own ashes to the employees of the Thread Emporium, unwashed except for a hurried stop in a Texaco. Charles's throat was too closed up to speak. He sat in a chair at the back of the store, drinking paper cups of water as one of the girls repaired the marks of fire on his suit, and I kept up an awful banter with the manager, a hulking, mono-browed thing called Dave. Dave had just inherited the store from his uncle, who was in only on Tuesdays and Fridays.

"What day *is* today?" I asked.

"It's Wednesday. You want to come back Friday?" he said, his brows lurking above his face like a dirty word. "You boys going to *make it* till Friday?" He rubbed a hand through the thatch of chest hair covering his head and sneered at me. Or perhaps he was suppressing a yawn. Afterward, Dave and his little corps of seamstresses tramped with us to the door and watched us pile into the Impala, marbled black and brown.

My friend's silence in the car had obviously become a matter of little choice. We bought a six-pack of cough syrup at a mini-mall and he cradled a bottle in his hands, inebriated, listening or not listening, for a kind of 4:00 A.M. exhilaration had come over me as we reached the open road again and made me want, at this of all times, to really talk to him. At this least expected juncture, in a manner I'd never dreamed, I had precisely what I'd longed for: that I might tell him all about my life, and that he would let me.

There was so much, so very much, unsaid, and as we trundled through a thin rain, without newspapers and distractions, following directions he'd scratched on a napkin, I talked about those things I'd thought, when we'd met in school, might one day become of me; and how—which was the remarkable part—they'd come true, in a reflected form, in the gallery. I talked about painting, and why he should come back. I told him what I'd only come to realize on this trip—that I'd made my gallery, in a way, for him.

"It's the room, Charles—it's *your* room, waiting for you." I was giddy—it was like drinking, talking. "You'd know, as soon as you walked in the door. You'd understand. It's right on the street. It's full of light. It just needs *you.*

"If you would just come back—I swear, I could make you rich." I glanced at him, but his face was impassive. "It's true—it is. I've done it before. Even your old canvases—if I only had your old canvases, I could show them and you'd see . . .

"But of course we don't have to talk about this now," I assured my friend. I recalled telling Charles on the phone I could join him for a week, two at most, yet it seemed arbitrary at this point, as if there had never been a time I wasn't driving around the South among the fires. We had all the time in the world, and there was so much to say. How little I'd said for so long. How little, for example, Caroline and I had really said to each other—how little we hadn't already said before, endlessly. I was reminded of her then, and how, over the years, as our lives became increasingly enmeshed, there came to be nowhere to take cover from each other but in plain sight. So I talked to Charles about Caroline, and all the reasons I was sure she wasn't coming back. I told him all those things about myself that had brought me this far, everything I'd lost hold of along the way. All the togethers coming apart.

. . .

It was late by the time we reached the town, and I'd become turned around, talking and reading his directions. The shops were closed on the main street, and on the side streets only solitary lights remained where a window in a house, an isolated lamp seemingly made of water, burned.

"Where are we staying?" I asked.

"A few blocks farther," he told me, voice like rust, speaking for the first time in hours. "The next block"—searching down the broader avenues; and later: "the next."

We drove beneath the sashes of trees, past another shuttered commercial district, and then he was telling me to pull into the parking lot of a large hotel—a sprawling high-rise such as I'd never imagined he might choose. When I examined the blue and white signage, it turned out to be a hospital.

"I hope we're not," I kidded, "staying here. Are you all right?"

"I don't think so," he whispered.

I spun through the nearly empty lot. "Was it the smoke? Is it your hands?" I asked, wondering how I'd overlooked the seriousness of his condition—why he hadn't said anything before now? All day, preoccupied with myself, I'd been lulled by his silence. He waited, face glistening in the halogens, until I cut the engine, and then he got out.

"Charles," I called, following him. "Charles?" But he walked doggedly toward the main doors, ignoring the orange signs for the emergency entrance. I caught up with him as he shouldered inside, one bandaged hand held protectively, and we found ourselves before a receptionist who was just rousing herself with studied indifference from a romance novel.

"Are you looking for emergency?" she asked. "Because this is not the emergency room —"

She pointed with the thick paperback down a hall through several windowed doors, beyond which could be read a sign for triage.

"People have a hard time with this, for some reason," she said. "So you're going to go through those doors, and someone will help you."

I thanked her, or the cover of the book she raised into place, and we filed into the hall.

"Would you please just tell me if you're all right?" I asked again when we were out of earshot. He coughed in a ghastly way.

"I told you —" he said, glancing back. I followed his gaze and saw the receptionist tugging at her hair as she fondled her pages.

"The bitch —" I began, but, hand to his lips, he drew me by the sleeve into a little hall that ran to the right, away from our destination.

"We're not going in there," he said, presumably of the door to Emergency Services.

"Don't be a fool, we have to."

He shook his head. I noticed he was no longer clutching his bandages. As I considered my obligations, he walked along the corridor in the opposite direction and turned through a set of unmarked swinging doors.

We passed into another corridor, shiny with lights and scuffed vinyl tiles; rounding a corner, we found ourselves in a hall banked on one side by windows onto the emergency room but with nothing telling how we might find anyplace but lab services and radiology. If it wasn't apparent before that we'd made a wrong turn, the conclusion was now inescapable. Charles, however, stood staring through the windows until I joined him.

Though our view was incomplete, blocked and bisected by blue sheets hung on rings from tracks on the ceiling, it was clear there wasn't a lot happening in emergency at this hour on a weekday. We moved along the windows, hatched with internal wire, discolored by traces of yellowed tape. Looking inside the various sheeted chambers, I wondered, briefly, if he'd brought us there to look for someone in particular, but I can't imagine how that could have been the case.

At last, in one of the blue cloisters, we found a small hive of activity. Surrounded by nurses, doctors, and residents, a man lay fully dressed on a steel gurney, face invisible to us. One of the doctors had a gloved hand on the man's bloodied chest, and the hand and chest trembled together while the scene moved slowly around them. Encircled by walls and eyes, the touch had a publicness and an intimacy that I can only describe as matrimonial, and I felt a stab of something like jealousy for this person in whatever pain, whose agonies had drawn these men and women wanting nothing else, right then, than to save him.

I looked at Charles, his attention pressed upon the scene, and then watched these people in their scrubs confer — even seeming to confer with the man, who'd obviously been in a wreck. Periodically, his chest heaved. His face, when I caught a glimpse, was black with blood. It nodded again and again for what was, I realized, no reason at all. As for myself, standing not twenty feet away, divided from all this by a sheet of glass,

I was becoming increasingly nervous. Surely we weren't supposed to be there. It seemed impossible we wouldn't be discovered; and still, I felt something was about to happen, and couldn't leave.

An orderly wheeled a tray of shiny instruments up to the gurney. The doctor who'd been compressing the man's chest glanced around at his companions in some silent affirmation, and then gently lifted his hand away. Everyone paused, and we stared for perhaps ten, fifteen seconds at the place where the hand had been. The chest heaved, but no one stirred. Some equilibrium had been attained. I was so glad that I'd stayed — I wanted to wave or otherwise sign to a pretty nurse who stood facing me with her eyes glazed upon the scene — until a dark clot of blood bubbled from the wound, a little geyser, and the doctors and nurses rushed forward and hid him from view. Turning from the window, I discovered Charles gone.

I cast a last look into the emergency room. It was sad — not so much that the man was obviously dying, despite the best efforts of these well-meaning people, although this, of course, was a shame, but that I, the two of us, were supposed to do nothing. We weren't even supposed to be there, and I thought, fleetingly, that I should have waved during that moment in which we could have done no wrong, because anything we would do from this point forward could only make matters worse. Fear closed over me again, and I headed toward the door at the end of the hall, past sections of blue, serene and empty of drama, into a nurses' station, where I found Charles alone behind a Formica desk, leafing through files.

He barely glanced up. There was a model of a human ear on the desktop, and thinking of the man we'd left to die, I was idly examining the sea creatures from which the inner ear is apparently composed when a doctor in a white coat swept in. He stared at us briefly, before, without a word, sweeping out the door through which we'd arrived. Charles, who'd frozen in place, put away his files. Laying the ear back down, I followed him toward a little plastic sign on a wall beside another door, illustrating stairs.

"Where are we going?" I said. Though even after we'd left the stairwell on the second floor and found ourselves in another hall, fluorescent and sallow, he hadn't replied.

"Did you see how close we were to being caught back there?" I whispered as he glanced at me sternly, and my voice rustled down the sanitized distances. For several minutes we stood listening. There was almost no sound, just the hush of central air, until, far away, there came to us a door closing, a scuff from a scuffle of footsteps, the vinyl squeak of a night nurse. The beating of my heart had grown so loud that by the time we began moving I felt I could hear nothing at all.

"They will call the police if they find us here," I whispered.

"They'll throw us out," he said. "Now be quiet . . . don't make me start coughing."

Around a corner, behind a laundry trolley, we paused. Patting the pockets of his jacket, he came up with a bottle of cough syrup and took a swig. After a few minutes, once more, there was the far-off opening and closing of a door. This time the footsteps were clearer, and we heard them drift closer until they stopped, and another door opened.

As soon as the door shut, he started forward. When the corridor T'd at an intersection, he read from a plastic plaque posting room numbers and headed in the direction we'd last heard the night nurse circulating.

"Do you *want* to get caught?" I said, trotting after him. "Is that what this is all about?"

He stopped walking and looked at the numbers on a door, then the next; and I watched in despair as he twisted the handle and went inside. Hearing another door opening farther along the hall, the squeak of feet, I was forced to follow. I closed us in as silently as I could, blinking in the unlit room, then blundered into his back and stood stock-still, listening in the meticulous black as the nurse moved on, accompanied by the rattle of her cart.

It is a terrible thing in my life that a fear of the dark has done nothing to spare me from such moments. I feel, moreover, that every crisis I have suffered has occurred not only indifferent to my fears, but in direct antagonism to my health, without the benefit of light; I have in the past few days begun to wonder if perhaps I might have done better, all told, had such a simple thing not been denied me.

I discerned in these moments the nearby beep of life support. I felt giddy, sick. I wanted to tell Charles to stop, but I was too anxious to raise my voice. Several times, in an undertone, I repeated his name. He ignored me, and when at last he threw a switch on the wall, we were both surprised to find the room whirling dimly to life as if inside a carousel, blue horses ghosting over every surface.

A bed made up in white sheets glowed not three feet from where I stood, and peering into its folds I saw, to my horror, a little girl, sleeping. I couldn't have imagined anything more frightening. Even after I'd confirmed to myself I hadn't screamed, I was terrified she'd hear us, wake up, and begin screaming herself; nothing happened, however, and as I watched the utter stillness with which she proceeded through the night beneath the dancing shapes, I understood.

"It's her, isn't it?" I said. "It's Margaret Duffey."

As my pupils expanded, I took in how thin she'd become. One can read about such things, fathom intellectually that a disused body wastes away, but the only picture I'd known of her was that one black-and-white image, of the child as she was before the accident — and that small face that once, in surprise, had looked at me through glass.

By the foot of her bed stood the magic lantern. On a cart beside the sleeping girl was a vase of flowers and around that, photographs — framed photographs, solitary snapshots, images cut from other images. I gazed into the class photos, little wallet shots and Polaroids of grown-ups, other children, pictures of her together with her family, rimmed in silver light. As if they hoped reminders of love would be the first things to greet her were she to awaken, and would hold her to the world.

"Do you think she knows we're here?" Charles asked.

"I don't think she'd want us," I told him. Out in the hall, I heard the night nurse again. There was a drip line running into the girl's arm. In one of the pictures on the stand, she was straddling the bicycle with the translucent grips.

I imagined how we must appear to her, sunk in that sleep in which she lay, and in which she'd become lost, like a swimmer in a blue world who no longer knows up from down and circles around nothing. Perhaps, I thought, standing above her, we reached some inner faculty she still possessed as shadows staring into the refraction of a swimming pool, into the bottom where she curled, nearly drowned; and if she hadn't noticed us where we watched her in her fading struggle, perhaps glancing up by chance and seeing where we waited, she'd go on feigning death rather than strike for the surface. Perhaps she hoped that if she could just go on sleeping, the evils of the world might pass. We were those evils, I thought. We hovered tonight above this girl like predators in her very dreams.

An idea so bleak I choked shook me from this trance: Had we come here to murder her? Was that to be our end, in fear of her finding a voice again? *In fear.* In my mind's eye, I saw us there beside her, unknowable. *I am not that man,* I told myself. *I will kill him first.*

"Don't be afraid," Charles said, but I wasn't afraid anymore. I came and stood a few inches from the bed.

"I'm not," I replied. "It was the shock."

"I wasn't talking to you," he whispered gently, turning to me before he looked back down at her. "I had to come, so she could see. Can you believe that three people so lost might ever meet?

"Now don't be afraid," he told her once again.

SOMETHING HAPPENED THIS MORNING, quite early. During the last couple of days I've been watching a lot of television—those dark stations. I watch Thales's channel as the hour grows late, with its silent images of bombers unloading clusters into the clouds above the blur of continents, men in helmets rustling through the rain. I sit bewildered amongst infomercials, a heavy infusion of programming devoted to the amateur metal-detection enthusiast. I've begun to think the woods must be teeming with individuals combing their lands and that of their neighbors for remnants of the Civil War. And as I've sat up later and later, these programs replacing my sleep, they've begun to seem to me like dreams.

There are again three stations, the remaining two composed of "Eileen's channel" and a program with a terrible, recurring drama of strangulation among the flames, of two hands and a dim, swollen face falling back into darkness and fire—it frightened me last night until I turned off the TV and lay down in bed. There are so many subjects, however, to keep one awake, even without the television — so many internal stations — for the mind of a sleepless man may rove from idea to idea, finding in nothing a refuge, in everything a fascination as deep and wide as himself. I'd set out to sleep, I'd lowered down and down the stupefied face; still, there in the dark, I'd recalled Emily's voice asking about the friend — "the other fellow" — and this friend began to work on me, an invisible companion, as Jane became in those final days of our flight through the South. Perhaps they were the same, Jane and this stranger, though more likely there had never been any rhyme or reason to Emily's musings from the start.

Moreover, once the *idea* had stuck, I couldn't free myself; over an hour passed as I dragged open the drawers of fixation and phobia, as if my brain were a child that might be distracted with a more glamorous but in the end merely diversionary toy. And this is precisely why I at last took my place beneath the veranda, flashlight in hand, contemplating the dark walk to the house. *Dark* — for though there was a moon above the trees, gleaming on the ground, it was the sort of walk I tremble to make. And yet if there was ever an hour I might speak to the old woman alone — I'd been told repeatedly that Emily *never* slept — it was at hand. I went to the edge of the veranda and shone my light among the weeds until I discovered the smudge of the path.

During the previous afternoon, Queen Anne's lace had erupted in the wasteland, pale faces floating in the moonlight, filling the air with a close, sweet smell, of old rooms abandoned long ago by old women. I walked quickly, shivering, feeling the pressure of darkness on my shoulders, a multitude of hands, grateful to at last discern the windows flanking the front door reflecting back at me. I turned off the flashlight as I rounded the Masculine Porch and made my way along the clapboard to the room at the back where Emily "sleeps." Her window was open, and built as the house was by a man scarcely over five feet tall, I had little trouble peering in through the screen at her bed. She lay in a shaft of moonlight, eyes gazing up and blinking from time to time, face perhaps two feet from mine.

"Emily," I whispered.

"Mr. Menger," she replied, no hint of surprise in her voice. "How nice of you. It must be quite early, or late. It's so difficult to sleep these days — don't you think? And the hours *can* grow tedious . . . I think I've thought tonight of every person I met in my whole life."

At these words, I recalled something:

"Charles told me you actually spoke with Isaac Singer, once. Is that possible?"

"It isn't polite to ask a lady her age, Mr. Menger," she teased. "Remarkable gentleman. Very funny gentleman."

I was unsure how to inquire about the missing "friend," and so I suggested, "He said, in fact, that Singer talked to you about his fears, of all things."

"A memory like a steel trap Charles has," she replied. "I've often thought about that afternoon, because Mr. Singer told me of his fear of the dark. *Strange* gentleman. This was long before I went blind, but still — you can imagine I've had occasion to recall it since."

"I have a fear of the dark," I murmured.

"How brave of you, coming out just now! We have nearly a great deal in common, you and I, Mr. Menger." She seemed prepared to say more, and then equally prepared to settle back upon her memories. I waited some time, then asked:

"Was there, though, another fear he mentioned?"

"Another fear," she repeated. "You're spooked, aren't you? But no — in fact, he helped me with a small fear of my own.

"I'd overheard, you see, from my great-aunt, that the way she'd been taught as a child to tell — absolutely know — one had *passed from this life* was that one would suddenly find oneself in a place without strangers. She was from Memphis, and perhaps strangers were an ordinary affair to her, but I was a little girl living in the country. Afterward, that days or weeks would go by without a fresh face . . . it gave me no end of worry, I can assure you.

"And then, the morning I spent with him at Torquay, Mr. Singer did me a great favor. My mother, who'd brought me along, was off with his charming wife, looking at curtains, and there Mr. Singer was, giving me tea in one of his gardens. We were already in a friendly way: I'd confessed a fear of spiders, and he'd reciprocated with his fear of the dark. So it was, wanting most likely to outdo him, I *told* Mr. Singer: We were sailing back from England the following day, and I'd already begun to dread my rural home, free as it was, if not of spiders, certainly of strangers.

"He was quite old by this time. Just from the way he poured tea, one could see he was not much afraid to die. My mother came to retrieve me a few minutes later, and I rose to go; but before we took our leave of one another, he called me round to his chair and said that he'd certainly remember me; and when he asked if I liked him, and I said that I did, he told me that when he saw me next he'd be sure to hold my hand. Then he said good-bye. I only understood much later, on the boat, what it was he'd meant — but isn't that a wonderful thing, Mr. Menger?"

I imagined it was, though I was silent, and my silence seemed to encourage her:

"So you see, it isn't hard to guess how happy I was to discover *you*. I remember telling Charles, 'What a nice man he is. A lovely man' — I'd forgotten, I think, what it was like to meet someone — and that's exactly what I said." Her face possessed no expression other than the contentment usually found there. "It was while you all were cleaning out the parlor for supper," she told me. "And *he* said: 'Em, do you remember that friend I told you about, when I was at the hospital — the one I said was going to come visit for a while?'

"He whispered this to me, and I thought he was being shy. 'You're so popular,' I kidded him. Anyone can tell *you* think heaps of Charles — why, everyone does. 'And here's poor Milton,' I said — I didn't mean anything by it — 'thinking he's your best and only friend in the world. Does he know?' I asked."

She was quiet a moment. I continued to look at her face, and she up at the ceiling:

"I remember," she noted, "he sounded a bit downcast at this, and he said, 'No, he's very smart — but *he's blind*' — and it was *this* I wanted to tell you, you see, Mr. Menger, because of course that was where I got my notion. But I suppose I must have misheard him, don't you think?'"

Perhaps it was the nearly toneless way in which she related news echoing things both distant and terrible that lent me a certain calm when I replied, "Did Charles tell you anything more about who this other friend was?"

"Well," she said, pausing, her face unruffled but her voice, for the first time, troubled, "he sounded like an odd sort of friend . . ."

"How so?"

"You see . . . Charles said he had a friend that he called his 'worst friend.' Not," she hastened to explain, "that he was a bad friend to Charles. Charles was emphatic that to the contrary, the friend had always been a very *good* friend to him, someone, even, that he could rely on — perhaps more than anyone else. It's just —"

I waited, the night behind me seeming limitless, rising and towering, swaying when I swayed, the room darkening around Emily as the street had that evening when I crouched beside the little girl on the verge.

"It was just that if he had to choose one friend, he told me, who mattered least in the whole world, who might even," she said, "die — because he was talking quite wildly, you know, when he was alone in the hospital, as if he didn't expect to live — but a friend whom no one, or the very least number of people, would think of . . ."

She trailed away and we were quiet together, each likely contemplating such a person and what had been asked of him.

"It sounds like a terrible business, doesn't it?" she said, allowing me to draw my own conclusions.

"Yes, I guess it does" — recalling Charles's words about the strangers who would complete our lives for us.

"I don't like to think of him mixing *you* up in all this, Mr. Menger — I was a little surprised when he mentioned it again after he'd found you to help out. The doctors, you know, had told him he'd be fine — but he's a man, of course, and men don't know what to do with pain. I'd put it from my mind, until he brought it up of his own accord. I suppose," she added, "it's fortunate we can never be as good or as bad as we imagine."

I wondered to whom this last remark was addressed, and in the end decided it was likely meant for no one at all. "He thought," I said, standing back from the screen, "that both of them might be killed . . ."

"Yes — or so he told *me*. Terrible business. You shouldn't worry yourself, though, nice man like you," she said. I could just see her now. "Do you suppose," she said in her very quiet voice, "that he's all right, Charles's friend?"

I have, as I've said before, a terrible memory. Yet there are things of which I would like to be certain, the certainty of which would make all the difference. There are factual matters, of course, but these are the least of my concerns; which is not to say they're worthless — it's just that one can make so many mistakes, even large mistakes, but to what end? People lose their lives upon mountains — piles of stone. And there are people who've happily given up everything for what we acknowledge are worthy causes, other worthy men; there are secret mountains — mountains in the dark, underground. Because I *did* admire him, and though the details elude me, remain inadequate, I wasn't alone. In the eyes of the world, I know this is crucial. Much as I hate to think greatness is no more than salesmanship — the ability to sway a crowd toward some anything — it does make a difference. We all admired Charles, those of us who knew him — and there is something wonderful in being even that least friend of such a person, though I think I can say it was more than that. For I think, whatever he believed of me, that he was my best friend; and I think I wouldn't be wrong if I claimed that I was also *his* best friend—the best friend he ever had. I think he saw I might do something for him that perhaps no one else would.

Still, whatever holds sway by day, by night I always return to the question: How can one be sure—for want of a better word—of *greatness*? Certainly, I can say he changed my life. Yet how does one know greatness when it leaves nothing behind? When it goes virtually unseen? It's difficult, at least in isolation; such people are few and far between, though I won't be so foolish as to pretend now, at the end, that such people don't exist among us—people nearly invisible, yet so much better than myself. But to know . . . to be sure one has thrown oneself into a great fire, having thrown oneself in a fire. That's the thing, having taken steps that are irrevocable. To know, all alone. How does one? It was a question I'd asked Charles, once, of Kennel. One of many questions he felt little inclined to answer. I would like to believe it comes to more than being someone of whom we could forgive a great wrong. I'm sure—I'd like to say I'm certain that it is.

I thought of him—of Kennel—this morning; and with little left, so few ends, I thought again of making that trip to the museum in Carthage. I thought of Caroline, then, and the consolation of excursions. Each night as the window darkens, and the nylon flowers in the curtains become one with the ground, I put off switching on the light for as long as I can, even the Singerlight, and instead, before I turn to the fitful dreams of the television, I turn to these consolations. I'm not unaware of how strange it is that I of all people would seek refuge in the dark, but I have, as I've said, a terrible memory: It was two weeks ago that my friend Charles died in a room not unlike this one.

AFTER THE HOSPITAL we drove west on secondary roads until, at a dim hour and pricked by poor stars, we crossed into the Florida panhandle and stopped at a gas station. As I stood at the bank of urinals, I realized the man down at the end of the line — the only other man in the room — was praying. The ground was covered in mole crickets, little griffins of insect and mouse living and dying by the million beneath our feet. I pumped gas, looking through the windshield at Charles haloed in exhaustion. We said little, and when he indicated where he wanted to stay, it no longer seemed important, much as it no longer mattered how long I'd said I was free to accompany him, or whether we'd ever gone hunting together; I did, however, remark the name of our motel.

"The owner," he whispered, "fancies himself a bit of a collector."

My postcard of the Artiste depicts a two-story quadrangle, the roof a checker of red and white asphalt tile, the façade a clotted blue. It's a nocturnal scene, a single, ground-floor window painted the yellow hue of the name curled in the sky. Between the road and the parking lot, frayed palms cut into the constellations, and a low, oval moon, much like the one beneath which we arrived, presides. There was a party in the courtyard that night — letters scattered on a marquee by the drive — but they had two rooms. Charles took the one on the first, I the one on the second floor, where an oppressive ensemble of odalisques decorated the halls. The air smelled of cooking, and the dark in my room was a corn silk of voices and laughter, though much to my surprise I fell immediately into a thin but troubled sleep.

When I opened my eyes, I didn't understand what had brought me to consciousness. The clock read 2:27, and after lying prone a few minutes, I sat up. It was a warm night. A glance out the window showed a milling mass, a commotion outside. Who, I wondered idly, had vacated these rooms? Into whose holiday had we slipped? I was thirsty, and got dressed.

At the end of the hall, beyond the ghastly nudes, a handful of men, collars wrenched open, stood in a box of smoke. They watched as I came in and out of the fluorescent islands; and then on the stairs someone brushed past, and I glimpsed a face, already gone, shoes clattering up, the plush lobby carpet beneath my feet. A clutch of women wove amongst the overstuffed chairs and flashed through the French doors at the opposite end of the room: a short white dress and her cosmopolitan friends, exotics to this place. And taking my orange fizz from the soda machine, I wandered after them into the garden and its oasis of chipped concrete and palmettos, a blue gem the ladies wobbled around toward a grizzle of male laughter and a fiery scene in the distance. The lights within the pool crawled the inner walls of the motel. The fire tumbled like liquor. In the midst of the blue, on an orange inflatable chair, floated a lone woman wearing a silver one-piece. The glow washing the little boat cast her in semidarkness, all except the coal that glowed before her lips, and I recalled that face, lit by a single flame, as her voice splashed up at me:

"If it isn't Mr. Menger." She smiled. How she seemed to cling to the edge of our world, as if she had none of her own anymore.

"I would have thought you'd given us up for dead," I said.

"I would have thought you were," she replied. Away, toward the fire, a circle of men began beating their chests and hollering like gorillas; a woman screamed, a bottle broke. The sounds dissolved in hysteria. She drew on her cigarette, and her face warmed the dark.

"Was he really so terrible to you?" I asked. When she only continued to watch me through her smile, I added, "I saw you the other night, you know. I saw you in the parking lot, watching—or believing you were watching us burn."

"And everything would be okay if it was me, wouldn't it?"

"You have," I began, "every motive in the world—" yet my voice fell away. I looked around. A sprawly, bearded fellow in a velvet suit was perched nearby on a camp chair, a travel easel erected between himself and the pool. He held a palette in one hand and a brush in the other. His beard was white and full; his coat pocket divulged a lime-green scarf. He looked like an aged dandy.

"What is your job, really?" I asked in a quiet voice.

"My job is lonely. It makes me curious about other people." The bottom of the pool swam with light. She wore metallic blue eyeliner composed of glitter or sequins, the facets of color large as pieces in a mosaic, lids heavy, like they were made of blue metal. "Now—what was it you said your job was, again, Milton?"

A figure on the far shore, visible against a shoal of orange-lit revelers, signaled to her then. A hand was tipped into the water, and as if feeling a touch she glanced toward the crackle of the bonfire. They'd blindfolded a man, a little fellow in a cowboy hat who tottered among the silhouettes, sweeping his hands as they scuttled away, squealing. A chill ran through me. And without another word, having apparently agreed that I wasn't going to answer her question, she set off, across the water. Glancing to where the dandy sat, our eyes met.

"Don't I know you from somewhere?" he inquired.

"It's possible," I replied, turning away, wondering if he'd been listening. In the water, upside down, I watched Jane receive a cocktail from the hand of a tennis-shirted sprat, the light from the floor of the pool wrapping the raft in a corolla of black.

"I've recently been learning to paint," the artistic gentleman broke in on my thoughts. "At the suggestion of a friend, of course. Have you ever tried your hand with the brush?"

I moved a few steps so that I might see what he was doing. It was a miniature of this same place, the size of a postcard, yet devoid of even the flicker of life around us. It was, in fact, the very image I described when we first arrived, but with a waxen, unlettered sky. I thought again of Kennel, and those worlds he'd fashioned in which he'd taken away and taken away until what remained of people was mystery, like a tool abandoned in a field.

"Are you acquainted with the painter Alsby Kennel?" I asked.

"Kenner?" He had a hawkish nose, a square-cut beard, and a perfect, snowy part. He shrugged and, reaching down, swished his brush in the pool before mashing it in a yellow lozenge, beginning to populate the sky with letters, one at a time. "Hard to say. Did you notice anything by him around?"

I understood. "My friend mentioned that you were a collector. I take it you know Charles . . ."

Across the water, the blindfolded man overturned a table of drinks. He'd lost his hat. For a moment he groped within a ring of darkened figures, and then he lurched toward the pool, feinting at the crowd. Only at the last instant, one booted foot twisting above the water, was he recalled by a collective shout. Yet in the interval before he wheeled, as he faced me, wrapped from his nose to the top of his head, I caught once more at the closing door of resemblance. Perhaps, I thought, it is only that I want so much to know anyone in this land.

The hotelier returned his brush to the pool, then hunched near the canvas to pick letters from the air. "I'm closing this place down, you see," he said by way of answer. "So I asked myself what I should paint, to pass the time. How I should fill the emptiness of empty days. I put the question to Charles. Everyone knows Charles. He was, I've been told, a painter once—"

"Yes," I murmured.

The hotelier leaned back for an instant: His letters looked nearly like animals, things that didn't know at their beginning what they'd become. "And of all the things in the world, Charles said postcards. Isn't that funny?"

"He loves postcards —"

"True, true. I can't read to save my life, and he insists on sending them to me, anyway." I wondered momentarily whether he knew what he was spelling. "Yet, of course, no one ever writes anything on a postcard. It isn't the point."

I looked away. We were, I found, both watching Jane where she rowed alone in the depths of the pool.

"Do you ever paint figures?" I asked.

In response, he took the yellow and illuminated a ground-floor window, just as it is here. "Say — was he any good?" he asked, cleaning his brush. "Was Charles any good, when he was a painter?"

"He was," I said after a moment, "the best painter I've ever met."

"Perhaps, then, when I'm done with this, I'll give it to him. He *does,* as you mentioned, love postcards. You did get some of Charles's cards, didn't you?"

"They're — I think they're upstairs."

"Shouldn't you be up there?" he replied, or I thought he did; I'd half caught on the barb of the words and begun to ask *what,* exactly, he'd said, but down our side of the pool the blindfolded man had reappeared, arms moving in slowing arcs, and we stopped to look. He'd recovered his hat. A bubble of laughter followed as he felt along the aisle of aluminum chairs. When he ran out of chairs, he paused to rub at his temples, seeming to laugh a little at himself before the hat slipped away again, to roll along the cement. The light from the water danced upon his western shirt, his wiry frame. And I became certain, watching him tip back on boot heels, paw the ground with his blind hands, that I knew him. The sensation leapt up before I even knew who he was.

"Harvey?" I breathed, scarcely aloud, as I began to walk toward him. "Harvey"—but in a voice that penetrated this private darkness. "It's Milton."

He turned to me, mouth open a little, trying the name. His tongue passed over his lips as if it made him thirsty. For a moment he seemed to lose me in the voices of the people around us, and again I called him. He took a step. It's as close as I've ever come to raising the dead. Someone rammed the hat down on his head, and he stumbled, then lurched the last dozen feet along the rim of the pool, until at arm's length he hesitated.

"It's all right," I said, stopping too. "You'd never believe the things I've believed. But everything's all right now"—laughing with the crowd as he started forward and caught his foot on a low table, the fool, lunging at me so we clutched in a fist as we once wrestled on the mats. The dead have that power. They can grant any wish. My hands tore at the mask. The hat sailed into the pool, and we pulled together at the cloth until I'd dragged it over his head—

But I looked, instead, into the eyes of a stranger: two small eyes that struck back at me between pale lashes. A face pocked from childhood. I watched him watch the joy fly around my face and out.

"You're it!" he gasped, and I sank away from the appalling hand he held out.

Pulling the cloth from his hair, he thrust it at me. "You're it," he repeated, a murmur beginning on all sides.

"I can't," I said; and when he didn't seem to hear: "I can't put it on—I'm afraid of the dark"—appealing to the crowd, this man I'd thought was my friend, anger appearing at the corner of his mouth like a tooth as the hotelier's voice, interrupted, urbane, charmed:

"But *I'm* afraid of the dark."

I looked at the old man, seated there beside me, brush in hand, his worn face like a grandfather's or a president's from a bygone time. And I thought, naturally, of my dream, and the dark night I shared with the boy, in which I, or the boy, are strangely unafraid. Staring around, my eyes wandered to a woman's face, a horse's features pulled tight into something like loathing, remembering another face, on another girl, or perhaps the same girl — a curious, wide-eyed face — and how I'd met her, once, weeks after I'd seen her features in a sketch tacked up in Charles's studio. And I thought again of Charles. I looked back to where the man I'd believed was Harvey was waiting for me, the blind held in his hand. I'd have to tell Charles, I thought, taking the blind. I would have to look at those postcards.

Then, eyes closed, very carefully, I brought the blind to my face and tied it over my head.

When was it that you first realized it doesn't matter whether your eyes are opened or closed? For when, as Thales so rightly pointed out, have we ever discovered anything, but what we were already looking for? I cannot tell you how long it was I knelt with the darkness pounding down, the voices pulling at me, magnifying themselves like light, then one by one turning away, fading into night; but I can tell you that as I let these things go, and stared at the cement where my hands were pressed upon the cracks, a pebbled texture, the tiny, jointed weeds pushing up, and an earring—a chunk of gold with a pin I slowly twisted between two fingers to catch a gleam, before I let it fall and roll over the lip of the pool—I saw, as in some of the deepest of our varied nights we can see. An empty basin lay before me, drained to a bed of leaves in which a single aluminum deck chair huddled. It was distinctly cold as I stood up in the motel courtyard; silent, as if an ocean had rolled back to a point on the horizon, so far that having risen, I was no longer sure even what direction that might be. Beside me was an easel with a postcard propped on it, damp from weather.

I was trying to remember the names of the motels as I climbed back through the empty halls. And then, standing in my room, rifling through the brown paper bag that now contained my life, I wondered if I *had* the cards anymore. I might have lost them in a previous fire; I might have left them in the car. They were, I found at last, in the pocket of my denim jacket.

I counted six, one of which was the postcard for the museum. Turning over the next, the name on the back clutched at me — *Cozy Rest* — because it was the name of the motel in Memphis. I gazed upon an artist's rendering, the cursive nominative dancing like fire upon a roof that now existed nowhere else, I thought, reaching for the phone. It rang and rang down to the front desk, and finally someone answered.

"I need an outside line," I said, wrestling past a description of long-distance charges, dialing the numbers on the backs of the remaining missives. I tried the Fairweather (duplex with deer head superimposed on foreground), The Hill and Dale (bleached mountain woodland reproduction, deckled edges), the Caravanserie (neon flying *V* glowering above highway), and the Plantation House (map of the state of Mississippi with you-are-here blood spot), until the cards lay about me on the sheets. Everything was out of service, the conclusion nearly inescapable, and in despair, to ensure the line wasn't faulty — the idea an oasis — I dialed my own home and waited for the murky sound of the answering machine. After five rings, I heard instead a woman's voice:

"Hello?" it said, thick with sleep. "Hello?"

My own voice blundered back, half forgotten: "Caroline," I said stupidly.

She moved among the covers of our bed. "Milty? Is that you? Where *are* you? I was trying to call all week. I was trying . . . and then I came over."

"I'm in Mississippi," I told her, "with Charles."

"Trembleman? That's funny . . . you've got some post-cards from him . . ." She got up, and I heard feet scuff across wood and grow soft on the Iranian rug. "Jesus, Milty — everything's brown — you didn't get anyone to water." She made a sound — she was disgusted — then seemed to forget. "Are you okay?" she asked.

"Charles was hurt in a fire," I said, carrying the handset to the window of my room. "He needed help driving. I thought it might clear my head." And suddenly it hit me: "You've come home."

She sighed or shivered. "I was picking up some things. I wrote you this note . . . Why won't you tell me what's the matter?"

Below lay the empty, leaf-laden pool. Raising the blind over my eyes, I found Jane in her little boat at the center of a drunken, burnished scene. The distant flames and the blue water picked out a limb, a face, yet it wasn't light by which I saw, and I snugged the blind back down.

"There's a woman outside," I said at last, "and she tells me that Charles has been setting fire to motels." I waited, but the line was quiet. "Well, not in so many words . . . it's ridiculous, though, isn't it? He's downstairs now, probably asleep. *I* should be asleep. It's just . . ." I heard my wife's breath. She was touching the corner of her mouth with a finger, as she always does when absorbed and unobserved. "It's so dark here. I can't explain how dark it is. Even the lights are made of darkness . . ."

"Milty, what have you done?" she said. "Tell me what you've done."

"What do you mean? I'm with Charles—"

"But you do things, Milty. *You always do things.*"

We both listened. "Yes—I suppose everyone knows that, don't they?" I closed my eyes. "There's a little girl . . . I need to go back out, you see, into that dark."

She considered this. Somewhere before her lay her reflection, and after a bit I heard her hand rub against the glass.

"I need to go back out," I repeated. "Just tell me something"—and I hung in the silence, staring down at the pool, the matted leaves.

"It doesn't look so cold," she said presently. "It looks like the beginning of a movie, when no one's spoiled it yet. It looks like sleep—white sheets of sleep." And I followed. We listened to the snow—I could hear the snow of nights gone by, nights suspended in nights. "The lights are off in the house, there are no stars, but the ground and the sky and the air are light. You can just see the tree line, and past that it all turns a blue that's also a very deep white. The roads are gone. The car is gone — it's a hill in the snow" — as I realized that of course, she hadn't meant to stay. She'd been snowed in. "It was snowing all afternoon, and it still is. Huge flakes — like fingerprints, covering the pines. If you walked out into the driveway, out by the lilacs, you'd think you were alone. The house, the woods, everything would be gone. Everything would be white, like it's all taken back.

"What are you going to do?" she asked.

"I don't know," I said. "Can I call you, in the morning?"

For a long time, I could hear her breathing across the line. I could hear her heart beating fast as she said nothing; and she thought, and she decided, and said nothing. I could hear the snow scratch the glass by her face, and I could hear all of the things that don't, in the end, get said, but become only a color — a color I'd never seen except in a dream — and I hung up.

I sat against the wall by the window, and then I lay on the floor, the side of my face pressed to the carpet. There was a clamor inside me, like the murmur of a vast crowd — like the gathered events of the night, of the week, of years; only when I'd gained some presence of mind and quieted my thoughts did I hear a tiny noise, an electronic bleat that pulsed on and on until someone — Charles, it had to be Charles — stirred down below; a light was switched on, and then there was silence.

I remember going through the vacant halls, my feet hushed in the orange nap. For a while I stood outside his door, wondering if I should knock, but instead I tried the handle and found it unlocked.

My friend was crouched in his patched-up suit between the sink and the twin bed. His back was to me, and he had the red can and siphoning hose before him on the carpet. Beside these, on the linoleum, was a pile of bedding. The room reeked of fumes.

"What are you doing?" I said.

He startled, but didn't turn. "What does it look like I'm doing?" he replied in his whispery new voice. "Please, close the door," he said, and I did.

He took a bedsheet between his good hand and his teeth and tore it lengthwise.

"Have you been walking the halls, enjoying the art?" he whispered, dipping a strip into the can. "I'd been meaning to bring you here. Show you I've kept a toe in the art world — something to take back and warm over with what's-his-name, your business manager —"

"Patrick —"

"— though I suppose you had other museums in mind. What are you doing up at this hour, Milton?"

"I was thirsty. I came downstairs, and then there was this party. There were all these people outside." For a moment I fell silent. "Charles — I thought I saw someone, by the pool," I said as he picked up another sheet. "I mean, he looked like —"

"I know," Charles said.

"No, no — he looked like Harvey —"

"Yes — I'd forgotten his name, the little fellow in the hat —"
I was confused. "You've met him before?"

The sound of a tearing sheet sheared the room. "A long time ago. But Harvey, you see, is dead," he whispered.

"Of course, of course —" though I struggled to recall where I'd heard or read this. I struggled to see more than a blue blazer in the snow. I remembered breaking the news to Caroline. It was, I saw now, perhaps her final reason to leave. "Did you ever visit him in Memphis, after we met?"

"He came to see me, once, when my tour took me to New Orleans."

My hand was still at the door. There was an open bottle of cough medicine on the floor, and Charles took a slug and reached for the gas can. I said, "What if we just get in the car —"

He looked up. "Don't open that," he said, hesitating as he took in the blind; and when he spoke next, something had shifted in his voice. "I know all of them, Milty. Stay with me."

I let go of the door.

"You were right, you know," he continued, taking another pull at the bottle, "when I met you down in Carthage. I was there to see the painting — Harvey's painting. I was lost — I think I *said* I was lost. I'd gone on and on, I'd become all turned around with this Singer business. Isn't it funny how you can see all the world in a drop of rain, and end following something that isn't the beginning of anything, anymore, just a ripple —"

Upon the nightstand lay a pack of matches. My head swam in fumes.

"And then I saw this wonderful painting. Harvey's painting. That was the day before you arrived. I remember there was a sort of celebration at the museum—an anniversary—and I'd stood in line, wandered in with a crowd to see what it was all about. I was lucky, really—I didn't know where I was going; and there, off in a back room, was *the painting*. We were alone together, and it came to me, what he'd said—what Kennel said—about Sherman. One doesn't imagine, of course, where the thread might lead . . . but it was only because I went back in the morning, when they'd thoughtfully closed the museum, that I met you. The brightness was nearly unbearable. A fire like that—it's the light by which you see. Though after that first fire, I knew I wasn't ever going to find my way out. No—not even if someone else found their way in. Not even Harvey. You know how he is—poor Harvey, who said he knew a place I could go, who said it wasn't too late; who closed his eyes at the end. But you understand: When was it you realized you'd never stop? I think for me," he whispered, "it was when I first admitted to myself that I wanted to. It was like hearing the world call my name. Everything," he told me, "they say will come true, comes true."

It had been a terrible journey, by any standard. I'd believed for so long that something might be salvaged, I had left open every possibility; but sometimes only fire can make perfect.

There is something gentle about killing someone, once you've decided to do it—such a tremendous relief in undertaking an action if it is, as it indeed was that night, without rage, without fear of recrimination, with a mind like a large, soft hand. I would never, I think, have been able to properly articulate my technique for sleep until I took Charles around the neck and choked the life out of him in that burning room.

I'd cast a match into the pile of gas-soaked bedding. The gesture caught him off guard, and he started to get up, which was when I stopped him. And this is not to say he didn't struggle — it surprised me how much he wanted to *live;* his resistance — really a raging, furious clinging — nearly put me off. He bloodied my nose and tore one of my ears before he dragged the blind down my face. He was done, though: His hands were damaged, and he'd planned badly, lacking in that final stretch the strength to get more wind. His thrashings weakened until his fingers buttered over my arms. The imperfection became an accord, and I can say that when he knew he would die, a look came into his eye — a recognition, a wild swing of the pupils that had nothing to do with me, but lay about the room where the flames were already busy in the carpet and the baseboards. I didn't know, then, what it was. I lifted him and laid him on the bed.

There had been, though, that imperfection. I couldn't entirely rid myself of it, even when his mouth opened blue and his eyes stood out. It lay like grit in our happiness as I rose, leaving the room shortly before the red can exploded, in my fuddled state making a wrong turn and finding myself in the empty lobby. We had an obvious problem with the alarms in those first seconds — fire safety seems to be shaky in these old places — but then, pleasantly, this corrected itself, and everything was working as it should by the time I'd headed back through the now-burning building to my room.

I wanted to see the postcards again — they would, I thought, restore the brief clarity I'd experienced when I glimpsed what I had to do. The flames, however, were already gaining enthusiasm as I hurried past my friend's door. Preoccupied as I was, I'd neglected to close it. First going the wrong way, then forgetting the door. It was the beginning of a sad snowballing of mishaps.

I retraced my steps through the smoke, past the people who appeared in their nightclothes, faces shifty with fear, to get to the stairwell jammed with guests. Misunderstanding, they tried to convince me to turn back, and I had to physically shake off the most well-meaning. All the same, by the time I gained the second floor, I found myself alone.

The doorknob to my room was too hot to hold, so I took off my shirt and, wrapping my scalded hand, wrenched the knob around; at which, in a belch of heat, I was thrown back by the fire. Crowning the various failings of the last five minutes, it seemed that the blaze had crept out of Charles's window, scaled the veranda, and swarmed into my own room and those on either side. There was nearly an intelligence to the act, and I stared in dismay at the flames painting the walls and swirling upon the ceiling, gusting into the hall to lie upside down over my head. For a moment I watched, and then, as the fire seemed to recollect itself, I ran, the watercolors hanging on either side becoming little cocktails of glass. At the top of the stair I turned a last time to see the open door of my room gouting fire into the corridor like agony, and then I vaulted down: There was nothing to do — I'd lost everything.

And yet it seems I remember standing again outside the door to Charles's room, the air a curtain of sparks. I stood in that carpeted hall, among the beastly odalisques, fire like golden paper on the walls, firemen passing to and fro about me, like angels in the furnace; and I looked in upon Charles where I'd laid him out in his forever room. The flames flickered and held, and dead he moved inside them, like the old Muybridge frames, blind with light and youth.

Here we were at the end, my friend and I. I watched him enter the fire I'd made as if entering the garden in the jewel, his room within the room. Here we were at the end, my friend and I. Or nearly.

I DON'T KNOW WHAT, exactly, I believed I might find when I drove out to the museum this morning. I hadn't slept at all the night before—I'd been up writing—and then, when the sun rose, and I sat back from the typewriter and the demons closed their eyes, I thought about Harvey, and I got in the car.

It was tomb cold inside, behind the pillars and the polished copper doors. I waited for my eyes to adjust. The foyer is a grand octagonal chamber whose only source of illumination, apart from four iron lamps at compass points on the floor, are four small oculi set into a dome. Sun stood in volumes of dust and lay in ellipses across a double staircase ascending to a mezzanine; arched doorways on either side led into further seclusions. Beside the entrance I discovered a desk, and perched by a wooden box and fan of pamphlets, a little man with brown paper skin and a worn brown suit—by the shiny buttons that fell down his chest, an antique military uniform.

When I turned back to the room, armed with a new, more elaborate pamphlet, my eyes involuntarily rose along the walls, thick with portraits, landscapes, and still lifes; and finding little purchase among the grave faces, vistas of summer foliage, and slain fruit and game, I again glanced into the space like a darkening sky beneath the dome. From far away came a clatter of footfalls, perhaps from a child. I heard the scrape of a chair, and I was just hastening forward, afraid the museum attendant might take me by the sleeve to impart some half knowledge, when my eye was caught by the enormous canvas placed high on the wall above the landing of the double stair.

The painting at first gave only a dim scene, composed of blacks, earthen hues, and densely worked patches of ochre, but containing in places thickets of brightness — licks of yellow and red. And then, as I stared, I realized that of course *this* was the painting. It could be none other than *The Fall of Atlanta*. Excited, I flipped through the pamphlet, expecting the picture and artist to be prominently displayed, as the work itself was, but the ink was frail and information perhaps five years out of date. The only descriptor that applied remotely to this section of the entrance hall declared: *Venus Arising from the Sea*.

"Excuse me," I said, turning to find the little man at my elbow, watching me with expectant spectacles. "What is the title of that painting? The one of the fire?"

His mouth opened and he paused impressively. "*The Fall of Atlanta*, commissioned by Eleanor Francis Bateaux and painted in 1865 by Alsby Kennel," he replied, "one of the true American masters." Our eyes met, and he drew fresh breath. "Kennel was present at the siege of the city, and witnessed these destructions with his own eyes." He lingered blackly on these words, then unexpectedly lightened: "A gift to the museum by the Bateaux estate in 1967, the painting was damaged by fire in the summer of '79. We are," he appended sotto voce, "currently raising funds . . ." and fell into some elaborate calculation.

"Damaged by fire, you said?"

"Yes—this work, and one of the galleries under renovation at the time. We were celebrating our centennial when the blaze broke out, and it seems to have been a cigarette, let smolder in a can of varnish rags—filthy habit"—at which he returned to his calculations and I returned to the painting.

The light in the foyer was poor enough that it was difficult to make out more than a general theme: a rambling, blackened skyline seen from above, as if from an elevation in the land, with a thick tide of flames coursing across the roof of the town. In the distance twinkled the campfires of what was presumably Sherman's besieging army.

I began to climb the curve to the balcony, toward a better vantage, though as I approached, I discovered the landing to be too narrow to allow a proper perspective. Pressing myself against the marble rail and ignoring the twittering of the attendant below, I was, however, able to inspect the lower portions of the canvas. The painting must have been forty feet wide and nearly twenty-five tall, and it was nothing like any Kennel I'd ever seen; though it was, beyond a doubt, a Kennel.

The darkness of the work—deriving in concert from the poverty of light, the fire and smoke damage, and also the fact that it was a night scene—was relieved only in those places where the flames devouring the town maintained their freshness, forming a halo above which everything seemed carbonized. While consuming some of the highest structures, the fire otherwise sat lightly upon the roofs and eaves of Victorian Atlanta. It rolled above the city as a mass of hair might roll from a woman's head across a bed; and beneath the tarnished surface there was something sensuous in the curls of color, a luxurious and organic outgrowth of the buildings. Applying my eye, I noted that below the rooftop nest of the fire, through little windows, were further flecks of color, further illuminations. It was then that I discovered within the houses, beneath the conflagration, a multitude of views upon tiny domestic scenes; and finding some of them near eye level, I gave my attention to the vignettes of urban life that Kennel had, quite typically, so lovingly and minutely portrayed.

My glance fell at random upon a room in which a man could be seen reading a book, pipe clutched in one hand, his parlor a refuge of Oriental rugs and wallpapers of mythological theme; in another room, paneled and hung with tiny oils, supper was being served by black maids in bonnets and aprons to a large family, perhaps entertaining, as one gentleman in evening dress seemed to be holding forth to another while several women and children looked on above a table loaded with porcelain. There was a faint scene by lamplight in which a mother placed an infant in its cradle, while downstairs, in an empty room, a bird in a silver cage sang beneath the gaze of a cat on a coil rug. People might be seen knitting, playing the piano, conversing quietly, or drinking claret. Strolling slowly along the landing, my eye traveled the streets of the canvas in proverbial seven-league boots to what was evidently a poorer part of town, where roofs were also aflame beneath the same striving mass of light. There was a bar with a shoe hung out for a sign, and a bordello where ladies might be seen dancing through the windows, skirts drawn high. Men were drunk and fighting amongst themselves, mouths grimaced in rage. A woman in a kerchief stared sadly out from her room; below, in the quiet pool of a streetlight, a boy petted a lean dog.

Looking from these mean streets to the avenues, carriages drove about, the coachmen's whips suspended in air. A cop forever gave directions with his baton to a matron on a corner; down a neighboring street, a handful of children in short pants were playing, running together with a red ball between them. They were all gazing at the ball, and it gave me pause to note that none of them seemed cognizant of the fire just above their heads.

At first I assumed the omission accidental; but as I roved back across those scenes I'd visited, in vain I looked among these people for any comprehension of the inferno. Not even the pallor of the light cast by the painter's hand — a soft vapor of gaslight — alluded to the lurid disaster that had overtaken the city. In a church whose steeple was wrapped in flame, a quiet sermon was delivered to a half-populated hall of well-to-do townsfolk; in a room beneath the very roots of the fire, its windows blackened by soot and the feelers of flame, a woman sat before a sewing machine like a girl out of one of Vermeer's domestic scenes, intent, concentrating, even as the fire sent a spark reflecting in her eye. They had all been captured at the crest of a wave, lifted above the disaster that was enveloping Kennel's world in the next crashing instant.

Turning from the gigantic canvas and looking over the rails, down to where the little attendant in his petty officer's uniform gazed up from the first tread, I said, "Could you tell me anything more about the artist who made this painting?"—although I was confident that he could tell me nothing I didn't already know.

"Kennel was a native," the man replied in a voice that quivered with age or pride, "of the state of Georgia, and fought himself in the War of Secession."

"And afterward?" I inquired. "Didn't he move to France?"

"He died," the man said, shaking his head, "in The True South."

Dazed as one often is on emerging from a museum into daylight, I stood on the front steps, as I'd done long ago in the company of Caroline and Harvey. A breeze pulled what little heat remained from the day, and I walked with my hands in my pockets down the slope onto the green, heading toward the car I'd parked roughly where Charles had parked that afternoon nearly two years ago. I thought of how he'd stood up from that same car and then lain back, out of view, waiting for us to pass, afraid—how rightly afraid, it seemed to me now. Without really thinking, I went into the darkened bar and took a seat where my friend had sat when he followed us inside.

The place appeared empty. I ordered a drink, and for a while I sat thinking about Kennel: of a life that tailed away into lives, of all the things that didn't agree even in my own memory, like the ragged edge of a flame; and how perhaps greatness, if anywhere, lies in a life that takes more than one life to complete. That the lives of the great, wherever they begin or end, breed ghosts.

An hour must have passed before I noticed someone seated at a table beyond the silent jukebox: a woman in a gray skirt suit, like a moth among the furnishings. The bartender brought me my drink and vanished; only then did I make my way into the back.

"Jane," I said. She was rising to go.

"They say arsonists always return to the scene," she replied, putting on her gloves. "It's a crime of place, after all." She fished in her bag for her cigarettes. Noticing the pack on the table, I hesitated, took one for myself, then handed them to her. She stared at me as if I'd said something she hadn't quite caught.

"What's the matter with you?" she wondered aloud, continuing to stare as I lit a cigarette. And then she shook her head. "Please," she said, "don't think it's cruel of me to say I'd hoped it would be Charles who came through that door."

I took a seat, but she stepped away. She made a beautiful widow—I think I told her as much. What most struck me, though, was how amazing it was that I'd ever found her frightening. Yet I think I was right in believing we'd both been lost in this place, once, together.

"'The supreme consideration,'" I told her, "'is man'"—a quote attributed to, of all people, Mahatma Gandhi. "The machine should not tend to make atrophied the limbs of man. For instance, I would make intelligent exceptions. Take the case of the Singer sewing machine. It is one of the few useful things ever invented, and there is a romance about the device itself."

"How does it feel," she said, "to have become the thing that you most admire?"

"We both came from the same little town—Elizabeth," I replied, as she began to walk away, and I turned to the drink I'd brought with me; hearing no word from her, but noting that she lingered at the end of my voice, I took a drag from the cigarette, then continued: "I'm sure he's mentioned his home. If you ever go there, tell his mother — tell her that I killed him — but tell her you're his wife. Tell her there are some things that belong to him that you'd like to see. Someone should take those paintings out of that damp garage; and there's a beautiful place — the Charles Street gallery, of all the names — with a beautiful room. Because I don't think," I explained as she hovered at the end of the bar, the kind of ghost that could only scare another ghost now, "that Patrick ever really believed me . . ."

After she left I loitered in the back. I eased my feet from their shoes, then took off my jacket, but even so, the suit remained hopelessly small — after all, there are some things you can never let out enough. I had no plans, hardly a thought in my head I could call my own. I raised my hand for another drink. It was getting on evening by the time I stuffed myself back into these clothes and made my way to the door to begin the return drive to the Idyll.

It's a long, straight road, and in the failing light — and why, I ask, does the light in the South always seem to be failing, as if sliding toward some total and final night? — I could see from several miles a wavering glow. My first thought, naturally, was of fire. Only when I drew nearer did I realize the colors were throbbing in the parking lot of the motel, and a few seconds later I made out the men in blue, hats tipped back and shotguns perched on their hips.

I pulled off the road, into a wallow, and cut the engine. For some time I sat in the car, and then, when the sun had sunk low enough, I got out and slipped along the roadside through the cane. It was raining lightly. I could hear thunder in the distance, eating up the land. Looking over my shoulder, I saw that the Impala was invisible in its ditch. By the time I came to the place where Thales's mowing begins and the cane cuts back to ragged grass, the lights had died and the cruisers just shivered. I waited for a while in the lee of a bush, wishing I'd had breakfast. After most of the vehicles drove away and the weather let up a bit, I looked out again.

Thales and Eileen stood in conversation with some local officers. The door to my room was open, and I crouched at the edge of the light cast by the motel sign, unsure of what to do, understanding with dawning sadness that I might never return to the life I'd so carefully manufactured for myself in this place. It had never seemed like much, but now that it was slipping away, it meant a great deal.

I was soaked, and once more I'd removed the cruel shoes, yet glancing up into the clouds, the rain was lifting. There was a tear in the storm, a smattering of stars. The police milled for a moment in the driveway before they went back and closed my door, and then three of them drove away while the remaining two accompanied Thales and Eileen toward the house, presumably to await me in comfort. Seeing the way clear, I went back to the car for something, then drifted to the edge of the lot and crossed the veranda.

My room had been hastily repackaged from its ransacked state — it looked like a store — and for a moment I saw myself as I must seem to them: an animal, a madness or blindness, a creature that wouldn't notice that its home had become a trap. I took my papers from my desk, the postcards and photos from above the TV. I was afraid — my fear, I knew, would drive me out, if not that moment then the next — but I also felt lucky, as I'd not felt many times on this trip. It's the kindest coincidence — luck. It ripples sometimes in the sky like thunder, like the echo of other coincidences, and I hurried out with my good fortune before it soured. At the threshold I set down the emptied can and, giving the place a final, fond farewell, threw a match, closing the door gently behind me. There had been a moment when I thought that this might be the one — *my room*. It was ridiculous to pretend as much now; better to be certain, and, again, fire would make perfect.

I found the car as I'd left it, but only then noticed that in coming down from the road, a sapling had lanced the driver's-side headlamp. There was little to be done. I had to cut the lights, anyway, as I blew by the old motel for the last time, the windows of my room yellow and alive.

And so I kept driving. The sky opened, and the mist rose away from the land. I didn't want to leave the sewing machine behind, or the typewriter for that matter — I would have brought everything; yet I was cheered by the thought of the road, and of where I was going. There is, after all, something cheering about all excursions, even if there hadn't been something remarkable about the road itself.

For I'd begun the wonderful road — the one Charles once assured me was the most beautiful road on earth. At first gently, then in grander and grander passes, it started to sway in the shelter of little hills. Someone had planted tall poplars on either side, and in my single headlight they flared and tapered into the dark like a colonnade. I remembered what Charles had told me, and this, too, was true, for I found myself taking the turns tight and very fast, the order of the trees giving way to a disorder of live oaks, branches nearly black with time, that seemed to offer space for additional speed. I thought of Charles, on fire in his room, and I thought to myself that I would probably never find my room — the room that awaited me. I thought of how there is something alike in beginning a fire and in going to sleep: There is, in each, that moment the whole stands in the balance — when it might turn over, all turn to fire and dreams, or all merely fade back into the old world one knows so well — that is intolerable. One waits for sleep to catch and run out of control through the mind. One wants to help a dying fire — Charles was entirely right — one wants it to burn forever.

Around a tight corner, a deer (there is an identicalness to all these creatures at night — eyes become reflecting disks, legs impossibly long in the distorted field of the headlamp) advanced into my single beam, and in swerving to avoid the animal I drove the car into a glittering meadow, wrecking the remaining lamp and part of the grille on an old stump.

Cutting the engine, I got out to survey the damage. The deer ambled to the roadside, and three of its fellows followed, a silent train through the suddenly silent night. The moon is very bright and the mist has all but lifted, but the darkness in the woods around the clearing is like the darkness around the dashboard lights.

It's cold in the car. I can't stay here. Glancing at the clock on the dash, I'm surprised to see that hours have elapsed since I left the Idyll. Somewhat pointlessly, the clock reads 2:27, as it did that night I woke in my room at the Artiste. I *am* very tired, but The True South can't be much farther, I reassure myself, although I'm unable to entirely erase the thought that perhaps I've passed it. I can scarcely remember what I've been thinking, let alone looking at, for the past five hours. Perhaps there was a fork in the road, some sign I missed. There's little to do but keep going. Somewhere in the night through which I've come, the police are stirring. They've no doubt already climbed into their cruisers, headed this way, their minds blank of questions, full of violence, and without fear — least of all fear of the dark.

Still, there is one thing more I should like to put down before I drive on. The night is a vast place. It preexists us, and it will survive us easily. It will survive every fire. There are people in each night who drive directly into their dreams, like ancient heroes; and there is something endless in that, deathless, even — far from frightening anymore. That we might be given a chance to close every door, wipe clean the map, burn out every star but the few, the very few — perhaps even the one, and the night sky would become again a road. I'm not sure when I'll have another opportunity to stop.

I AM ALWAYS SURPRISED to find myself there, even in memory. I hadn't expected to be invited to the wedding, held on the Hurleys' grounds for their son Kevin and his fresh and covetable wife — I believe her name was Incline — both nonsewers; and once I arrived, I began to see that I'd known Kevin even less than I'd imagined. Not that I'd pretended to know him to begin with, but setting foot upon the strange pastures of his nuptials, I understood that I *really* didn't have the faintest idea.

My brother, who'd rented a car when he arrived in the country, was my ride across town. They'd been school chums, Ted Jr. and Kevin (I picture them together, my brother and his cronies, cawing on a car in the driveway), and Kevin's parents and my own were also sometime friends, so my entire family had been invited. Together in our parents' house for the first time in years, granted a cushion of innumerable rooms, my brother and I had avoided one another beyond the most perfunctory exchanges — and lulled by this mutuality, I hadn't seen coming until too late his invitation to drive in his company to the wedding. My mother (a sewer) would, I knew, be renewed in her misapprehension that we'd even the slightest affection for one another; my father (a nonsewer) would be chuffed because he knew that we did not. I, for my part, found my brother unchanged by his time in Indonesia — nearly twitching with his sportsman's vitality, if reddened and made more leathery by the equatorial sun.

I've sometimes thought of Charles as a Rimbaud, but it's the sort of association too easily made; it seems to lie on the underside of every man of sides. Wasn't my brother, for example, also a kind of Rimbaud? Yet, once again, it is a weak analogy. My brother was — is — no genius, merely a used car salesman gone off into some distant and unknowable miniature of inhumanity where his insignificance can loom enormous. My father had already informed me that Ted had set up a sports equipment factory — "*the sneakers*," said my father, for whom sneakers were an exotic thing, something in which a man could speculate. Ted now informed me that he'd played a lot of tennis. He had "two hundred men under him" — grinning as if some bits of those unfortunates might linger between his teeth. He wondered if Dallas Peabody would be at the wedding. "God, she gives good head" were, I think, his final words on the matter. I don't think I've mentioned that my brother was, against all odds, a sewer (he'd been bedridden as a child — a sporting injury — and had only my mother's company for several months). As we got out of the car and he gave his keys to the valet, he asked how the gallery was doing as if it were some sort of private joke.

I complimented his shoes. We parted amicably and without a word at the first beverage table, having arrived at the wedding as one always does, with the newlyweds the farthest thing from one's mind.

I read in the papers the next morning that there were two thousand people loafing around the Hurleys' preserve that humid August afternoon. Whole towns had worked nights to feed us; their sons and daughters were there that day, serving. At first glance, the gathering was composed of generations at least as advanced in age as our parents, many of whose numbers have since, I'm sure, died. It was these people alone I seemed to know, people I hadn't seen since I was twelve, and wouldn't have recognized in any other setting; their eyes lustered like a ruffling of the wind as we passed with a quiet hello on the lawn.

As for members of my own generation, I knew few; but if I had feared I'd feel the odd man out, I needn't have troubled myself: The wedding was, as I mentioned, gargantuan, and no one I met seemed either discernibly closer to the bridal duo or to know anyone else. Wandering the golf course–like pastures of the Hurley estate, with its small artificial lake, rose garden, hedge maze, rococo-playboy fountains, and several gazebos, I blundered into dimly recalled classmates at least as lost as myself. I was at no point that day even able to find, let alone say hello to, the groom — except, which I'm getting to, for one brief glimpse, toward the end.

While I'm sure a cluster of handpicked friends and relations circled in a lazy Susan before the rich young couple, the newlyweds had otherwise decided to deal with the impossibility of such numbers by ordaining a fleet of bridesmaids their surrogates. I've since been told it's a common approach to handling such Olympic affairs. I'm reminded of Isaac Singer's funeral in 1875, in Torquay, England, his final place of exile — he was attended by a mile-long procession of seventy-five carriages and as many people as I saw about me that day on the lawn — but I'd never before or since been to such a betrothal or wake. It was Sunday, and having arrived home from California only the preceding Thursday, I was freshly cognizant of the world in which my parents lived — a world in which this *wasn't* extraordinary. I staggered in the sun for an hour, grasping hands, drinks, and hors d'oeuvres indifferently, at last taking refuge indoors with an old man everyone simply called "Andrews" — he'd given me a golf club, once, when I was nine; a nonsewer. And it was here, to approach the point more closely, that a young stranger bore down from across a ballroom in which I'd prepared to hunker by the bar for the duration, salting away sedative materials. I think it was the fierceness of her smile, as if she might hit me, that made me release Andrews's arm (he sailed gallantly into a crowd of older women, and from there, some time not long afterward, to his death) and reach out a friendly or protective hand.

"Milton? Milton Menger?" she said, looking at my chest as if I might have a tag. I transferred my drink to a safer place. She was wearing a low-cut dress grouped in a sort of lariat around her ankles, with a white corsage, itself like a tiny wedding cake, that I'd noticed on several young women but recognized only now as an emblem of embassy.

"Are you . . ." I began, finding (fortunately, as it would turn out) that I'd forgotten the name of the bride, as she said, "Yes—I'm one of the bridesmaids." And then we both laughed. She was pretty. I felt gifted. "Of course it's you. Kevin told me what you'd look like (He did! I thought). He warned me—he told me you were shy," she added to my reddening expression. "And look—you've been hiding with the warhorses. You're my last one—I've found everyone else."

I felt like an egg.

"I just wanted to welcome you, you know, on Kevin and Judy's behalf. They're so lucky! Isn't it a beautiful day?" she asked, as far as I could see spontaneously, whipping a glass of champagne off a passing tray.

"Completely," I agreed, speaking with as little shyness as I could muster, adding with fluent use of the recovered name, "Judy must be so happy. And who are you?"

"I'm one of Judy's bridesmaids."

"But *who*?" I said, finally catching her eye.

"Oh, right," she said, placing the empty glass on another tray and returning to actually looking at me. "Caroline Metcalf. I'm *horrible* at this—I know I am. *I told them I would be.* I missed the rehearsal and everything. Do you know Judy?"—No, I didn't.—"Well, it doesn't matter much how *I* know her then, does it? I take it you're a friend of Kevin's . . ."

"No—I don't really know anyone here—"

"So you were kidnapping that old man?"

I remembered Andrews. By the look of things, he was holding forth to his audience of women about his tie. I admired the way he could entertain so many with so little.

"I'm crashing," I said; and then, when she smiled: "Well, there must be someone here who's crashing. No one would even notice . . ."

"I would," she said. "I've received special training—or I *would* have. I had a sort of GED instructional last night from a maid of honor. It all seemed to be about underage drinking"—though in truth, she barely looked old enough to drink, herself.

"What does a crasher look like, exactly?" I asked.

She glanced covertly around the room, and evidently finding no one suitable among the ancients, led me to the picture windows that dominated one wall from floor to ceiling and through which the entire Hurley wedding revealed itself to the eye in its various articulations and subplots, like a painting by Brueghel.

"There," she said, jabbing at the glass. I followed her directions and found an unassuming man in navy jacket and taupe trousers mooning around near a liquor stall. Was there anything to distinguish him? His clothes fit acceptably; he seemed sober; he wore, I saw as he kicked up a heel to lean against a tree, spotless loafers. He . . . I peered more closely . . . but then I perceived he was dressed just like me. I turned and Caroline laughed.

"I'm sorry," she said. "But *really*, if you *really* look at him you'll see I'm serious."

I gave her a second glance, yet she assured me, and though doubly skeptical, I looked back at the mark, and she voice-overed: "Notice how he just stares into the distance. He doesn't even peek at anyone who comes to the bar. He'd have to make out a friendly face at two hundred yards. And watch—here's a fellow ambling up to him right now . . . see how he sidles away? He just turned another direction completely . . ."

"That's right," I said, smiling at the poor man. "They

taught you this at the GED? . . . He doesn't know anyone, does he?"

"And he's afraid somebody's going to come up and talk to him, because then he might have to make something up—"

"Which you obviously have no trouble at—"

"—when all he wants to do is get a drink. He's probably a guy from the papers. He's supposed to cover this for the society column, but he isn't really a society columnist—just look at him. He'll load up on booze, imagine he glimpsed some famous faces across the lawn, misremember as much as he can, and then—oh, quick!" she cried, pushing at my shoulder. "Look away! He's staring right at us!"

"He must have noticed his ears were on fire," I said, half turning, for he was, in fact, staring directly at where we stood in the windows. But we'd clearly looked away too late—discomforted, he revolved and blundered off toward a protective screening of hedges.

"See?" she said as we both burst out laughing.

There was a stir behind us, then, and we glanced around to find a battalion of white-aproned caterers carrying in what were presumably elements of the dinner to be served following the ceremony. I was relieved to find that things weren't quite as torpid as they'd seemed, and I was also actually enjoying myself for the first time all week. Caroline held a gloved hand over her mouth as they proceeded to drag in various roasts—what I took to be an ox, an enormous boar of some sort, what may have been an ostrich, something not unlike a porpoise—mounting them on tables. The old people, sensing they'd somehow placed themselves behind the curtain of spectacle, drew back to the far wall.

"I didn't know the Hurleys were so primitive," I said.

"Father Hurley is an amateur renaissance enthusiast," Caroline offered. I still wonder if she made that up. "But now it's your turn. You pick one," she told me, drawing my attention back to the window.

"A crasher?" I asked.

"Or anyone. What about her?" she said, indicating a woman my age in the middle foreground. She stood in a circle of companions, men and women, though I knew exactly which person Caroline meant: She was a bit the outsider, and she watched her companions from beneath a wide straw hat, laughing sometimes with them but saying little. Her eyes, one could tell even from this distance, were roving the lawn, settling on other groups, other clusters. It seems to me now that these were often our choices down the years: other lonely people; but at the time, I hadn't played the game before. It was all new.

"She's a widow," I said.

"She's dressed in floral prints!"

"Even the dead can't wear black to a wedding, Caroline."

"You're *terrible*," she replied. "I mean, a widow — do you have to *kill* someone just to tell a story?" she said with a smile. She was tipsy.

"Hold on," I protested. "My brother *did*, in fact, tell me that the best man died recently, leaving a sort of awkward vacuum" — her raised hands disowned any such knowledge. "All I'm suggesting is that, however innocently, you've *chosen* the widow, because if you look at her, just the way she's watching everyone and saying hello to anyone who comes up — well, there you have it. She knows most of the people here, and she's not a Hurley — I'd recognize all of them." I was suddenly quite pleased with myself. "These are her people, you see, only she's used to finding her husband among them. She just can't stop herself from looking —"

"Because it always looks incomplete?" Caroline made a face. "I suppose they all know what's going through her mind, then."

"Everyone in that circle is in fact thinking only of her. They all feel sorry for her, and if they appear to be having a good time, it's for her benefit alone."

"They're all terrified of saying the wrong thing, aren't they?" Caroline said. She was quiet, but only for a moment, for behind us there was another hubbub. Lights pricked against the inside of the windows. The caterers, after covering and stuffing everything with fruit in homage to the fertility gods, had now thrown a switch, revealing that each of what I'd taken to be a culinary object was in reality wired full of hundreds of bulbs in varying shades of blue. Each table became a brilliant machine, a city. "Screw this," Caroline said. "I don't want to do them anymore, Milton. Pick somebody else."

Out on the lawn, caterers carried a swan boat down the grassy slope into the distance, toward the artificial lake. Arriving in our view were two men conversing haphazardly over drinks. The larger had a round, red face that seemed happiest when it could make angry shapes with its mouth. It was my brother. I knew the smaller man, too, from high school (a struggler, presumably a nonsewer) outfitted casually and apparently aware of as much from the way he fussed with his batiked shirt. The smaller man was doing most of the talking; periodically, my brother made a comment or sign that his companion would then take up as a sort of fuel. My brother put his hand to his angry mouth and yawned.

"What about that one?" I said.

"Ah"—placing her nose trimly on the rim of her glass as if sighting along a scope—"he's a mean one."

"The little fellow?"

"'Course not. The other one." She poked my shoulder. "He's a big ol' fellow like you. But he likes to hit people. He'd like to hit that guy he's talking with—"

"But they're both smiling."

"*Sure* they are."

"And the big one really seems like a bit of a natural coward—"

"Hold on—I'm not done with him," she interrupted, placing her hand wonderfully on my arm again and leaving it there. "It seems to me that if we're after specifics here, the little fellow's asking him for a favor—it's just neither of them knows it yet. They're still deciding who it is, exactly, that they're each talking to. The little guy has *schemes*. He keeps throwing things out, to see if anything sticks." She squinted at them. "The other fellow's done his scheming. He has opinions. It's nearly like he's just letting the little guy go on until he finds an out . . . but I think it's not so simple. They're both hoping for something."

"The little man wants to borrow money, for instance . . ."

"Well who doesn't?" she said. "But *he* thinks—the big guy—that this fellow might be able to do something for him. That's why he's still listening. It's not that he needs anything, but it seems to him sometimes, when he's gotten a few drinks, that there's something he's missed."

"The little one is more of an optimist, then?"

"Optimist, euphemist," she said. "He's in real estate. Overseas real estate," she said without missing a beat.

"What do you do, anyway?" I asked.

"I'm an actress."

I was distracted, however, by the awareness that truly strange events were occurring behind us. There was a faint hum, and all the reflections shifted in the glass. Turning, I discovered that the grotesque and lavish tables were rotating. Each display, like an engine in a glittering, high-tech factory, spun ponderously about, lights gleaming, full of mysterious purpose. I realized that this was in fact the entrance hall between the outdoors and a formal dining room only now being revealed. The guests would need to pass through this museum of food automatons — likely resembling at least superficially the manufacturing plant my father imagined for my brother in Jakarta — before they went to their seats. I thought then of Charles, and of his paintings of the refineries in northern Jersey glittering like a fairyland as one circled them on the throughways. I'd have to look him up again, I told myself, thoughts touching the gallery before settling once more upon the room around me. Caterers were folding away the walls at the back with stately gestures. Two busied themselves at the windows at which we stood — also doors, as it turned out: a bank of glass French doors leading into the afternoon.

"Excuse me, sir," someone said, placing a white glove upon the door in front of me. The heat of the day touched us.

"My," Caroline murmured, and then she squeezed my arm. "But hold on, hold on: The big guy . . . the big guy is an oldtime businessman, see. It's the old versus the new, Milton — do people really call you Milton?—and that's why he's such a brute. Everyone used to be. Though he has nice hands," she decided, her mind wandering between him and the scene around us. "That's really our clue. He runs a sewing machine factory in Southeast Asia," she said suddenly, shockingly, so that I turned and looked at her. "He's a sewing magnate." She laughed, and I laughed, relieved she wasn't entirely correct, unaware of that darkly glimpsed coincidence.

"He's my brother," I said.

"You're shitting me."

"His name's Ted. He actually owns a *sneaker* factory in Indonesia, so you get a B, I suppose."

She squinted at me, then at him. Giving in, she admitted, "There *is* a resemblance."

"I try to put it from my mind."

"I guess I haven't been saying the kindest things about your brother—but you haven't been such a nice guy, yourself. And by the way, that's cheating, you know. It's not the same if you have all the answers already. I thought you said you didn't know anyone . . ."

"I don't—but you had him there very nicely. Only he doesn't have opinions, really, just things that resemble opinions."

My brother at this point extricated himself from the gadfly companion's clutches and strolled down, away from us, toward the lake. We followed his progress until he'd reached the waterside, visible beyond some shrubbery. In the midst of the waters was the stage where the wedding was taking place, rising in concentric tiers of round, cream-colored platforms on an island—a symmetrical mound of grass. There was a boat—the swan boat—with two men in livery ferrying people back and forth. I lost him for a moment in a swirl of suits, and then he reappeared, at the water's edge, hailing the craft on which the attendants balanced and pushed with poles like gondoliers.

"It's really quite something, I suppose," I said, acknowledging what was obviously the pièce de resistance.

I watched as he boarded the vessel and was drawn out toward the marriage epicenter. The grass was black with people clear down to the shore. Both Caroline and I now examined the bridal pyramid, or whatever that ziggurat is called, hung with scoops of soft draperies and buttons of what were probably frosting, culminating in a little arena upon which a man in a tuxedo and a woman wearing a long white gown had drawn up side by side before a tiny priest. My brother gained the island and hastened up the slope, as if approaching some waning gate of the heavens. Glancing around us, I became aware that everyone else was watching the spectacle of the cake, and that the two people so like a bride and groom atop it all were, in fact, the bride and groom.

"Jesus, it's so detailed," I murmured.

My future wife looked at me — she batted her eyes, afterward following mine to where the tiny bride and groom leaned into one another to the distant shush of the crowd. My brother had vanished into this larger perfection; yet I now saw there was, in the fantastic order and symmetry of it all, a gap — it was so pleasing to discover — to the left of the bride, like a missing tooth. Several people around us began clapping, but it didn't seem entirely right, as when a person in a restaurant joins in with a table of unknowns for a chorus of "Happy Birthday."

My future wife had her glass half in her mouth. I caught her looking at me, then, and we both looked back at the ceremony, a little fire suddenly surrounding my every thought.

"Aren't you," I asked after a moment, "supposed to be up there?"

"Aren't you," she replied, "supposed to ask me something else?"

ACKNOWLEDGMENTS

I owe many thanks to the generous and long-term assistance of Bill Clegg, and to Arlo Crawford and Chris Parris-Lamb for their patience and thoughtfulness in developing *Singer* from its very (cloudy) beginnings. I'd like to thank Rebecca Wolff and Greg Lichtenberg for their attentive readings, and thank Robert Polito for providing me with workspace at the New School while in New York City. To Miah Arnold I owe a wonderful story from her own life, kindly lent; and to Adrienne Brodeur and Tina Pohlman at Houghton Mifflin Harcourt, I owe thanks for editing and support in seeing *Singer* through to completion. To Chris Stackhouse, Erica Gorn, Anthony McCann, and Kent Matricardi I owe various debts for unspecified services they may or may not recall.

I am, finally, beholden to *The First Conglomerate* by Don Bissell and *Falling from Grace* by Katherine S. Newman for research regarding the genesis and sociology, respectively, of the Singer Sewing Company.